WOLF UNTAMED
THE WHITE WOLF SAGA - BOOK TWO

VALIA LIND

SKAZKA PRESS

Copyright © 2023 by Valia Lind

All rights reserved.

No part of this book may be reproduced in any form or by any electronic or mechanical means, including information storage and retrieval systems, without written permission from the author, except for the use of brief quotations in a book review.

This is a work of fiction. Names, places, characters and incidents are either the product of the author's imagination or are used fictitiously, and any resemblance to any actual persons, living or dead, organizations, events or locales is entirely coincidental.

Cover by Anika at Ravenborn Covers

WOLF UNTAMED

THE WHITE WOLF SAGA - BOOK TWO

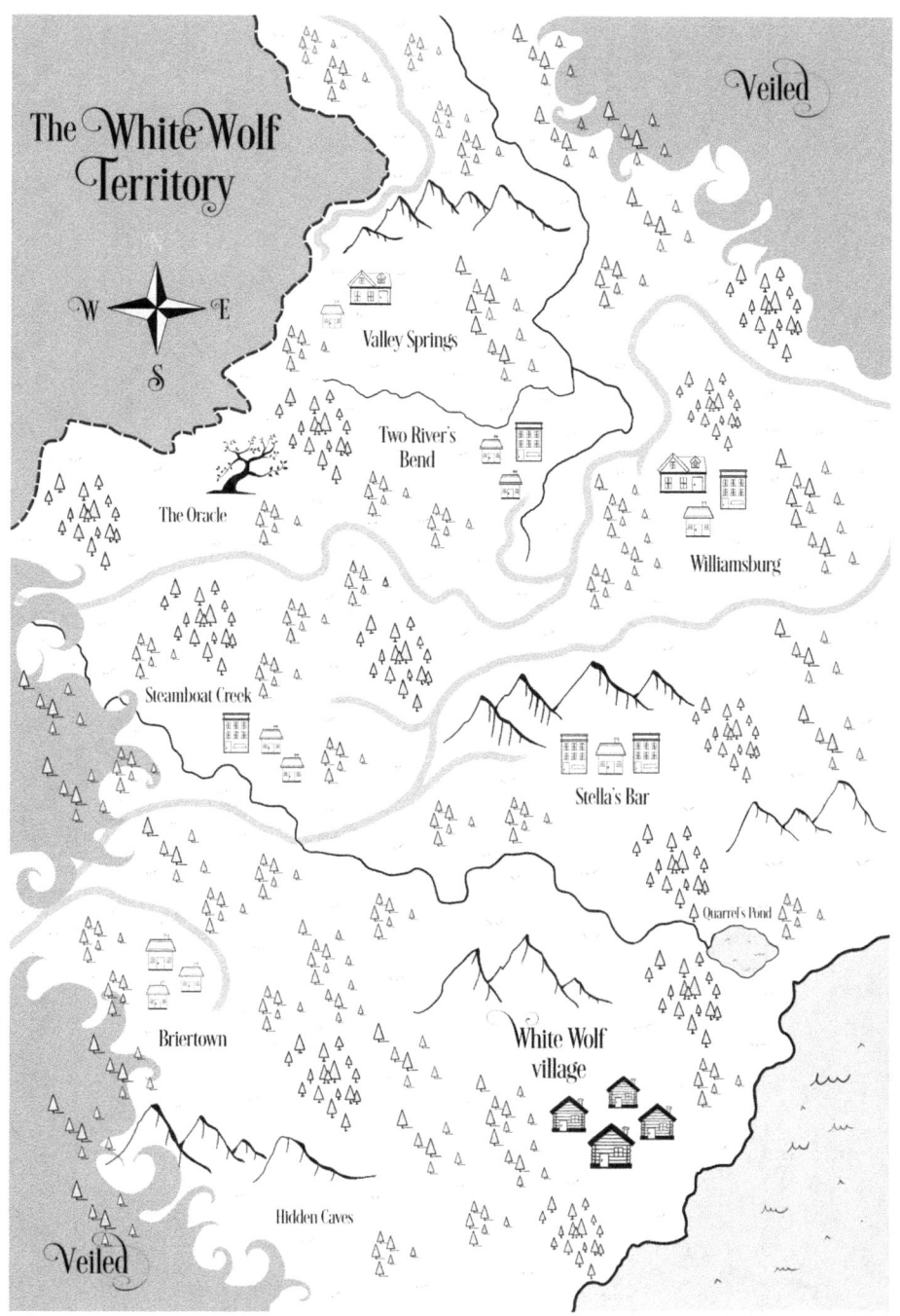

CHAPTER 1

It's been five days, and we're no closer to finding a starting point for our many to-do lists. Like figuring out if someone messed with our memories. Or deciding on the direction to go to find the first shifter. I'm getting antsy…very, very antsy.

Stella has been a gift and has given us a safe haven. As the resident witch of Holden, the town which sits about fifty miles from the edge of our wolf village, she has taken upon herself to help us. Which I am grateful for, considering I actually trust witches and think they are an asset in tight situations. Stella has also warded the bar against basically any kind of assault, besides the actual physical kind, and I can handle that, no problem. I would really love to have someone walk in and start a fight right about now, because I could use something to do.

"If you don't stop with the pacing, Stella is going to kick you out," Rylan comments as he comes into the room carrying a giant box, which he places on the table. Since we've been here, he's mellowed out about the whole witches thing. Although, I think it might just be Stella. She's been feeding him good food. I think Rylan enjoys her fussing over him—I don't think he's had anyone do that since my mom's disappearance. She was the only mother he knew, after all.

I try not to think about them, even though I want to think about them all the time. If my memories are truly messed up, then maybe my parents aren't— no, I can't let myself think like that. If they were still alive, they would've found me by now.

But since I was summoned back by the Oracle as the vital piece of the puzzle in protecting the shifters, it's been one surprising thing after another. It's difficult not to have an outrageous kind of hope. Between the vision quest and the possibility that I might be a True Alpha—something I'd always believed was a fairytale—we've been faced with more questions than answers.

It's only been a couple of days since the wolf village was attacked and we sent everyone to the caves to hide. Rylan and I are still trying to assess the threat and sniff it out. Since then, all we've been able to figure out is that the Ancients have human followers and that there's a compound nearby with some medical labs. Oh, and we were attacked and shot at, while coming to terms with the fact that maybe Rylan and I shouldn't hate each other quite so fiercely.

Now, we're waiting. The witches are trying to find any trace of the first shifter, a creature that would've been the first to be experimented on, and someone who, we hope, can give us some kind of insight on who is experimenting on magical creatures now and how we can stop it. This all has been a great adventure, I tell myself in the most sarcastic way possible. I might also need more sleep than I'm currently getting.

"I'm going crazy in here. I already restocked all the utensils and wiped the bar down at least five times. I need something to do!"

Rylan and I have been helping out at the bar as much as we can so that Stella has more time to help us. She's been spending a lot of time on the phone with the Hawthorne witches, and they're cooking up something—just not fast enough for my liking.

Everything is too quiet. No one came after us after shooting at us at the compound, and no more attacks have happened at the village. Nothing. It all makes me very nervous, because I'm just waiting for the other shoe to drop. That weird saying is courtesy of Jay, who apparently picked it up from Harper. Some of the things the witches have taught the pack are just plain weird.

Rylan doesn't comment on my complaining, but I know he feels the same. We'd both rather run into danger headfirst than sit around and wait, and yes, that's probably going to bite us in the butt, but we're working on it. Rylan and I are working on a lot of things.

"How about we spar?"

His question takes me completely by surprise, and I turn to find him watching me steadily. This is not something we've done since we were kids, and I'd be lying if I said my heart doesn't speed up with anticipation at the prospect. Without giving him time to change his mind, I push the table closest to me out of the way.

We work in silence, moving the tables and chairs to the corners and creating a circular space in the middle of the bar. We could've gone outside, but since the bar is protected, it's better if we don't. The way Rylan and I anticipate each other never fails to amaze me.

"So, how do you want—" But before I can even finish my question, he's on me. Zach and Ezra were the last two wolves I sparred with, and they were good. But Rylan? Rylan is incredible.

There's a fluidity to his movements, a dance which he perfected. I dodge the initial assault, spinning around as I bring my own arm in a backhanded motion, which he blocks. I keep to the balls of my feet, shifting forward when he goes backward and vice versa. My punches follow a pattern of left, right, uppercut, left, and he matches me for each one. Neither one of us is holding back, but our movements compliment each other in that otherworldly way that's very much all our own.

When Rylan catches my wrist, I'm not ready for him. Instead of a typical block, he wraps his hand around my hand, yanking me forward, while his other arm wraps around my waist. There's a moment of stillness as our bodies collide, before I go slack in his arms. The movement drives him downward, and I use that momentum to twist around, landing on top of him.

He doesn't move his hand from around my waist, or the one holding my wrist between us. My other hand is in the space near his head, so I can prop myself up, but my heart is beating against his chest, as my body buzzes with awareness.

There are always a million unsaid words twirling around us, but when he's this close, I can't think of a single thing I want to say—only a dozen things I want to do. His gaze drops to my lips before flickering up to my eyes, and I think I see the same kind of confusion and awareness there that I carry within myself.

"I think it's time I checked on the pack," Rylan says, breaking my silly fantasies with that simple sentence. I push back from him immediately, and he lets me go. Jumping to my feet, I rearrange my clothes and command my heart to stop trying to escape from my chest.

"What do you mean? We checked on them a couple of hours ago." My voice comes out strong and completely unbothered, so go me.

"I meant, I need to go and check on them. With my eyes."

I've only been alpha for a week, so the whole being in charge of a pack mentality is new to me. It's strange on many levels, one of which is that I worry about them constantly. It's this nagging sensation of sort that won't leave me for even a moment. I want them safe. I want them healthy. I want to be the one to provide that kind of comfort. But Rylan has a different perspective. His relationship with them is a learned behavior, acquired over years of respect and care. It isn't just a magical calling that we don't understand. It's his heart.

I can tell that by spending five seconds with him. If nothing else, he has grown into a very good alpha.

"So, we go—"

"I go, and you stay."

"No."

"Trin, you said yourself that there's two of us now. We can't both keep going out there and putting ourselves and the pack in danger. I'll go, I'll keep the link open, and if anything happens—well, you know where to find me."

"I don't like it."

"And I don't like arguing with you about it." He holds my gaze, and I stare right back. We're like a ship in a midst of a storm, constantly being thrown around by the waves. Except in our case, the waves are made of emotions and stubbornness and neither one of us is going to yield.

"So we're just going to stare at each other?" I ask, sighing.

"Whatever it takes," Rylan replies. I narrow my gaze, but he's unrelenting. I don't tell him that I would also feel better if he checked on them with his own eyes, but it would probably help me keep my cool a little better. It's a new experience, having the whole pack's well-being on my shoulders, and it's taking some getting used to. Even without the True Alpha aspect to this whole situation, I've been chosen to be their alpha by some mystical power, but with no guidance to see me through. There's a lot of emotional baggage attached, since I'm finely attuned to the pack now. I am unprepared, to say the least. But at least Rylan knows what he's doing. I'm learning as I go along.

"I don't need your permission, Trinity"—Rylan's voice is slow, his gaze hot on mine—"but I am trying to be civil in this newfound partnership of ours."

That just makes me all kinds of ticked off, because I want to be the mature, levelheaded one! Ugh, annoying. He knows it, too, the way that simple phrase is now driving me nuts. I roll my eyes and give in.

"Fine. I can use a break from looking at your face."

He smirks. "Don't miss me too much."

He doesn't say anything else, just turns and disappears out of the door he came through earlier. I feel him shift, almost as if I'm watching him do it, and then he's racing for the trees. Thankfully, he didn't ask me if our five-minute sparring match helped, but I'm sure he can tell that it did. And he also left me to put all the tables back myself. Double annoying.

Rylan pushes my buttons in every way possible, but when we were sparring, it felt like the old us. Before the exile, before the million unsaid things that now stand between us.

Somehow, we need to learn to coexist, because right now, we're in a midst of a war, and it's going to get worse before it gets better.

I just hope we're ready for it. I hope *I'm* ready for it. Because I don't have a choice but to fight.

* * *

"Come. Sit. You're going to wear a path in my wooden floors." Stella's voice reaches me, and I turn from putting the last chair back in place to find her coming out of the back room, her ever-present journal in hand. What is with everyone being concerned about these floors?

"No offense, Stella, but these floors have already been tarnished by all the bodies and spilled drinks that have been through here. Isn't there some spell you can use to prevent that from happening?" I ask. But I come and sit at the bar as she steps behind it.

"Don't be sassy with me, darling," the witch replies, pulling a glass bottle from under the bar and handing it to me. The sparkling water fizzes as I pop the top off, but I take a good swig with a smile. "You should know witches don't do magic for their own benefit."

"But they can."

"Yes, they can." Stella sighs. "We just try not to."

"Why is that?"

I didn't mean to ask, but now I kind of want to know. When I lived in Hawthorne, I noticed that the coven there rarely did any mundane spells or magic. They lived like they didn't even have magic at times, only bringing out the big guns when the town was in danger.

"I'm sure you've heard of the Salem witch trials."

"I have, but I thought no actual witches were killed during that time. At least, I'm almost positive that's what Harper told me." She's one of the more scholarly witches, although her eldest sister, Brianna, can give anyone a run for their money (another phrase Jay learned from them and then taught me). Brianna is going to be the next coven leader, so she must know all the things.

I would've known more of the things if Rylan hadn't summoned me away.

Ugh, Rylan.

Anyway.

"You're correct," Stella says, and I can tell she's a little surprised, "but what that time taught us is to be careful. Ever since then, we've minimized our everyday use of magic, and only focus on spells that are for the good of the society."

"There's more to it," I narrow my eyes at Stella, as she polishes a glass. Her hair is back in its signature braids, her turquoise necklace always front and center. I glance down at my own amethyst bracelet—the one I made with the witches before I left Hawthorne—and smile. Much like her necklace, my bracelet brings me comfort.

Nothing else about Stella brings comfort. She's wearing black jeans and a band t-shirt, her arms are covered with bracelets, and her fingers are covered with rings. She looks more like someone I wouldn't want to meet in a dark alley than an approachable aura-reading witch, but I love it. She changes her style whenever she sees fit—three times since we've been here—and for someone who loves style, I'm learning a lot from her.

She puts the glass down and meets my eye, giving me a thorough study before replying.

"You are a perceptive girl, Trinity."

I grin at her, but don't comment, waiting for her to go on. She sighs again, sounding more tired than before.

"I'm not sure how it was with the Hawthorne coven—I know them by reputation only—but where I grew up, magic was looked down on. I didn't have a safe place, like their town, where I could practice and learn. We met in secret, and we learned in secret as well. My town was full of magic users who believed that power corrupts and there was no changing that. They knew of the Ancients long before the stories became reality, and they sought to keep us from becoming like them."

I'm silent for a moment, as I process her words.

"You're telling me they thought you'd become like the Ancients if you used your magic? But how does that make sense? Magic isn't bad in itself."

"No, it's not. And the fact that you know that will help you." Her gaze takes on a faraway look, then she shakes herself and turns back to me. "But Trinity, there are many people out there who will use magic until the world is completely destroyed, all because they like the power. You and I both know just how magic can corrupt someone."

She's talking about the wolves. This all started when wolves disappeared, only to return missing their vital human nature. Whatever experiments the humans are running at that compound is turning humans into wolves…and shifters into rabid animals. We have no answers, which is why finding the first shifter is so important.

Not for the first time, my mind travels back to my visit with the Oracle and that pointless vision quest I went on that provided me with zero answers and a bunch of forgotten information. According to the Oracle, who is directly responsible for me being summoned back, the memories of the vision quest will return, and I will have much needed pieces of the puzzle. But none of them have returned. Granted, the witches think the vision quest unlocked my access to my True Alpha calling, but what has that gotten me? Has it provided me with any help with this big mess we're living in? No. Of course not. Why would it? All it's done is bring me back into Rylan's life.

I do a quick check on Rylan, but he's fine, still racing through the forest. My wolf is a little bit jealous as we watch the trees rush past him. It's been a minute since we've been in the woods.

"Where's Rylan?" Stella asks, as I take another swig of the sparkling water.

"He's checking on the pack."

"Did he drink the tea I made him?" she asks. I nod. Stella made a healing potion for Rylan, something we hope will also block whatever tracking spell the bite had left on him. Another wonderful side effect of me being back is that Rylan had to come get me, which got us both attacked by the very problem we're trying to fix. Those rabid wolves are something to behold, and when we arrived at the White Wolf village, they weren't that far behind, even though we made sure we weren't being tracked. The only way they could have found the village was if they had a way to follow Rylan's bite. With Stella's help, I hope that's no longer the case.

"And you let him go alone?" I roll my eyes at Stella's mock outrage.

"I didn't let him do anything. We argued, and then decided to compromise."

"You mean, he decided to compromise, and you had no choice lest you look ridiculous." She chuckles, and I narrow my eyes.

"I don't appreciate that at all."

"Darling"—Stella reaches out to place a hand over my wrist, where my arm is resting on the bar—"there's a lot going on between the two of you. Even a blind man could see that. But you should remember that, no matter how much you don't think so, you both have each other's numbers."

"I don't even have a phone," I say, raising my eyebrows as Stella laughs.

"Not in the literal sense. I mean that you know each other much better than you think you do. He knows how to push you, and you know how to push him. Imagine what you could do if you both put all that energy toward working together instead of against each other."

I sigh, frustration rushing over me like a cold shower. She's right, of course, but it doesn't mean I have to like it. I've carried a lot of pain and resentment toward him for years. It can't all be washed away in the one storm we had to weather together. It'll take more than that.

"It's not that simple," I say, and Stella nods.

"No relationship ever is. Especially not the important kind."

"We don't have—"

"I'm going to stop you right there, darling. Because whether you like it or not, you do. And you need to figure out your role in it. He's doing his part. Admittedly, he's doing it reluctantly. But he's trying. Are you going to try?"

I hate that I can't argue with her, because my hurt eleven-year-old self certainly wants to. But there are so many things at play right now. I can't afford to be a child about this. I have to use my wits and my strength, and yes, also my emotions. That last one is the hardest, considering I've buried them so far down it's going to take a while to dig them up.

But maybe, I'm just lying to myself because I want to believe I'm this tough she-wolf and not someone who still carries pain in her heart. If I'm going to truly become who I'm meant to be, I have to work through my trauma... however unpleasant the process may be. So, I give Stella a tight smile and say, "I'm going to try."

CHAPTER 2

RYLAN

Running though the familiar woods brings a sense of clarity. And a pang of regret that I had to leave Trinity behind. Ever since I saw her in that diner, it's like every thought and dream I've had over the years is resurfacing. Now, we find out that some of my memories might not be what I think they are, that someone actually had the audacity to mess with our heads on the most personal level possible and keep us apart—well, it makes me want to shed some blood, that's for sure.

I'm almost hoping one of the wolves or the humans involved in whatever is happening at that compound come find me because I am itching for a fight. So is my wolf. I freaking love it when we're in agreement on that.

However, I guess I'm not that lucky today, because the woods are quiet. I circle around the village a few times before I weave my way to it. I could go straight to the caves, but I don't want to give the enemy any advantage in finding them. I'll enter through one of the village houses—there are a few—and head for the pack.

I'm close. Meet me. I send the words through the pack link, and Ezra and Zach immediately perk up. I haven't been away from them this long before, and I'm excited to see them.

When I step into one of the houses closer to the middle of the village, I shift back to my human form. It'll be easier getting to the door that way, so I pull the cabinet doors open and slide the back panel to the side. The cabinet blocks one of the entrances to the caves, the smell of the damp earth reaches toward me through the darkness. I climb in, feet first, before pulling the cabinet doors closed and then shift back to wolf. I wonder if I can ask the witches to create some kind of an early detection system for us, to help keep the village safer.

I nearly stumble over myself at the thoughts. Never in a million years would I have thought I'd be contemplating asking the witches anything. But here we are, in a new age apparently.

Instead of dwelling on that interesting development, I open up the link and check on each pack member individually. I'm not ready to let them know I'm here yet, but I want to make sure everyone is safe. They are, and my wolf and I breathe a little easier at that. When I reach the meeting spot, I shift to my human form and meet Zach and Ezra's eyes in turn.

"Status report," I say.

Zach chuckles. "It's good to see you too. We weren't worried at all. Or feeling in any way useless or abandoned," Zach says, folding his arms in front of him. I narrow my eyes at him, before I look at Ezra.

"What he said," the other wolf comments, surprising me.

"I did what needed to be done. I'm not going to apologize for it," I say.

"But you can understand how leaving your betas out, when we're used to having your back might make us feel a little—" Zach stops and looks at Ezra.

"Useless," Ezra supplies.

"I didn't know my betas were a bunch of emotional saps." I roll my eyes. "Should we hug it out or are you going to put your big boy pants on and tell me how the pack is doing."

"I could actually use a hug," Zach says, shrugging. I can't help but laugh, because I missed them too. Even Ezra cracks a smile.

"I left you in charge because I would trust no one else. How's that?" I raise an eyebrow, and Ezra nods.

"It'll do."

They're ridiculous. But they're brothers, so I wouldn't have it any other way.

"The pack is fine. They're emotionally traumatized, of course. A new alpha and an attack aren't exactly events that will leave anyone untouched," Ezra begins, his voice firm as he delivers the updates. "The younger ones have never had to leave their home behind like that, and everyone is concerned for the village's safety. But they have complete trust in you and understand that you will do whatever it takes to protect them—even if that means not being here right now."

I study the betas, the drawn lines around their eyes, the disheveled hair. I hate that I'm putting them in this position, even though, strategically, I know it can't be helped. They're carrying my burden for me.

"Have you gotten any rest?" I ask.

"We sleep in shifts," Zach replies, and I nod at that.

"The guard?"

"They're healing up just fine. No one was bit, just slightly torn up."

I nod, grateful for small favors. We have no idea how the deranged wolves' bites would affect us. I came out fine, except for that part where Trinity thinks the bite led them to the village. Hopefully, Stella's potion works.

"Where's Trinity?" Ezra asks, bringing my attention back to them.

"Back at the bar. We're dividing and conquering," I reply, receiving a raised eyebrow from Zach.

"It must be a day for miracles for you guys to be working together."

"We do what it takes to keep the pack safe. And the rest of the wolves." I'm not sure if I'm trying to convince myself or them, but saying it out loud makes it true. Or something like that.

"Yeah, okay, keep telling yourself that." Zach chuckles. I growl. It's menacing enough that he shuts up immediately, but the amused look in his eyes doesn't go away. Zach and Ezra are the only two who know just how messed up I was after her exile and just how much her coming back has affected me, even though I won't verbally confirm it. They know me too well for my own liking.

"What's next?" Ezra asks, keeping us on track for business types of conversations and I'm thankful.

"The witch is trying to find a spell to help us clear our minds or recover our memories, I'm not exactly sure. But we're staying put for now."

"And working with witches." Ezra is just as cautious about them as I am. One day soon, I'm going to take him and Zach to meet Stella. I think they might like her…which makes me think that *I* might actually like her. Zach called it; it is a day of miracles.

"Let me see the pack, and then I need to get back."

Because like it or not, I'm worried about Trinity. Even with us connected over the pack link, I still need to be near her. I'm not sure what to do with that. As usual.

* * *

TRINITY

IF ANYONE ASKS, I will deny it till the day I die, but Rylan being gone is driving me nuts. I mean, I'm already pacing the rooms, but this adds to it exponentially, which is something I'm not exactly ready to deal with. He's supposed to be firmly in the I-don't-like-you category and he's wedging his way into Okay-I-probably-have-missed-you-more-than-I'd-like-to-admit and it's annoying.

I keep thinking of opening up the pack link and seeing what he's up to, but that feels a little like eavesdropping, and I'm trying to be a mature responsible alpha, not someone who uses her powers for her own benefit. But, oh my goddesses, it would be amazing if I could just get a glimpse of what he's thinking. Our partnership—or whatever we're going to call it—is so different than what I thought it would be coming back here. I can't seem to figure out my emotions or my runaway thoughts or anything going on inside of my head while we're trying to save the wolf community. I mean, this is definitely not where I thought I'd be.

The bar will be opening to the public in about three hours, so I've been restocking Stella's available snacks. I have no idea when Rylan will be back, but he's been gone most of the day and I—nope, I'm not going there.

"Trinity, darling, if you don't stop wiping that one spot, you'll tarnish the wood polish," Stella's voice reaches me as she comes back into the room and I glance down to find myself still wiping the bar top. Here we are again with me tarnishing things. This seems to be a running joke. I drop the rag and place the bowl of individually wrapped crackers in the spot.

"He'll be back soon."

"I don't know what you're talking about."

Stella simply narrows her eyes and takes a seat at one of the bar stools, holding her trusty journal. Immediately, I know something is up.

"You found a spell?" I ask. She opens her mouth to reply, but then I feel it.

She glances behind me, and I don't have to turn to know Rylan is there. I felt him the moment he stepped into the building.

Immediately my body goes into overdrive, sensations racing over my skin. My breathing hitches, and I tell myself and my wolf to stay in control. The strange response to Rylan is making my head woozy, but I do my best to turn and meet the other alpha's eyes.

He looks tired after traveling at high speed all day, there and back. Fifty miles one way is already a long day, and he's done it twice. His hair is a complete mess. I have the urge to reach over and run my hands through it. Instead, I curl them into fists. Rylan doesn't miss anything.

Stay focused, Trinity.

"The pack?" I ask, as Rylan comes around the bar, stopping near Stella.

"Safe. Ezra and Zach are on top of things."

I can tell he feels better after being with them, more balanced in the same way that I'm more unbalanced. Just a week ago, I was firmly in the hating Rylan category and now I'm all over the place. What is happening?

"Rylan, you're just in time," Stella says, completely oblivious to my inner turmoil. She hops off the barstool and motions to one of the tables. "Before we go any further, I would like to point out that what we're doing here may be unusual for you, but please try and keep an open mind." She looks over at me at that last part and I narrow my eyes.

She definitely cannot be looking at me when she says that, because I am clearly the most flexible she-wolf around. I'm even compromising with Rylan! Someone should give me a medal.

Stella motions for me to come around the bar, and then turns to Rylan.

"I need you to sit here, and I need you to pay close attention."

Rylan narrows his eyes at her, clearly not liking all the instructions she's giving out. As an alpha, he usually is the one who makes the rules, so I can see how this could be frustrating for him. It's why I'm so frustrating to him. Well, among other reasons. I'm sure he has a whole list.

"Must we do this now?" he asks.

"Yes. Now sit."

That earns Stella a growl, but she's not swayed. Taking the lead, I walk around the bar and head for the table. Rylan meets my eye briefly, and I simply raise an eyebrow. He huffs but comes over to the table as well.

Even with the distance between us, I'm far too aware of him. I stare at him, and he stares at me, and I think we're both feeling the weird imbalance between us. For the millionth time, I ask myself, what is happening? This is way too confusing for my liking. And for my wolf's liking. She's a little frustrated with me as well. But she's also a little confused about why she wants to run through the woods—with Rylan.

"I'm glad you can communicate without words but sit." Stella's voice breaks through our staring contest, and this time I growl.

"Yes, yes. I know you both are big and bad. But please, we don't have all day." Stella gives us a look that leaves no place for argument. While my alpha really hates taking direction from anyone but…well, myself, I take a seat. I have learned to trust the witches, and I'm not about to stop now.

Rylan stares at Stella as if he can't believe she would speak to him that way. Points to her though, because she doesn't flinch. She just stares right back, and I wait to see which one will win. Finally, Rylan glances at me, and when he finds me sitting down, he sighs in defeat.

"That's better." She sounds a little like my mom. The thought comes uninvited, and with it, the pain. Rylan's eyes fly up to mine, his whole body going rigid with alertness as he looks me over. When his study brings him back to my gaze, we stare at each other in confusion. It's like he's ready to go to battle for me because I'm—in distress?

Whatever our connection may have been as kids, it has grown exponentially since I've been back. As if years of being apart were nothing but a blip in time. I have no idea what to do with that information, so I turn to Stella instead.

"What did you find?"

CHAPTER 3

It's difficult to keep my attention on the witch, but I must. I don't miss the way she studies the two of us before she opens the journal in her hands.

"The Hawthornes and I have been doing research, as you know. That Harper really is a wiz at the library. And I heard the town librarian, Miss Myla, is even more so. I'd love to meet her." Stella gets a faraway look in her eyes, and I can't imagine what it would be like to be so cut off from the magical community—so alone. Well, actually, I guess I can imagine. My heart goes out to her for sure.

"Stella?" Rylan nudges her with that one word, and she's back, giving us a quick smile.

"While we don't know what kind of spell was used to mess with your memories, we definitely believe that's what it was. The girls and I have been talking it over and it makes sense for the discrepancies in your recollections." I try very hard not to look at Rylan. "But since we don't have a starting spell, we have no idea how to counteract it. Our best bet is similar to what the Oracle performed."

"You mean, the vision quest?" Rylan asks. This time I do look at him because we're both thinking the same thing. The vision quest was a complete waste of time. How many times can I lament over remembering next to nothing? Let me count the ways. Unless I take the witch's words into consideration and believe that it opened up my alpha powers. But I can't tell if the Oracle knew it would do that or if it was only a side effect of messing with my mind, after it's already been messed with. Clearly, this is all a big jumble of madness.

"Similar, but yes. Except you do it together. This will rely heavily on you performing—" she stops for a moment, trying to think of a correct terms. "I would say, trust falls. Into each other."

"You want us to practice trust falls?" Rylan looks adorable when he's confused. The way his forehead scrunches up— And I need to stop that train of thought before it develops any further. What is with me? My emotions are completely wild right now. My wolf huffs, as if in agreement.

"Not in a literal 'you get up and fall back into Trinity's arms' kind of a trust fall. But I was thinking, I could do a grounding spell that would open up and clear your mind, and then guide you through a few steps of channeling your inner memories. It won't be a one and done solution, however. Even if we uncover something immediately, you have to continue."

"Continue how?" I ask.

"By talking." She meets my eyes first, then Rylan's. "You have to basically do mental trust falls. Remembering together. Talking about what happened. You have to communicate."

"Well, that's my least favorite pastime," I grumble, and Stella chuckles.

"I know. Both of you would much rather run headfirst into whatever dangerous situation is out there than talk about your feelings, but tough luck, darling. You have no choice."

I sigh, very dramatically, before glancing at Rylan.

"Do you want to fight it out instead?" I ask. He sends a smirk my way.

"Absolutely."

"Knock it off, you two," Stella rolls her eyes, before stepping closer to the table. "But do keep that bonding energy up as we do the spell. Now, hold hands."

My whole body sits up straight at those two words.

"Why?"

"For bonding purposes." Stella is definitely done with my attitude for the moment. I don't want to look at Rylan, but it's like I can't help myself. We've held hands before—it's not like it's that big of a deal. But everything in me is screaming that it's a big deal, and I have no idea what to do about that.

Rylan doesn't seem to be freaking out the way I am, because he holds my gaze steady as he places his hand on the table, palm up. I stare at it for a long moment, as if I've never seen a hand before. Then, he wiggles his fingers, making me jump. I glance up and find him trying not to laugh. The combination is so absurd, I huff once, and then reach over to place my hand over his. The moment our skin touches, I feel that electrifying connection that I can only assign to Rylan, and then his fingers curl over mine.

I feel steady and grounded immediately. Which is incredibly inconvenient for me. My wolf even sighs in contentment, and I want to punch something at this ridiculous response to skin on skin. I really liked my fighting idea better. That way when we touched, it would be purely for training purposes and I wouldn't have to feel like I've just been cut open and am bleeding all over the place because a boy is holding my hand.

I am dramatic. I am okay with this.

Stella clears her throat once and I glance up to find her motioning to the table. I reach out with my other hand and take Rylan's hand like it's a chore, all the while hoping he can't read the raging mess of emotions inside of me.

It's a freaking hand, Trinity. Calm yourself.

But my wolf and I are both on edge, and it's all because of Rylan. I force myself to stay as still as possible while Stella places various crystals and herbs on the table around our hands and then behind our chairs and on the opposite sides of the table. She makes sure to step out of the makeshift square before she speaks.

"Maddie helped me with this, so it'll have a little bit more a punch behind it. It won't be a true spell, like she would do, but it would be a very powerful guidance," she says, and I think about the youngest Hawthorne sister. I never met her, but I heard she has the story spell casting power and it's very rare among witches. Clearly, the Hawthornes are pulling out all the stops to help me. I can't help but feel unworthy of all this fuss.

Rylan squeezes my hand once, and I glance up at him to find him already looking at me. It's like he's anticipating my emotions, and I can't say that I like it. But I also don't hate it. So basically, that is also right there in the confusion state, along with everything else.

He runs his thumb gently over my skin, sending a thousand goosebumps over my body, and it takes all of my self-control not to whimper. It's such a small gesture, but my wolf is going absolutely ballistic at the gentle touch, and it's becoming increasingly difficult not to react.

"Close your eyes, darlings. It's time."

I give Rylan one last long look, and then I close my eyes as Stella begins to talk.

* * *

THE WORDS POUR out of her like a gentle fall of rain, a barely-there caress on my skin. At first, I can't understand what she's saying. She might be speaking another language for all I know, but it doesn't matter, because my body relaxes.

"Focus on my words. Let your mind free."

There's a pause, and then she starts again, as Rylan's hands tighten slightly on mine.

A STORY OF A PACK,
 A journey of two wolves,
 Whose minds interlap,
 Whose hearts beat in two.

THE LIVES TORN APART by words of a witch,
 Is the friendship intact or the loss too rich?

I SINK DEEPER into my mind with each word, but I'm not going alone. Rylan is right there with me. It's like I can see him, even with my eyes closed. He feels so unsure of it all that I'm the one who squeezes his hand in reassurance, and then it's like a door is opened up, and suddenly, we're racing through the forest together.

It's so vivid in my mind's eye, I feel the need to look around. But I keep still and I keep the focus on the words.

NO MATTER THE DISTANCE, *no matter the pain,*
 The souls beat in rhythm,
 And time heals the way.

THE MEMORIES COME, *unashamed, unafraid,*
 No veil of forgetfulness,
 No reason to be dismayed.

ALL DOUBTS STRIPPED AWAY,
 The path made whole,
 If only the souls would choose to walk it
 Together, never alone.

SO CLEAR YOUR MIND,
 And let your heart speak the truth.
 The two souls are ready,
 To know what is true.

STELLA'S VOICE fades with the last word, but maybe she speaks again, and I just can't hear it. I'm watching a memory unfold—and experiencing it at the same time. It's like I'm in two places at once, the past and the present.

. . .

I'M ABOUT ten years old, sitting in the middle of our old house, a bunch of different books open in front of me, and I'm holding a collection of flowers. My brows are furrowed in concentration as I clean off the stems, one leaf at a time.

"Please tell me you're not seriously going to do that whole flower pressing thing?" Rylan asks as he walks in, not even bothering to knock. He's thirteen and already much taller than me. Overnight, he's grown bigger and stronger than he's ever been. And cuter. But I refuse to admit that, even to myself. It's been about a year since I started noticing what he looks like, and not in any annoying "eww" kind of a way, but in that way that girls do when they first start noticing a boy. In that way that makes them all giggly and flirty. I, of course, compensated for all the giggling by beating him in every training session.

"Of course I am," I say, without taking my eyes off the flowers. "Mom said it was all the rage when she was a kid."

"What are you going to do with them once they're all squished?" Rylan asks, sitting down cross-legged in front of me. I glance up, just taking in his sheer size. Even sitting down, he towers over me. He leans closer, over the books, and glances up at me with his hair falling in his face. I feel my face heat up at his proximity and I lean back immediately. I can't tell if he can tell that I'm blushing, but I'm really hoping he thinks it's just the light playing tricks off my red dress.

The dress is one of my favorites. My parents got it for me as a birthday gift, and I've been wearing it as much as I can. The skirt flares out around me when I twirl, which I have only been doing behind closed doors—I have an image to uphold, after all.

"I don't know," I reply, keeping my attention on the flowers. "I think it'll be cool to put them in a frame. Mom's got one of those *glass ones, from her time living with the humans. It presses the picture inside."*

"When did you get so crafty?" Rylan chuckles and I take offense immediately.

"When did you get so annoying?" I throw back.

"Whatever. You love me and my fantastic personality. I'm the coolest."

"You can't be the coolest. That spot has already been taken by me."

"Oh, is that right? Who said?"

I'm still keeping my attention on the flowers, but it's like I can feel him moving closer.

"Me, obviously. No one else's opinion matters. Duh."

"Not even mine?"

"Especially not yours."

This time I do look at him, and we're both cracking up, as he reaches for me, like he's going to grab me. This is his typical move before we wrestle.

"No! Keep your stupid hands to yourself. You're going to crush the flowers."

"How can my hands be stupid?" Rylan laughs, raising them up so he can flex. "They're amazing. Because I'm amazing."

"You're dumb. And your arms are dumb. Now, stop distracting me."

Rylan laughs again, but then I feel him move. When I glance up, he has settled into a comfortable pose, leaning back against the couch, his eyes on me.

"What are you doing?" I ask, narrowing my gaze on him.

"I'm not doing anything."

"You're doing something."

"Fine. I'm keeping you company. Now, shouldn't you be working on your flowers?"

I stare at him, as if he's lost his mind.

"You're just going to sit there until I'm done? Why?"

He takes a moment to respond, his eyes on the books and the flowers, as he seems to think it over.

"Because this is important to you," he finally says, looking up at me.

THE MEMORY ENDS ABRUPTLY, and I'm back in control of my body. The emotions I felt back then—how significant those simple words were to me—slam into me with intensity. Opening my eyes, I meet Rylan's gaze. He looks just as unbalanced as I feel.

"The flowers," he says slowly, "Your tiny obsession of pressing the flowers into books. It lasted maybe—a week. But you were so proud of them and the way you decorated the frame after. I didn't—" He clears his throat. "I forgot all about that."

"So did I."

My voice is barely above a whisper as I try to calm my racing heart. Such a simple memory, but it's such an important one. Our friendship—it was my whole world. It made the exile so much worse when it was delivered by the one person who made me feel—everything.

My wolf is in as much of a distress as I am, and I take a deep breath to calm her, trying to focus my mind on why we're doing this in a first place.

"I don't understand. Why would someone care about making us forget such a small innocent moment in our childhood? It has nothing to do with what happened." I turn my attention to Stella, who's sitting on one of the barstools, facing us. She gets down now, and comes forward.

"Because whoever messed with your memories wanted to break your bond. And it looks like they succeeded."

Rylan squeezes my hand, pulling my attention to him, as I try to keep the sudden tears at bay. He looks just as confused and broken as I am and somehow that stitches together a small wound in my heart. I nod at him, and he nods at me. When I retract my hand, it feels empty immediately.

"So the spell worked?" I ask Stella.

"It did."

"But this wasn't the memory we needed to clear up," I say.

"It's what your mind needed to clear up," Stella replies. "Now it'll be up to you to make sure it continues to do so."

"How?" Rylan asks.

"You'll know. When the time comes, take each other's hands and remember."

These instructions are so simple and vague. I thank Stella and stand, needing the space away from everything to think.

CHAPTER 4

I don't go far, considering we're trying to keep as close to the bar and the protection it provides as possible. I don't have to ask Rylan if he ran around the whole town a bunch before making his way back to the bar when he returned. It's what I would've done. Our scent is all over the town, and we're leaving it that way to make sure our pursuers are at least a little bit confused.

I dodge one of the couples standing in the middle of the sidewalk, taking a picture. While I don't find Holden as picturesque as Hawthorne, it does carry that small town charm that people seem to like. Plus, the mountains in the distance add something special.

The main street is filled with window shopping displays, and there are flower planters on the edges of sidewalk. But unlike Hawthorne, this town doesn't have the multicolored buildings, mostly brown and white. Which looks very intentional but makes me miss the warmth. Granted, I probably miss my friends more. And considering this town and the surrounding area just holds a lot of hostility for us, it's okay that I don't get attached.

It is a bit weird that we've been left alone. They do know where we are, so I have no idea why they haven't returned to Stella's bar for us. Maybe they think we wouldn't be dumb enough to make a safe haven where they can find us. But she is keeping it protected, so at least I know if they do return, they can only do so as humans. No mutated monsters for them. It's honestly the only reason I'm okay with staying in town. My wolf and I would like nothing more than to run straight into the forest and meet those wolves head on.

Actually, maybe that's exactly what I need to do.

My other option is trying to process the emotional hurricane currently raging inside of me after the spell, and I am definitely not in the mood for that.

Ignoring emotions, Trinity Whitewolf specialty.

I'm going into the woods, I open up the pack link, because I am trying to be better about working with Rylan instead of against him.

Not a good idea. His response is immediate, because of course it is. I roll my eyes even though he can't see me.

I wasn't asking for permission. Okay, maybe the working together needs some work.

Then let me come with you.

No, I think it be best—

Trinity.

Rylan.

Even though he's back at the bar and I'm in the middle of Main Street, I can feel his frustration with me. But it only makes me grin. I am much more comfortable with us being at each other's throats than when he's holding my hand and trying to comfort me.

Is this your way of running from what we remembered?

There's nothing to run from, I say quickly, trying to keep my emotions in check in case he can feel any of them seeping through. *I'm just tired of sitting around and waiting for something to happen. Why haven't they come for us, Rylan? They know where we are!*

So what you're actually saying is that you want to use yourself as bait?

Stupid wolf, annoyingly direct. He knows me way too well for my liking. It's like he's reading my mind. Because that is exactly what I want to do. I want to fight these wolves on my terms. It's impossible to do so because they can track us. Our shifter magic is something that can be honed on if someone is smart enough to figure out how and has some magic on their side. We can't exactly say the same for the rabid wolves, because I didn't feel magic in them last time we came face to face. Now I just feel like putting that to a test. My wolf and I really like that idea.

I'm going. You can either come with me and have my back, or— I don't even have to finish that because he's already growling in annoyance.

This is not my idea of working together.

Oh please, I feel his agreement even with the distance. *You're itching for a fight just as much as I am. Tell me I'm wrong.*

You're wrong. He says immediately, but we both know he doesn't mean it. I grin, probably looking like a lunatic to the people walking by, but I don't care.

Liar. I'm heading for the woods. Keep enough distance so they can't tell I'm not alone. I pivot into an alley, heading toward the neighborhood and the forest beyond.

I don't like when you boss me around. Rylan is definitely sounding extra grumpy, but I can't help the smile that won't leave my lips. It's the alpha in him. The confused part where he's the one who makes the rules, but there's also me, who makes the rules. It's a strange dynamic, to say the least.

Liar, I say again, and then I'm past the houses and in the backyard, shifting for the first time in days. My wolf is immediately ecstatic, and the moment I'm in the woods, I take off running.

The forest opens up around me with sharp clarity. My senses expand, picking up every ruffle of leaves and every buzz of an insect. I breathe fully for the first time in days, my wolf's joy mirroring my own. The feel of the dirt beneath my paws makes my whole body buzz as I weave in and out of the trees and bushes. The woods around me are my first home, the forest part of the White Wolf territory, even if it's a little far from our village. They're still my childhood woods, still a place I feel the most connected to the earth.

I run away from the village and the bar, heading toward the river. It separates the woods north of the town. There are areas past there that I haven't visited recently, and one of these days we need to take a trip. Our pack's territory is larger than many, which is why it's so important for us—for me—to make sure the wolves are safe. It involves many more wolves under my care than just my own pack.

When I'm near the major interstate, northeast from the town, I feel the sudden stillness. My link is still open to Rylan, but neither of us speak. I don't want to give away any kind of advantage, in case by some magical miracle they can sense the magic of the pack link. While no one can intercept a pack link, it just feels right to stay silent. But I can feel Rylan's caution, just like I feel my own. I'm near something, and he's farther away than he would like to be. I try to open my senses even more, searching for the rabid wolves, but there's nothing. Just silence.

So I slow down, still moving through the woods but no longer running. When I come to a stop, I search the space around me, but I can't see anything. However, the sense of tension creeps in toward me, as I try to pinpoint the source.

It's the growl that reaches me first.

* * *

Spinning around, I study my surroundings thoroughly, trying to pick up something through my shifter senses. The sound echoes against the trees, reverberating through the forest. It comes at me from every direction, making my heart beat faster in my chest.

When the wolf leaps out of the shadows, I'm almost a half second too slow. But I move at the last moment, sidestepping the jump. The monstrous creature lands beside me, saliva dripping from his open mouth. I can tell immediately that he's already gone—there's no human left in those eyes. Just like before, I feel no magic in him, not even a drop.

He crouches low, a growl deep in his throat. Past experience has taught me they never travel alone, there must be at least one more somewhere beyond my sight. The wolf in front of me snaps his jaw, spraying the area around him with his spit. I wait, keeping myself as still as possible. If I attack first, I'm done for. If these wolves operate at all how the pack usually does, the other one will flank me, and there will be no getting out of it. Even in this state, they feed off each other. Or someone is feeding them the information.

Either way, maybe this wasn't the greatest idea.

The beating of my own heart drowns out the next growl.

I can feel the danger surround me. Whatever this wolf is waiting for, I will have to fight with every part of me to get out. I tense, preparing myself for the attack. But when the wolf pushes off his legs toward me, there's a split second of fear, which is quickly replaced by another emotion.

Hope.

A white wolf barrels out of the trees and toward my attacker, intercepting him before he can reach me. Another two rabid wolves come from the trees, and I don't even have a moment to wonder how Rylan got here so fast, before they're on us.

Rylan swipes at the wolf in front of him, scratching him straight across his face. The other wolf howls, this time in pain. I force my own body to remain calm as I turn toward the others. They jump at me as one, giving me less than a second to decide my move.

Instead of running away, I launch myself toward them. The motion takes them by surprise, but they're already past me when they land. I twist my large wolf body, jumping straight on top of one of the wolves and digging my claws into his back. The wolf howls in agony as he goes down, and I don't let go until my nails are inches deep. I rip them out, as I jump off. The wolf drops straight to the ground, as the other leaps toward me.

But then Rylan is there again and the two of us flank the remaining wolf on both sides. The wolf glances between us, then he turns and bolts into the forest, leaving his fallen mates behind. We don't hesitate to take off after him, but his movement is much faster than we can keep up with, and that's saying something. The wolf almost blurs in front of us, fading in and out of sight, until he's completely gone.

Rylan and I continue moving for another fifteen minutes, but we can't find him. Gone without a trace, just like before.

We stop, and I shift, running my hand through my hair in frustration. Rylan shifts as well, and I can feel his eyes on me as I pace.

"That was entirely pointless," I say.

"It was."

"But a good workout?" I ask. Rylan almost grins. That was definitely better than sparring with him and worked off some of that nervous energy we've been carrying around.

I twist around, throwing a glare at Rylan, who's now leaning against the tree, his legs crossed at the ankles, looking like a GQ model. Harper had to show me some examples of what that looks like, since she uses that as her favorite way to describe her husband.

Rylan has always been gorgeous, but the years have done him good. His boyish looks have matured into those of a refined man, with dark hair that could use a cut, a strong jaw, and shoulders that are broad and capable of holding up the world. At least, that's how I've always thought of him, strong and safe. Of course, that's before he exiled me. There I go, being all hot and cold again. I'm giving myself a headache.

"It was a good plan," I sigh, turning back to the forest, hoping to see something that will give us a clue about where the wolves have gone. "Do you think they tracked us or we just stumbled into their guard territory? Maybe whoever is behind this is also testing things. Maybe—" I trail off, because I don't even know what I'm talking about anymore.

Rylan doesn't say anything, and when I turn back around, his eyes are still on me. Since I've been back—returned against my will because the Oracle said I'm needed—we've been at two different points. One, where we're constantly at each other's throats, or two, where we're not talking about whatever it is that's happening between us.

But now there's the fact that our memories were messed with and we don't even know where we stand. Also, we will not—and I repeat—will not be mentioning the kiss. I refuse to even think about it.

Here I am, thinking about it.

I am too worked up to be of any use to anyone right now, myself included.

"We should probably head back to Stella's," I say, because that's all I can come up with. My eyes are still on the forest around us, but I feel like that last encounter is all we'll get today. I can't tell if the wolves were actually tracking us or if we happened into their territory. We literally have no information when it comes to them. And it's beyond maddening.

When Rylan still doesn't say anything, I turn back around, stepping into his line of sight, and wave my hand in front of his face. His eyes fly to mine, sending me a glare. That's more like it.

"You done napping? Can we go?" I ask.

He rolls his eyes, a habit he's clearly picked up from me, before pushing away from the tree.

"We really not going to talk about it?" Rylan asks, and I'm shaking my head before he's even finished with the question.

"There's nothing to talk about."

"Right, which is exactly why you rather throw yourself into danger than look me in the eye."

He's got me there. It makes me want to punch him. Instead, I take a deep breath and turn to look him directly in the eye. He holds my gaze unwavering, a small smirk on his lips. What I wouldn't do to wipe that smile of his smug face. Or kiss it away.

The moment the thought crosses my mind, I squish it. But I'm not fast enough. Rylan's eyes darken, as if he can see the thought written in my eyes. A small growl resounds somewhere in the back of his throat and I hold myself completely still, afraid of what would happen if one of us moved.

This is how we are with each other—always at a standstill. Even though that should mean we have a solid foundation beneath us, in reality, it's the opposite. I want to throttle him, and I want to kiss him senseless. Now, someone, please explain that to me.

"Trin—"

"Don't." I don't want to hear anything he might say, because I'm afraid that he'll say exactly what I'm thinking, and then where would we be?

"We have to."

"No, we don't."

He finally breaks whatever spell he's holding me under as he reaches up to run a hand through his hair, sending it in disarray.

"You're driving me nuts. Why can't you have a normal conversation?"

"Oh, you want a normal conversation?" Now I'm fired up. He's absolutely not putting all the blame on me here. "You mean where we actually talk—both of us—about our feelings and thoughts and everything that's going on in that head of yours. Because if you're willing to share, by all means."

I cross my arms in front of me, cocking my head to the side, as I watch him. Because I know I got him on this. He doesn't want to be first to tell me how he's feeling either.

"You're impossible." He sighs, shaking his head.

"Right back at ya, babe."

We both freeze at my use of the nickname. I have no idea where that came from, but I decide I'm not backing down from it. I raise my chin a little, as if challenging him to say something, and he surprises me with that small smile again.

Then, without another word, he shifts and turns back toward town. I guess that's that. For now. I'm sure we'll be yelling at each other again soon enough.

CHAPTER 5

When we reach the bar, it's going in full swing. Stella has modified the hours, only opening it up to the public after five and going till two in the morning, but that hasn't hurt the business at all.

"I take it, it didn't go well," Stella says as Rylan and I walk up to the bar. She's changed into one of her dark pants and red corset outfits, leaving her hair braided, with a few wisps falling out. Honestly, she looks ready to take on anyone who might try to mess with her. It's the image I aspire to portray. Also, judging by her statement, I assume Rylan told her what I was doing before he left to come after me.

"The trap worked, but we couldn't follow," I say, taking a seat at the bar. The place is getting fuller by the minute, the music so loud I can feel it vibrating off my skin. Doesn't stop the sparks of awareness at Rylan's proximity, as he hovers at my back. He has this thing about keeping himself at my back, like a self-appointed bodyguard against anyone who might approach me. I have conflicting emotions about it. Part of me is offended, but a bigger part of me likes it. That second part is the one that's trying really hard not to lean back against him. I'm definitely losing my mind here. It's probably because I need rest.

"It was worth a try," Stella says, oblivious to my inner freak out. Or maybe she's aware, as I see her eyes squint for a moment in my direction. She hands each of us a glass of water, before walking into the kitchen. She comes back a few seconds later, carrying two steaming plates of food.

"Eat up," she says, placing the bowls in front of us. It looks like a potato and meat stew, and it smells delicious. My stomach rumbles and I chuckle at the timing. When I glance over at Rylan, he meets my eye, and I swear there's a spark of amusement there. I turn away quickly, digging into the stew.

Distance. Rylan and I need distance. But instead, he leans on the bar beside me, eating his own stew. There's barely any room, not with people pushing at each other to try to get drinks or food. Stella doesn't have a big menu at the moment, but she made food for us.

"Maybe we should take this upstairs?" I ask Rylan when two different people glance over at us and ask Stella for "some of that goodness." He nods, picking up both bowls and holds them over his head, which puts them way out of reach of anyone else as we move through the crowd. I give Stella a quick wave, and she only nods, before moving on.

Two days ago, I asked her if we could help during open hours, and she very politely told me that we would only cause a riot and she doesn't have time to deal with over-enthusiastic flirts, trying for Rylan and mine attention. Apparently, she remembers Rylan's possessive reaction to someone asking me to dance. Something I very much try not to think about on the regular. So we help behind the scenes, but she's got other people to work during business hours.

I silently follow Rylan upstairs to the room we've claimed as our own. I think all the adrenaline has left my body, and all I want to do is sleep. This day has been a long one.

When we step inside the room, I head directly for the bed. I flop right down on it, my dress pulling around my thighs. Rylan stays in the doorway, but I can feel his gaze on me. Tugging my shoes off, I crisscross my legs in front of me, rearranging my dress, before finally looking up at Rylan.

There's something in his gaze, some kind of an emotion he doesn't actually want me to see, and a shutter comes over his eyes the moment they meet mine. I stare at him, trying to process everything I've felt today. His being gone, the spell, his coming to my rescue…

"How did you get to the forest so fast?" I ask, and my voice tugs him back to reality, as he straightens from the doorway and walks over to hand me my bowl. Instead of taking a seat beside me, he sits on the floor, with his back to the wall and his legs stretched out in front of him. He's tall enough that in this cramped space if I put my feet back down to the floor, they'd be touching his.

"I was right behind you," is all he says, as he continues eating. I narrow my eyes at him, as I take a spoonful of the stew.

"Were you already tracking me?" I was gone for barely thirty minutes before I got my mad idea to dash into the forest.

"I was in the area."

That's all he says, and he proceeds to concentrate on the food like it's the most fascinating thing on the planet. Wasn't he just telling me that we need to stop not communicating? And what is he doing but that exact thing! I swear, this shifter is going to be the catalyst that actually makes me lose my mind. We're both being ridiculous, and neither one of us is going to own up to it. That much I know for a fact.

"Can we check on the pack?" I ask as soon as I'm finished eating. Rylan has been taking his time, as if that one bowl of stew will protect him from me. I'm not sure why that's the way I'm thinking about it, but it makes a lot of sense.

"Of course," he replies immediately. If it's pack business, we will put our differences aside and work on it together.

He places his now-empty bowl on the floor and takes a seat beside me on the bed. It dips immensely, shifting my body into his, and I have to pull myself away before I sink in any deeper. Because that's what my body automatically starts to do. Seriously, I'm going nuts.

Rylan places his hand, palm up, on his knee, his eyes on me. We can check on the pack without touching. But since I'm new to this, Rylan has been showing me how to access this particular alpha power. We've learned that somehow this helps the link to be united, and the pack feels better when it comes across as such. Maybe because they can tell Rylan is present through it, or maybe simply because I feel like I know what I'm doing when we're linked, and that translates to the pack. Who knows really, we're learning as we go. I've touched Rylan plenty of times in the last few days, and yet, every single time, I have to prepare myself.

I place my hand in his and his fingers curl over mine immediately. My hand fits so perfectly in his big one, and my skin turns hot at the simple touch. I try not to fidget in place, but then his thumb makes one gentle swipe against my skin, and I nearly jump up off the bed. A trail of sparks starts at that small touch, travels up my arm, and then spreads all over my body. I try to keep my breathing even, taking a deep inhale, before letting it out slowly.

Then, without a word, I open up the pack link. Rylan is already there with me. We feel a lot of uncertainty and some fear, but no distress, which makes me breathe a little easier.

Everything calm? Rylan asks, and I feel Ezra and Zach perk up immediately.

Nothing new to report. All quiet, Ezra replies, and there's a small pause before he asks, *Something happened?*

Maybe he can tell there's a new tension between Rylan and me, or maybe he's just that perceptive. I glance at Rylan, but his eyes are on our hands.

Nothing new to report. Just wanted you to know I'm back. He echoes his beta's words, but I don't think they buy it. They won't question him though. *We'll check in in the morning,* he says.

Understood, Zach and Ezra reply, and then Rylan cuts the link. He doesn't let go of my hand immediately, staring at it for a moment longer. Then, it's like he remembers where he is and with whom, so he uncurls his fingers from mine and stands. Without a look in my direction, he shuts himself in the tiny bathroom.

I stare at the door, as I try to process my own emotions. Sharing an alpha link is becoming like second nature to us, but it's also opening me up to a plethora of emotions.

Honestly, never in a million years did I think I'd be back with my old pack—back with Rylan. Growing up, we were inseparable. Until he separated us in the worst way possible by exiling me from the only family I had left.

That knowledge, that rift between us, is everywhere we go. The moment we start moving toward each other, start finding some solid ground, the rift opens up again, and we're back to being on opposite sides of it.

But then to discover that those blocks of dynamite that

were thrown at our friendship weren't thrown by us but by someone who wanted to manipulate us? Our connection is as strong as it was when we were kids, back when we were still open to the possibilities of who we would one day become. It makes me want to trust him, even though so much of me still doesn't because I can't get away from thinking he has his own ideas and agendas. But then, I see the softer side of him, the one who will race into the forest to have my back or hold my hand with the utmost gentleness.

I make sure to move the bowl against the wall before I pull up the covers and climb under them. I'm too tired to change out of my dress and too drained to process any more of today. With thoughts of Rylan, I close my eyes and give myself over to sleep.

I'M in the midst of the dream before I know what's happening. The darkness is ever-present, squeezing me from every side, as I try to make myself move from this one spot. The water under my feet is still and black, and no matter how much I fight against it, I can't move.

The pain comes next. It doesn't sneak up on me in little bursts but rushes in all at once. I nearly double over from it, gasping for air. It feels like someone is punching me, moving around my body to make sure to hit me from every side. It's the same as usual, and yet different somehow. More intense, more realistic. I can't catch my breath enough to clear my head.

Fear and pain fill every part of me. I turn to look behind me, just as another wave of assault hits me. I fall to my knees, slamming them down hard as I wrap my arms around my middle. It's like I'm trying to keep myself together, because it feels like I'm being torn apart.

The scream that finally rips from my soul shatters the stillness of the water. Suddenly, waves surround me, and I'm kneeling in the middle of a storm. The voices reach out to me, crying, and in agony, and I feel it all.

Trinity!

The voice—the one voice that I want to hear more than anything—pushes through all the others, and suddenly, I'm back to myself.

I sit up in bed, falling right into Rylan's arms. He pulls me to him, and I cling to his shirt, my body shaking. He must've woken me, because he's kneeling beside me. All I can do is gasp as the aftershocks of the pain rush through my body.

"Shh, Trin. You're okay." His words are lost somewhere in my hair, as he places his lips against my head. The shaking doesn't recede, and I can't seem to form a coherent thought.

"Forget this." Rylan mumbles. He grabs my thighs and twists his body backward. My legs drop on either side of him, as he places me directly on his lap, pulling me as tightly against him as he can. I don't hesitate to wrap my arms around his middle, burying my head in his chest, as he leans back against the wall.

I can feel his hand running up and down my back, and I concentrate my whole attention on it, as it travels down and then up. My breathing returns to normal, slowly, with each stroke of his hand.

When I think I can finally sit up without passing out, I pull back. His arms go still immediately, but he doesn't unwind them from around me. I lean back, finding his eyes on me. There's a rage of emotion there, worry and possessiveness—they fill my heart with more confusion than anything else.

He feels too right, too much like I belong right here in his arms. I have to put distance between us. It's my specialty after all. I push back farther, and this time he doesn't try to stop me. His arms come off me, and I swing my leg back over, so I'm sitting beside him instead of on his lap. I won't admit this out loud, but I miss his warmth immediately.

"That was different." Rylan finally breaks the silence, and all I can do is nod. He pushes himself off the wall, sliding down the bed, and then standing. He stalks over to the bathroom and returns with a cup of water, handing it to me. I gulp it down in full and hand it back to him.

"Stop staring at me like that," I say, when he doesn't move away.

"Like what?"

"Like I'm broken," I snap, but I can't help it. His penetrating eyes see too much, and I have to put my armor back up, because that simple comforting hug just broke it back down. Everything he does seems to get through my defenses.

"That's definitely not how I'm looking at you," Rylan growls and I finally meet his gaze again.

"Then enlighten me," I say.

"No."

That makes me laugh, and the sound surprises both of us. I'm more tired now than I was when I first went to sleep. My body feels like it's been through a fight.

"How long was I out?" I ask.

"About two hours." Rylan replies, finally moving back to the bathroom. He leaves the cup in there, then he comes out and leans against the wall again. I can tell he's just as full of energy as I am, but he doesn't know what to do with it.

Looking at him leaning like that, I have a few ideas. Immediately, I beg my face not to blush. Okay, wow, Trinity, you are all over the place.

"It was different," I sigh, trying to get myself back on track. "Typically, the dream is always the same. I'm frozen in darkness, with sounds and feelings of pain reaching out to me. But this time? It was like there was more." I haven't had the dream since I was a kid, but the first time I had it after seeing Rylan again, he had to use his alpha command to get me out. Much like tonight.

"More of what?"

"Of everything. The pain, the voices, the feeling of helplessness." Wow, my wolf really doesn't like me admitting that out loud, but I have no choice. She's just as agitated as I am.

"What do you think that means?"

"I have no idea, but maybe Stella will be able to tell us."

I can still hear the distance noise of the bar and the music. Stella didn't come up, so maybe she didn't feel my distress. Or maybe she can tell I'm fine. Since she reads auras, she's more attuned to emotions than anyone else I've met. I must not have put out so much emotional distress that she has to check on me. Either way, it'll be a question for tomorrow. Right now, even in this state, all I want to do is sleep.

Rylan watches me from the bathroom doorway, and it's like he knows exactly what I'm thinking. He turns the bathroom light off, then walks back over to the bed. He climbs up, lying down on his back close to the middle of the bed. He doesn't meet my eyes or reach for me.

"I'll watch over you while you sleep," he whispers in the darkness, which is the best reassurance he could give me. It was his voice that pulled me out after all. He's the best person around to do so, but I also can't help feeling just how intimate this is, and how much both my wolf and I are desperate for it—to have someone watching our back, even as we sleep.

So instead of ruining it all by saying something I'll regret, I lie back down on the bed, also on my back, with only a few inches of space between us. I can feel him, as clearly as if he was pressed up against me, and I focus on his breathing. It's calmer than my own. With his heat reaching out to me and his promise on his lips, I close my eyes once more and sleep.

CHAPTER 6

The next morning when I wake up, I'm alone. Rylan's side of the bed feels cold, and I have no idea how long he's been gone. Clearly, my dream knocked me completely out, because normally I would've known the moment he got up. I ignore the pang of disappointment and slide off the bed. Now is as good a time as any to take a shower and put on fresh clothes.

I picked up two new dresses, thanks to Stella, along with some other personal things. There weren't that many options, and I probably could've gone with something else, but the red dresses make me feel like myself—right now, I can use all the help I can get. My current option is a cotton A-line with a flair skirt, straps for sleeves, and a square neckline. It's simple but it fits like it was made for me, falling at mid-thigh. It also has pockets, which was the greatest discovery. I run a brush through my hair but leave it to air dry as I head downstairs.

Stella is behind the bar when I step into the main room, and there's a cup of coffee resting in front of a barstool.

"Good morning," she greets me, motioning to the cup. I make a straight line for it.

"Good morning," I say, before taking a sip. I'm trying not to look for Rylan, but my senses reach out around the building anyway.

"I asked Rylan to do a quick run for me." Stella says, as if reading my mind. I turn my attention back to her, frowning. "He needed something to do."

That's a loaded statement if I've ever heard one. Stella watches me for a long moment, as I pretend to find my coffee fascinating. She walks to the kitchen and comes back with a plate of food.

"Stella, you have already done so much for us. You don't have to go through all this trouble." I stare at the bacon and eggs like they've personally offended me, but Stella only waves me off.

"I enjoy every minute of fussing over you two, so you'd better not take that away from me."

She turns away before I can say anything else. Maybe that's for the best. Stella doesn't talk about her family or her coven. I asked Leah if we can trust her, since Leah is the only other Reader I know, and she said yes. But just like with everyone, I am cautious with my trust at the moment. Looking at Stella, I can't imagine her as anything other than who she is. But what do I know. Someone messed with my mind, so maybe I'm a terrible judge of character. But for now, I eat my breakfast…and resist the urge to reach out to Rylan through the pack link to see what he's doing.

When I'm nearly done, Stella comes back in. From the clipboard in her hands, I assume she's doing inventory.

"You ready to talk about it?" she asks, putting the clipboard down and giving me her undivided attention.

"I don't know what you mean," I say, before taking the last bite of bacon. Stella sure can cook! She's also as stubborn as I am, because she simply watches me with a knowing look in her eyes until I'm completely finished eating.

"You really think I didn't feel that incredible amount of emotional energy coming from your room last night?"

"It was nothing."

"I would've said it was you and your boy, but there was a lot of pain and darkness there. If I didn't feel your immediate calm right after, I would've been upstairs in a flash."

I completely ignore her "your boy" comment and focus on the rest. I thought she would be able to feel it, but when she didn't come, I—I don't know what I was thinking. But it was the calm after the storm that stopped her?

"It was a dream," I say, seeing no point of keeping it from her, especially since I wanted to talk to her about it anyway. "The same one I've had before, even back when I was a kid, but it was different somehow. More powerful? I don't know. I just—I felt overwhelmed by the emotions."

"Whose?"

I glance up at her, and find her eyes on me. There's a bit of comfort in them, as well as sympathy.

"I'm not sure. It feels like…everyone's. I'm standing on top of water, and it's pitch black, when the emotions of a hundred people assault me from every side. I can't move and I can't do anything but take the hits. Rylan—he had to use his alpha command to get me out."

"And that's not how it used to be?"

"No. I would wake up, sweaty and disoriented, but not like this. It's been years since I've had the dream."

"When did it return?"

I think back, trying to remember if I had any dreams in the last few years, but no. It came back recently.

"The day Rylan picked me up from Jefferson. I feel asleep in the truck and—"

"And you dreamed." Rylan chooses that moment to return. Suddenly, I don't know what to do with myself. The memory of his arms holding me close, tucking me into his embrace, is imprinted in my brain forever. Mixed with the kiss we shared in this very bar and the intense emotional rollercoaster that is our whole relationship, I have no idea how I have any coherent thought in my brain at this point. What happened to that tough she-wolf who can handle anything that was thrown at her? Her gorgeous best friend, that's what.

I push the brakes—or whatever Harper always says—as I try to keep my mind focused on the dream and not the walking dream in front of me.

Whoa. Who am I? I have been taken over by a very antsy and angsty hormonal teenager. Which is technically me—but I've been working so hard to appear anything but!

"So it started when you came back," Stella says, still oblivious to my current freak out. Either that or she's just careful about bringing attention to it for which I am grateful. When I meet her eyes, I don't miss the gleam in them. Oh, yeah. She's definitely aware.

"Yes, once I was back with the pack."

"It must be related to that...proximity." I can almost see Stella's mind working as she ponders it and try very hard not to move as Rylan takes the seat beside me. From what I can see, he's not carrying anything, so I have no idea what kind of an errand Stella sent him on.

"Maybe it has something to do with her being alpha,"

Rylan comments, reaching over the bar to grab a bottle of water. Stella and I both turn to look at him in surprise, as he twists the cap off and takes a swig.

"Explain," I say, when he doesn't continue. He meets my gaze then, and as it's become our typical fashion, neither of us looks away, holding the other captive.

"I've been thinking about it," Rylan says, his eyes still on me. "The first dream, at the back of the truck, threw out some crazy emotional waves. I mean, the guys nearly shifted."

"What?"

We both ignore Stella.

"And then, after we saw the Oracle, they became even more powerful. But still, after we returned to the pack and you were called alpha...it's like the dreams are out of control."

"You think the dreams are her alpha connection," Stella says, and Rylan nods.

"But my pack is not in pain, not the way these people are."

"Trin, if you're the True Alpha like your witches think you are, you won't be simply channeling our pack. You'll be channeling the wolves in the whole region." Rylan says the words carefully, as if he's afraid he's going to spook me. Good thing, because I do feel spooked. If the whole True Alpha isn't enough responsibility as it is, now I may be have a physical and emotional proof of it.

"It's only a guess," he quickly adds, leaning toward me as if he can predict my near freak out. He probably can. I'm close enough, I doubt he even needs to use any powers.

"It's a good guess, and I think a lot closer to the truth than you'd like," Stella comments. But I'm not listening any longer. My chest fills with that tightness I've come to expect any time I feel too much, all at once. My breathing shallows as well, my hands trembling as I try to process.

A slight pressure catches my attention, and I look down to see Rylan's big hand covering both of mine on my lap. When I look up at him, his eyes are full of comfort and focused entirely on me. We stare at each other, that constant awareness burning hotter, as if we've thrown some more logs on it. At this point, this fire is going to get out of control if we don't knock it off by feeding it.

A sound of the phone breaks the connection and I glance over at Stella, who looks apologetically at me, before reaching for her phone. Then she smiles at the screen.

"The Hawthornes have something for you."

As I wait for the video call to connect with the Hawthornes, I run my hand over my amethyst bracelet automatically, while Rylan hovers over my shoulder. I expect to see Leah when I open the call on Stella's computer, but it's the eldest Hawthorne sister that greets me.

"Hi, Brianna," I say, and she smiles.

"Sorry to spring my presence on you, Trinity. Leah is helping Harper with some coven business."

"Is everything okay?" I immediately perk up because I'm not the only one with magical problems. The town of Hawthorne has suffered plenty at the hands of the Ancients, and they continue to keep a strong hold on their borders. Hawthorne is built on a powerful nexus and that's not something the witches are going to give up to the Ancients.

"Yes, we're safe for now, but still cautious."

I've heard her say that before…or maybe it was her

mother when I was at one of the town's meetings. They may be safe but they're still fighting. A part of me really wishes I could be there for them, like they've been there for me, but I have my own battles to fight—more than I know, apparently. I try not to think about the shifter hovering over my right shoulder.

"What did you find out?" I ask, focusing on the witch. She reaches for something off screen. It's a book, a very, very big one. She can't hold it up, even with two hands, and moves backward to place it against the table and her knees.

"There are many human stories that talk about shape shifting. Often, in the olden days and especially in mythologies, shape shifting was used as a punishment by the gods… or as a way to infiltrate the human world without alerting anyone to their being higher beings. There are so many records of trickster gods and deities, of magical entities walking the earth for their own amusement."

"The Ancients," I whisper, and Brianna looks up, giving me a firm nod.

"Exactly. For generations, these were just stories used to entertain and teach children about the balance of good and evil. But now that we know the Ancients exist, we can look to these stories for the truth."

"But how do you know which parts are truth and which ones are just skewed stories passed down through generations?" Rylan asks, leaning over my shoulder so he's in the frame for Brianna. She gives him a warm smile, which isn't at all to my liking, even though Brianna has a soulmate. Okay, something to ponder later.

"We don't know, and sadly there isn't an easy solution. The best we can do is find patterns in all this information—something that stands out enough—and then investigate."

Brianna gives me an apologetic look. "I wish there was another way, but all I have are bits and pieces."

I take a deep breath. I knew this wasn't going to be easy. When is life ever easy?

"Okay, so what bits and pieces do you have?" Brianna gives me a proud smile before she glances down at her book.

"There's a god, Veles, who is portrayed as many different reincarnations throughout various regions as the god of the earth. He is also a god of waters and the underworld, with a love for theatrics."

"He was a shifter?"

"I believe so. Many stories talk about a great dragon. Others describe him as just a large serpent. He was both good and evil, depending on the situation."

I know what Brianna is saying. They recently discovered that not all Ancients are evil. I still find that hard to believe. I think that the Ancients just hold to a different set of rules. Their good and bad might be on a whole other scale from our definitions. But I'm trying not to be skeptical. Well, at least not out loud.

"So how does that help us now?" Rylan moves back into frame, and I feel the heat of his body as he leans closer. He's being skeptical out loud, but Brianna isn't deterred. He meets his gaze straight on.

"It helps you because I think he may be real, and you need to find him. While I can't promise that he's the first shifter, I think he's pretty close. He might be able to point you in the right direction."

"And how exactly do we do that?" Rylan is not letting up that easily, and I'm with him on this one. But Brianna is the next coven leader, and she's dealt with plenty of suspicious and untrusting shifters. She's a pro at this. She leans forward, making sure she holds Rylan's gaze before she speaks.

"I did a location spell with the help of my mother. No, I can't actually scry for an Ancient," she hurries to say, because Rylan opens his mouth to ask. He growls in response, but Brianna isn't done. "A few of the mythologies we found speak of a great willow tree, being sort of a conduit for Veles. So we searched for a vast amount of magical energy attached to a willow tree. One of our fae friends was able to enhance our magic to do a very specific type of search, and we sort of hit a jackpot."

Rylan and I just stare at Brianna, and she chuckles.

"A big win. The magic leads us to an area north of you, past the town of Valley Springs, near Williamsburg. There's a mountain range there and an area northeast of the mountain range that's…well, let's say it's a little fuzzy for us to see into."

"Like it's cloaked?" I ask, thinking about what Stella said about some of the areas around here.

"That's definitely a possibility. I can't really be sure, but the scrying spell was very specific, so it's the best lead I can give you."

I think that over for about two seconds flat because this gives us something to do. I'm all in.

"How will we know when we find it?" I ask, and I feel Rylan turn his attention to me. I think, if I'm picking up on his exhale correctly, he's just as ready to get out there as I am.

"There's no way for me to say for certain. It could even not be a tree for all we know, but it will have an incredible amount of magic pouring out of it. You'll be able to feel it."

Here we are again, talking about me feeling the magic. I still have no idea if that's all in my head, or if that's actually something I can do. Is it a True Alpha thing? Is it a me thing? No one knows. But there is something to it. Because while those rabid wolves definitely have no magic on them, I can feel Rylan's wolf. But I can't be sure if it isn't just Rylan and has nothing to do with my strange new alpha powers.

"I would suggest you ask Stella to create a protection pouch for you, in case you have to hide. Yes, Rylan," Brianna addresses him directly when he opens his mouth again, "the witches' magic can help protect you."

"We don't need protection," he says, the alpha in him rebelling entirely against any kind of direction. Before I can stop myself, I reach over, placing my hand on the arm that's leaning on the table in front of the computer. My fingers wrap around his wrist, and his eyes jerk away from Brianna and toward my touch. I'm nowhere near restraining him, but the simple touch seems to have calmed him. When I glance back at Brianna, she wears the same smirk I've seen on Stella's face. I have no idea what it means.

"We'll keep working on our end," Brianna says, her attention back on me. "Considering we all believe the humans are working with the Ancients, I would suggest keeping yourselves out of the towns on the way. Stay safe, Trinity. Both of you."

"You too," I reply. I click disconnect, then I let go of Rylan's wrist and turn my head to look up at him. He's much too close, still hovering over my shoulder, and I can see the gleam of determination in his eyes. He's just as ready to get moving as I am.

Finally, something we both agree on.

CHAPTER 7

It takes us nearly no time at all to get ready. In fact, Stella already had the protection pouches ready to go and gives me a quick rundown on how to use them, while Rylan goes upstairs to take a shower and change. He didn't get to do that earlier this morning.

"You sure you don't want to take anything else with you?" Stella asks as I place the pouch in my very handy pocket. Seriously, all dresses should have pockets.

"We'll be fine. Thank you."

"Of course. I'll keep working on my end. Please come back safely." She reaches over, taking me into her arms, and the gesture is so maternal, I nearly start crying. My emotional state is definitely not a fortress. I need to work on that.

I step back just as Rylan comes downstairs. Stella surprises me by stepping over to hug him as well. He freezes for a moment, as if unsure about what to do, before he hugs her back gently. She doesn't even try to hide the worry on her face as she sees us off.

I want to say that we will be fine; I want to make promises I can't keep because Stella is important to me. It surprises me too. But as I glance at Rylan, I think that he may be thinking the same thing. Who would've thought a shifter would become attached to a witch, but that's exactly what I think Rylan has become. It's probably because he's just as starved for parents as I was when Jefferson took me in. I'm not sure how it is with other people, magical or not, but that hole that opens up when your parents are no longer part of your life is not something easily filled.

"Should we let Ezra and Zach know where we're going?" I ask as Rylan and I leave Stella's bar behind. The streets are filled with people, likely tourists passing through and enjoying the scenery.

While they smile for the camera, I'm curious about what they see when they look around. Do they just see a pretty town? Or can they feel the danger brewing in the sky like dark clouds rolling in? Because I can feel it everywhere.

"We should. They're going to hate us even more for leaving them behind again."

"Just tell them they can come on the next run. I'm sure we'll have plenty of them."

There's no way we'll be one and done. The first shifter has kept a low profile for a long, long time. His knowledge of how the Ancients work and how they've created shifters in the first place is what we're desperate to find. If he can provide us with some insight, maybe we'll be able to help the shifters which are being tortured and stripped of their magic now. I don't expect our luck to be so good that we stumble on him on our first try. But I do trust the witches to know what they're doing, so that means that even if it's not the first shifter, we'll be able to find something. The magic they found in that area must mean there is someone or something there.

As I step around a couple walking toward us, Rylan reaches for my hand. His fingers are warm and strong as they wrap around mine. He tugs me against his side, and for a moment I think he's going to wrap his arm around my shoulders. Instead, he opens the pack link.

Get it together, Trinity. Of course, this has nothing to do with us. It's the fact that the link is stronger when we're touching.

It's about time, Zach says. I have to chuckle. Since I'm not walking by myself, at least I don't look like a lunatic laughing at nothing.

I was just there, Rylan replies, and I can almost feel the brotherhood between them just from their simple interaction. I saw this same sense of comradeship with Jefferson's pack, and I'd be lying if I said it doesn't warm my heart to know this pack—my pack—has the same type of a relationship with their alpha. Now I'll just have to work to make sure they have that relationship with me as well.

Wow, that is a weird thought to have.

We wanted to let you know that we're heading out, I say, trying to keep my mind on the business side of things. *We have a lead.*

I can feel Zach perk up immediately.

You need backup? Ezra asks, because of course he does. Zach teases, but Ezra gets right down to business.

Not this time, Rylan replies, and I can feel the betas' disappointment immediately. I nudge Rylan in the ribs and he narrows his eyes at me before he says, *But next time, you're coming with us.*

Their mood shifts immediately once more, and I have to

grin. They're something else, that's for sure. It probably would be better to have them with us this time, considering we have no idea what we're walking into, but they have a job to do as well.

We might not be able to reach out, I say now, just in case we're all thinking it. *But we will as soon as we're able.*

Stay safe, Ezra says. Rylan shuts off the link, because we've reached the alleyway that'll lead us straight into the woods, and it's time to shift. I don't want to let go of his hand, and that's why I do it first.

I can't help but think about his arms around me, chasing away the nightmare last night. The gentle way he held me, which is so uncharacteristic to the tough alpha he portrays to everyone else. I want to say I'm surprised, but in reality, Rylan has always been different with me. Even when we were kids, I got to see parts of him no one else ever did, and it's like we're falling right into that, before I even realized we were falling.

The way my emotions keep ping-ponging from this to that is confusing to say the least.

"Ready?" Rylan asks. For some reason, it feels like he's asking another question. I meet his gaze, keeping mine steady, and nod. Whoever this soft Trinity is, she needs to be put away. I have a job to do.

MY WOLF IS happy to be back in the forest. Any amount of time she spends inside Stella's bar is like a punishment to her. Not because she doesn't like Stella—she actually likes her a lot—but because we *have* to stay there to stay protected, and that feels like a prison to a wolf who thrives on being free.

I'm not going to ask, but I'm pretty sure Rylan feels the same if his increased speed and near playfulness is any indication. We were born in a forest, and we feel the most ourselves here. The fact that we have to hide away from it is just one more reason I'd like to teach these meddling humans a lesson or two about playing with magic...preferably with my teeth and claws.

Clearly, I need a good fight. Thousands of years of instinct to fight first and ask questions later is difficult to ignore, even while trying to be more civilized in my approach. But that second attack in the woods did nothing to calm me down. Obviously, I know I shouldn't be looking for danger, because danger will find us anyway. But it's almost an instinct, and I can't help it. My wolf and I are in agreement when we say we want to get our hands and paws dirty.

How far are you thinking we should go? I break the silence, reaching out to Rylan through the pack link. From the sun's position, I guess we've been moving through the forest for about two hours, and we're not running at full speed. Even though time is of the essence, we have to be careful. Which means being purposeful with our movements.

Maybe another hour? If we can cross the highway, we can camp on the other side, before heading into the veiled territory tomorrow. Rylan sounds like he's been thinking it over, and I'm sure he has. He's much better at the planning end of things, which makes sense considering he's had to take care of others since he was a kid. I could use a lesson or two in how to take the needs of others into consideration. Yes, when I ran into the compound on our last recon, I was thinking of protecting

Rylan, but I forgot the part where he feels like he needs to protect me too. Even when he doesn't want to.

That's a good plan, I say instead of saying all of my thoughts out loud. I'm not sure I'm ready for him to know exactly how confused I am right now.

No argument? That's a first, he replies, and I go on the defensive automatically.

What did you want me to do? Arm wrestle you for it? Even in my wolf state, he can tell I'm rolling my eyes at him.

It would probably make me feel better, he replies, and I have no idea how to take that.

Because I'm all about making you feel better, I say, a hundred other questions on the tip of my tongue. What are we doing exactly? Why doesn't this feel like normal griping? Why does it feel so playful?

My inner walls come up immediately, the need to protect myself nearly overwhelming. I'm letting him in too fast and it's too much. I don't understand why it's happening, but it's leaving me unprotected. And we can't have that.

Where did you go just now? Rylan's voice pushes through my mini panic. I glance at him, trotting parallel to me. We've slowed down some now that we're closer to the highway, but we're still moving faster than an average walk.

I'm not sure what you mean, I reply.

I think you do. I think you know exactly what I'm talking about, but you don't want me to know.

Rylan, none of that even made sense. I sigh and almost wish I was in human form right now, just so I could run my hands over my face or push my hair back—do something that would make me feel more grounded.

Yes, it does. The memory spell spooked you and you've been running from me ever since.

I nearly stumble. So graceful for a wolf. But he can't know. He can't see me like that. This is too much...again. Too much, too soon. I'm drowning in this newness of us—and yet, it's not so new, is it? We might have been fighting our connection, pushing each other more than we should have, but we both know we're still us. Maybe, that's why we're fighting so much. Because fighting is safer than...

I don't want to talk about the spell.

Well, we don't always get what we want, do we? I'm not really sure I'm supposed to hear that, but when I look at him, his wolf looks like an impenetrable statue. Eyes focused forward, legs moving in sync. I think he's going to drop it, but I should know better.

Someone messed with our minds, Trin. We can't ignore that.

I'm not ignoring it! The shout vibrates through our minds, and I can't take it anymore, I stop and shift. My body shakes with memories pushing at the corners of my mind, and I move my hands up and down, trying to work some of the blood flow through them. It feels like all of my blood has gone straight to my head.

"Trin, hey—" Rylan is beside me when I turn, catching my shoulders to stop my hectic movements. He always seems to be catching me, even when I don't know that I'm falling.

"I don't know what you want from me," I say somewhere in the vicinity of the middle of his shirt because I can't look at him right now. "I'm trying, okay? I'm trying to make sure I keep it all together, but being alpha, the memories thing, the spell, the wolves, you—" I swallow the words before I can say them and take a deep breath. "This is not how I pictured our reunion going."

He sucks in a gasp of air, and I realize what I said a little too late. I can't help it as my eyes fly to his and the intensity there nearly brings me to my knees. We stand frozen in this in between time, where we're not friends and we're not enemies, and I can't figure out what we are. But we're here, and we're together.

"Did you?" Rylan's voice is barely above a whisper, but it sounds like a shout in my mind. "Did you picture our reunion?"

There's a pause in the air, as if the forest around us is holding its breath just like I am. Very slowly, I take a step back, and he drops his arms at his side. I want to lie to him. I want to say that I didn't mean it. But if we're truly supposed to be working together, if we're supposed to be doing this as a team, I can't keep doing that to him. Or to myself. So I settle on the truth.

"More often than I'd like."

CHAPTER 8

RYLAN

"More often than I'd like."

I can't keep those words from replaying over and over in my head as we cross the highway and look for a place to settle for the night.

The more time I spend around Trinity, the more I can read her. She hasn't changed as much as she thinks she has. Sure, she's rougher around the edges, but so am I. When cornered she goes for the jugular, and I can't say I blame her. What happened—what I did—it would break anyone.

Except it didn't break her.

Regardless of the truth that someone messed with our minds, I can't shut off the feelings of mistrust and hate I've carried for her all these years, but I also can't lie to myself that those were the only things I carried.

Sometimes another being is so much a part of you that it's like losing a part of yourself when they're gone. Trinity has always been that person to me. Exiling her ripped my own heart out just the same.

But pain and anger fueled my resolve then, and they fuel my resolve now, because I can't let myself fall apart in front of her. Holding her nearly breaks me every time.

If anyone could see the inside of my brain, they'd call me soft. Weak.

I should focus on all of the mistakes she's made.

But that's not the kind of a leader I want to be. I have made so many mistakes in my time, and so have the wolves in the pack. If I can forgive them—if I can lead by example—then I can't just ignore my own convictions when it comes to Trinity.

I should keep myself hardened against the pull I feel toward her, but I've never been able to. Even with years of misunderstanding between us, I still feel it. And I have no idea what to do about that.

So while I usually give myself the space to process my chaotic array of thoughts when I'm away from my pack, I know I must put it all away. I can't let myself sit with these emotions and while my wolf doesn't seem to like that, we have a mission to accomplish. I have a job to do. No matter how much Trinity seems to bring out those long hidden parts of me to the surface, I am no longer that young pup in touch with his feelings. I've buried them a long time ago, and it's better it stays that way.

* * *

TRINITY

I THINK we should stay in the woods tonight, Rylan says just as we reach the outskirts of town. We've shifted back to our wolf forms, but kept our pace careful as we travel through the forest.

Williamsburg is similar to Holden in many ways. Same small streets, same packed main street full of eccentric shops. But while Holden has Stella's bar, we have no idea what this town holds in the way of magic. Brianna's warning to stay away from people rings in my head. It would probably be better not to announce ourselves.

That's a good idea, I say, keeping my voice even. I still can't believe the confession that escaped me—I've tried many times to convince myself I wasn't thinking about Rylan throughout the years. But it's like trying to forget one of your limbs—while they're still attached to your body. It was so much easier when I hated him.

I realize right then and there that maybe I don't hate him quite as much as I think I do. Or thought I did. Even without knowing our brains were messed with, I've lived with his betrayal as the truth for so long, hating him until it felt like second nature. Now I have to deal with that in a completely new light, and I have no idea what to do with that.

You're being very agreeable, Rylan comments, and I huff.

Don't push your luck.

He chuckles, the sound vibrating through my mind. I'm thankful he's in front of me, because even in wolf form, I'm probably showing way too much on my face. I have to stop this. Somehow, I have to get my confusing and conflicting thoughts in order, because I won't be good to anyone if I'm this type of a walking mess.

Stella gave me a protection pouch, so if we find a good place to rest, I can set it up, I say, trying to stay on the productive side of things. Rylan only grunts, but I actually do think he's coming around to the whole witches thing. Stella is winning him over, for sure.

When the bullet comes, we're not prepared.

The first one hits the tree right next to my head, sending splinters from the bark to rain down all around me. The second one zooms over Rylan's head as it lands on the dirt behind him.

Scatter! Rylan yells, and we separate. I open up my senses, trying to pinpoint where the assault is coming from, but I don't find anything.

They must be protected by magic! Even though I communicate through the pack link, I try to keep my voice calm. I guess that answers our questions about magic in Williamsburg. My senses track Rylan's movements. He circles back toward me in a large arc.

My eyes scan the area, finding nothing to alert me of the danger, which sends a wave of panic through me. We're not prepared to fight blind. I should be able to pick up something. I should be—and when a bullet finally hits me, I don't see it coming.

My howl rips out of me as I drop and roll, blood splattering around me. When I glance at my shoulder, I see a large gash, and then I see the bullet stuck in a tree a few feet behind me. It's just a graze, but it's a deep one.

Trinity! Rylan's voice is a mix of control and panic. I gasp, but I answer him as calmly as I can.

Just a scratch. We need to lose them.

Where?

In the woods—

Where are you hurt?? His voice in my head is so strong, it nearly makes me stumble.

Focus, Rylan, I snap, because he needs to keep that balance and not give in to panic. If he gives in, I'll lose it.

Highway. Head back to the highway and veer west. I'll meet you near the mountains.

Without a second of hesitation, I turn. My shoulder is screaming in pain, but I push it down. It's easier than trying to control my responses to Rylan, and I have no idea what to do with that information, so I file it away for later.

I keep searching the woods behind me, looking up into the trees, but even with my supernatural eyesight, I can't seem to locate the shooters. They had to have been close before, and I didn't see them, but I do feel Rylan moving closer, as he weaves in and out of the woods.

There's an overgrown area of forest in front of you. Head there.

I don't argue with him, turning in the direction he's pointing with the pack link, almost like a string guiding us there.

What was that? I ask, and I can feel Rylan's frustration through the link.

I have no idea. But we clearly don't know what's going on in Williamsburg.

Isn't that the understatement of the week? In the next minute, Rylan is beside me, and we've reached the spot he pointed out. There are fallen trees here, which have overgrown with ivy and have sprouted new trees. And behind the trees, there are rocks...with an opening. It's a cave, small from the looks of it, but it'll do. My pain has mostly numbed, and I see Rylan studying me in that intense way of his. I shake my head, and he sighs, then he leads me into the cave.

CHAPTER 9

Even though the last thing I want to do is hide, we both understand the importance of it, so I follow Rylan's lead without question. He's surprised I go so quietly, but it's a day of miracles, I suppose. I mean, we did come out of there alive, so there's that. Sometimes I forget humans have some of the best ways to hurt us, and they don't even need magic to do it.

Once we wiggle our bodies through the narrow opening, we find ourselves in a small cavern. There are so many running under and around the White Wolf territory, it's impossible to know them all. This space is maybe about ten feet across, with a flat wall on one side and an oval wall on the other. The sound of running water reaches my ears, so there must be a stream here somewhere. I notice two other openings, but there's no way we're fitting through there. The cavern isn't as dark as it would be if it didn't have an opening at the top. I lean back to follow the direction of the sloping wall, until it almost funnels out at the top, barely visible moonlight coming through the opening.

"Cozy," I mumble as I shift. Rylan follows suit, his eyes on me and the gash on my shoulder. "It's not as bad as it looks."

"We need to bind it. We need—" We both know we've got nothing with us and nothing here we can use.

"Me first," I say, before taking out the small pouch Stella gave me to keep on myself. I open it, pouring out four quarter-sized crystals. Black and green weave together in patterns on each crystal, and I position them across from each other, one at each wall. I step back into the center, glancing between the four gems. From what Stella told me, I have to set an intention as I place the crystals, so I send out a protective intention, before I grab the tiny bundle of lavender and set it down where I stand.

"Is that all?" Rylan may have decided to keep an open mind when it comes to witches, but even I have to say that sometimes I'm skeptical. I just have more faith in them than I do in their rituals, so I nod with confidence.

"Stella said it should keep us protected, but only for a few hours at the most. Especially if they're close by. It's a one-time use because she would have to cleanse them…or something. But it'll work for tonight."

"Just long enough for us to do something about that," he motions toward my shoulder, but I'm already shaking my head. I'm purposefully ignoring the sting from the bullet graze, because it makes me want to whine a little, but we do need to bind it.

"I don't have a bandage," I say, raising an eyebrow.

Rylan's eyes meet mine, and then, as he holds them, he reaches down and yanks on a corner of his shirt. The sound of the material tearing echoes around us, but I can't pull my eyes away from his. There're just as many emotions brewing behind his midnight blue eyes as the ones currently rushing through my body.

That was close. That was too close.

Rylan moves toward me, his eyes never leaving my face. If this was a month ago, I would've pulled away. But now, I just prepare myself for the way my body will react to his proximity. Maybe I should be used to the way my skin ignites at the touch of his fingertips. Maybe I shouldn't be so affected by the way his breath warms and cools my skin as he leans closer.

His hands find my shoulder, and I inhale sharply as he lifts it, ever so gently, using his other hand to place the piece of his t-shirt over it. The material feels rough against the wound, but I can't tear my eyes away from Rylan. His whole attention is on my shoulder, his hands moving with familiarity, his brow furrowed as he concentrates. I have the sudden urge to reach over and smooth out the small space between his eyebrows, but instead, I curl my hand into the skirt of my dress. This constant need to touch him is new yet familiar somehow, and it's driving me nuts.

Rylan ties the makeshift bandage at the top of my shoulder, and steps back. We exhale together, as if both of us have been holding our breath the whole time. He doesn't go far, since the cavern is small. I feel exhausted. I should probably shift to help the healing, but I don't. Instead, I plop down on the ground, my back against the wall, and stretch my legs in front of me. Rylan gives me one long, heated look, and then he sits opposite me. Even so, our legs are nearly touching.

I'm too aware of him, and it's sending my whole body on hyperdrive.

"The pack—" I begin, my alpha powers reaching out, but Rylan is already nodding.

"They're safe. We're too far. I don't think the attack had anything to do with us specifically. It was as if they were protecting their territory."

"Human territory."

Rylan nods.

I expand my senses as much as I can, but I don't feel any threats. I'm hoping with all my might that Stella's charms are holding. Suddenly, I feel incredibly exhausted, and so I slide down the wall, twisting around so my head is in the middle of the cave, looking up as I settle on the ground on my back. After a moment, I feel Rylan follow suit, except his feet are pointing in the opposite direction. So now, we're lying shoulder to shoulder, looking up at the tiny opening at the top of the cavern. If I turn my head just a little to the right, I'll meet his eyes. So I keep staring up.

Maybe we should be talking about what just happened, but I feel so tired, I simply don't want to.

There are a million things I want to say on the tip of my tongue, but I can't bring myself to be that vulnerable. Neither of us does vulnerable well. We're too proud for that, too stubborn. And I'm too scared.

Maybe it's silly that I can run headfirst into danger, but I'm terrified of telling Rylan just how much I missed him. How much I missed us.

The mistakes and miscommunications of our past weigh heavily on me, but even so, it doesn't diminish the fact that he has always been my best friend. Even when I hated him.

"Do you remember"—Rylan breaks the silence, his voice low, barely above a whisper. My whole body locks up, too afraid to move lest I make him stop talking—"that giant tree near the Quarrel's Pond, with the—"

"Hollowed out center." It doesn't take much. Memories rush in just at the mention of it.

"We hid there from the storm that one night, and the snow piled up so high it covered the entrance. Our parents couldn't understand why we didn't just brave the snow before it got so bad, but we wanted to stay."

"It was the first night we spent away from the pack," I whisper, picturing the two of us huddled against each other in our wolf forms, listening to the wind howl outside of the tree. Even though we were still connected to the pack with the link, it felt like we were explorers, on our own, braving the world we knew nothing about. We even talked about going on adventures, before Rylan had to become alpha, leaving the pack to see other parts of our realm.

"What was your life like?" Rylan asks, his voice still barely a whisper between us. "With Jefferson's pack?"

I don't answer right away, letting my mind and heart fill with the images of the people I left behind. But even across distance, they're still with me, still helping, still having my back. I am blessed beyond anything I could've imagined as an exiled pup.

"They were amazing," I say honestly. "They saved me, Jay in particular. He threw himself into being my best friend and my big brother all at once, with no reservations. The others were cautious around me after Jefferson brought me in, but Jay didn't care. He saw how lost I felt, and he worked to change that."

Rylan doesn't say anything for a while, and I finally turn my head to look at him. His brow is furrowed again as he stares up at the cavern's ceiling, and I wonder what has him looking so intense.

"The pack got close with the witches when the whole

Ancients thing happened," I continue, and then I smile. "The library in town had the best graphic novel collection. I was sad to leave those behind. I started my own collection."

"Of graphic novels?"

This time when I turn my head, Rylan is looking at me. Our eyes are in line, even though his body is facing the opposite direction, and this feels intimate somehow, like it's another level.

"Yes," I smile, and Rylan blinks, as if something blinded him. "They're very entertaining. And the artwork is amazing."

"I'll take your word for it." He gives me a half smile, and I shake my head a little at him.

"When this is all over, I'll take you to a bookstore. You might even find something you like. You have to learn how to read first, though."

"Oh, shots fired. Like a ten year old."

But he laughs, and the sound burrows into my chest, making a place there. I know we're not back to where we were, but these little moments of comradeship are there and no matter how unsure I may be of him, or us, or the rest of the world, I can't lie to myself and say I don't eat them up like birthday cake.

"Shall we try?" I ask, lifting my hand and watch his eyes zero in there. This seems like the perfect moment, or maybe I want it to be the perfect moment because I have the sudden urge to touch him.

He doesn't move from his position, but he bends his arm at the elbow and wraps his fingers over mine. No matter how many times we've held hands, it always feels like the very first time. A little nervous, a bit mind spinning, and somehow precious in the way not many things are. I turn my head to watch him through the little triangle of space left between our arms and he's already watching me. My inhale sounds loud in the small cave, but Rylan doesn't react.

I try to focus on the memories, I try to push my mind back to that day, but it stays right here, in the quietness of the moment, with Rylan's steady eyes on me and a weight of a million emotions on my heart.

* * *

WE STAY safe through the night, and I'm able to shift so that I can heal proper. The memories didn't come, and neither one of us are talking about the intimacy of the moment or the fact that it was a failed experiment. We're just compartmentalizing the heck out of it, as usual.

Rylan is once again wearing a t-shirt that's ripped and it's getting to be a habit. We're definitely not going to be able to waltz into town looking like we do. After yesterday's display of hospitality, I'm thinking we should steer clear of the town anyway, unless we absolutely have to visit.

"Best bet is to head east, parallel to the highway," Rylan says as I make my way out of the cave. The sun is barely waking up, and the forest is covered in morning dew. Even though we're not near our village, these woods are still part of the White Wolf territory and I can feel it in the air, in the way the leaves shift in the breeze. I take a deep breath, holding it in my lungs for a moment before I let them out. When I look over at Rylan, I find him watching me.

His expression is unguarded for a split second, before the mask falls back in place. But I saw the hint of a smile, and it does things to my insides.

Better stick to business.

"Parallel to the highway, and then?" I ask.

"North, once we're past the town's boundaries. We'll have to try and come around from the west, and it'll take longer but—"

"But better to be on the safe side."

We stare at each other in agreement, keenly aware of the tension between us. Every moment I spend with him breaks down yet another brick in my well-erected wall. I think it's the same for him.

I can't get the image of him lying beside me on the cavern ground last night nor his recollection of our childhood antics out of my mind.

"Let's get going then," I say, turning in the direction of the highway.

"Too easy," Rylan mumbles, and I grin because he can't see me. It makes him a little crazy when I go along with his plans, and I'm using that to my advantage. I can't help it; it's who I am.

Keeping Rylan on guard is my favorite pastime. It was back then, and it clearly is now.

"Here," he says, coming up beside me and handing me a bundle of leaves. I take it, realizing it's actually a single leaf filled with berries. I glance up at him, but he's already turning away.

"Thank you," I nearly whisper and watch as he nods his head, keeping his attention in the opposite direction. I eat my breakfast quickly, grateful, considering we don't really have time to hunt right now. And we're not about to give away our position with a fire. He must've gotten up way earlier than I thought to go find food. I try not to let that affect me, but I'm just being stubborn. Everything about Rylan affects me.

I finish up the berries, and we make sure we don't leave a trail behind as we shift and move toward the highway. We'll keep enough distance between it and us not to alert anyone who might be patrolling the area, but we'll use it as a guiding point, since the veiled area is beyond it to the north.

I didn't really give myself time to think about it last night, but we should've been able to sense the danger when we got closer to town. Rylan said they must be using magic, but what kind of magic hides them from all of our senses? It's too similar to the rabid wolves, and that doesn't sit well with me at all. I would like more answers, instead of all the questions that keep getting thrown at us. Maybe we do need to visit this town and see what information we can dig up. If these people are some of the ones working with the Ancients, there might be some evidence of that. I file that away to worry about later, because one thing at a time, Trinity.

You think keeping our distance from the town will keep them from knowing we're here? I ask through the link, glancing over to where Rylan is walking a few feet ahead of me. He's put himself between me and the highway, and it's not like I don't know what he's doing.

It's our best bet. I have no idea if we crossed some supernatural alarm system before or what—

He trails off, but I feel dumb that I didn't even think of that. We must've. Or were they just going to shoot any wolves that walked into their territory? What about wolves that live in town? Would they have wolves living in town?

If they have magic, does that mean they have shifters? I ask. *How would they know who's who?*

The more I think about it, the more it feels like we should be going into town to figure out what's going on. I can't just let it be, but I also can't tell if it's just my stubbornness or the alpha magic in me that needs to fix everything at once.

The magical alarm could tell them, right? Wouldn't your witches know?

They would. Too bad I can't reach out to them with a pack link, because that would be very helpful right about now.

I know what you're thinking, Trin. But one problem at a time. First, we look for the tree. Then, we play detective.

I can hear the smile in his voice, and it makes me happy even though I shouldn't let it. It's difficult to reconcile my two-faced emotions when it comes to him. When he's like this—like the boy I knew—I fall into our old dynamic without thinking. But he's not just that boy, he's also the hardened alpha who abandoned me.

I can tell that he's just as boggled by these conflicting emotions as I am. It makes me feel slightly better that I'm not the only one suffering. I know, that's so mean of me.

Now is really not the time to be processing any of this, but anytime I'm around Rylan, I can't help it. And since I'm around him constantly—yeah, here we are. We have to have a conversation about this, a logical in-depth conversation, because we cannot keep running from ourselves or from whatever is growing between us.

The highway comes into view through the trees before I can have any further inner emotional turmoil. Rylan and I both grow quiet, as if whoever is out there can actually hear our conversations through the pack link. He glances at me for a moment, and I nod.

We speed up, racing parallel to the highway for another half an hour, at least, before we finally pivot. We'll have to cross the highway now and then double back, but it should work. I'm not feeling any danger around us. Granted, I didn't feel anything yesterday when we were attacked either.

Rylan and I stay on high alert as we move toward the veiled area, and I hope with all my heart that, this time, we get farther and we stay safe.

CHAPTER 10

*T*ime seems to go by faster as we reach the space behind the town, closer to our destination. I keep searching the trees, looking for any sign of ambush, but there's nothing. I'm surprised, considering I wasn't expecting this to work. If they're protecting the entrance to the town in one direction, shouldn't they do so in all directions?

Something isn't right.

Rylan's words sound too loud through the pack link after all the silence, but I feel it too. Something is different in these woods. Even the insects seem to chirp quieter. There's no absence of other creatures, but they're more...timid somehow.

I don't see any imminent danger. Doesn't mean it's not there, I hurry to add, and Rylan makes a grunting noise of agreement. *I think I—*

I trail off as something shifts in the air. It's like an air of oppression has settled over us, pushing us down. My body feels ten times heavier, like it's being literally pulled to the ground, and I fight to stay upright. Rylan is watching me, waiting for me to continue, but then his eyes round. He feels it too.

My senses are being overwhelmed, but we keep moving, albeit much slower than before. There's magic all around us, and it's not happy we're here. I don't have to be a witch to tell; the moisture in the air is potent, a heaviness just before the skies open up and a downpour starts.

I take another step and my chest grows heavier—so much so that I can't seem to get a full breath in.

"Rylan, I—" I say, shifting back to my human form as I drop to all fours. My wolf is whimpering inside of me, the pressure becoming too much.

Rylan is beside me in a blink of an eye, shifting as he drops in front of me, his arms on my shoulders. I'm panting. My vision is swimming. My eyes latch onto Rylan's worried ones for a moment, but then a wave of pain slams into me. My whole body jerks, and it's only Rylan's hands on my shoulders that keep me in place.

"Trin, what's happening? How can I help?" His voice sounds far away, as if he's at the bottom of a hole, and I'm fifty feet above him.

"I—" I try to push the words past my lips, but I can't. Another wave of pain hits me and then my vision blurs. Suddenly, I'm in that dark space in my dream, feet frozen to the spot. But this time I'm not alone. At least a hundred people and wolves crowd the space, their voices rising in panic, as they cry and shout. I raise my hands, slapping them over my ears as the shouting becomes unbearable. My body continues to shake and I—

Trinity! The voice—Rylan's voice—attacks whatever is assaulting my brain. He's pushing against it as he tries to get to me. It's almost a visual image inside my brain.

Come back to me, Trinity. Come back.

His voice—it's shouting louder than the rest. Louder than the pain. Louder than the despair. I push the air into my lungs, and when I raise my head, I'm back in the forest. Rylan's face is barely inches away from mine as he holds me in place with his strong arms.

"I'm okay, I'm here…"

I trail off, as another wave of despair hits me. My hands grip Rylan's arms just above his elbows as I try to physically hold on, so I don't go back to that place. I don't understand what's happening, I can't focus my mind long enough to figure it out.

"That's it," Rylan's voice is full of something—I can't keep my eyes open as another blast of pain hits. The voices return, and it takes everything in me not to cry out. I shut my eyes, falling forward and then feel myself being lifted.

Everything is darkness—and then it's not.

My heartbeat races in my chest as I try to take in calming breaths, pulling myself out of the black hole. Pushing the air into my lungs, I hold it there for a moment before exhaling. Only then do I open my eyes.

That's when I realize that I'm pressed against Rylan, who carries me through the woods. His footing is sure, and he moves quickly, keeping me cradled tightly against him. My limbs feel heavy, the nearly-healed wound on my shoulder throbbing with renewed pain, and I simply have no energy in me to protest. My hand curls against his shirt, and he glances down at me, his gaze unguarded.

In his eyes, I find a protectiveness that makes my chest hurt. It's a look I've never seen before, not when it comes to me. There are layers there, layers I'm not ready to unpack. My automatic response is always to fight against this, to show him that I don't need to be taken care of. I can take care of myself. But I don't respond as I typically do.

Instead, I curl into him a little more and give myself the space to process what's happening while giving someone else the chance to help. Especially if that someone else is Rylan.

* * *

RYLAN BACKTRACKS to the other side of the highway, east of the town, weaving in and out of the standing trees and the fallen logs. Even though we've just come through here, my sense of disorientation makes everything look more ominous. He holds me close, as if he can protect me from whatever it is that's happening to me. It's minutes that feel like hours before I finally get a grip on myself enough to speak up. I hate feeling this helpless, but for some reason, not as much as I used to. Something else to unpack later, that's for sure. That list is getting longer and longer every day.

"I'm good. You can put me down," I say, lifting my head so I can look at Rylan directly as he looks down at me.

"Are you sure? I don't mind." His voice is barely a whisper, but his gaze is intense, and I nod. He places me gently on my feet, and I take a moment before I uncurl my hands from around him. We've definitely reached a new level of comradeship between us, and I can't really tell which of us made the step forward. Maybe we're both doing it.

I take a step back from Rylan and his embrace, trying to regroup. Whatever happened back there was strange. It would be nice if I had any idea if it was alpha power related or magic cast by the town or the Ancient we're searching.

"Want to talk about it?" Rylan's voice pulls me back, and I turn to find his eyes on me. His face is clear of emotion, much different than the care I glimpsed in his gaze while he was carrying me. But that's to be expected. We're very good about not having open communication. Which means, no, I don't want to talk about it. But I still need to say something.

"There's nothing to talk about. There's some kind of a strange magical forcefield here. We need more information about this town and the kind of magic they carry." My brain is in full problem-solving mode. "There has to be something that's causing the reaction—"

"Trinity."

"They're protecting something, that's for sure. Or they wouldn't have shot at us in the first place."

"Trinity."

"Stop saying my name like that!" I snap.

"Like what?"

"Like—" I don't even know how to finish that because it's just affecting me and I don't want to admit to it. It feels like every time I have found some semblance of a sure footing, everything goes spinning again—with Rylan always in the middle. I can't deal with him when he's like this—concerned, caring. I need us fighting, pushing each other, because that dynamic I understand. Everything else feels like too much with my current emotional state—which is unbalanced, to say the least.

"Look, we've clearly walked in on something way more complicated than we initially thought. There's magic and men armed with guns. Whatever is going on, we're not the only ones on a mission. Clearly. So we need to determine what they're doing, so we can figure out what we need to do and, finally, move forward with this instead of walking around like lost puppies."

I'm nearly out of breath as all the words tumble out of

me, and I don't want to look at Rylan, but I do. He's watching me steadily, not moving any closer, but also not moving away. That's something, I suppose.

"What happened back there?" he asks, his voice gentle. He can tell I'm spooked, and he's treading lightly. This is really not the kind of pushing I was thinking about, but I sigh, because I also know I have to give him an answer.

"It was like my dream, the overwhelming pain assaulting me from every side."

"Except you weren't asleep."

"No." I meet his gaze. There's no rhyme or reason to these weird dreams that I've been having. The only thing we've come up with is that it's tied to my alpha powers and whatever I saw on that quest. It could be a dozen explanations that we haven't even thought of yet. "Maybe it's tied to what the Oracle had me do, and this is how my memories are coming back to me, how I'm breaking through whatever barrier's been placed in my mind."

Rylan doesn't comment right away, keeping that steady gaze of his on me. When he gets this silent, those eyes lighting up in the way that makes me feel as if he's looking straight into me, I have a difficult time not bolting. Running from him and the emotions he evokes with me has always been the easy path. I should stop trying to take the easy road, but it's not like I want to even though I should. This is a never-ending cycle of doing what I should and what I want to. They never seem to coincide.

Except when they do and cause a whole other slew of problems.

"That's what I've been thinking," Rylan finally comments, taking a deep breath. "Whatever happened to you in that quest, and everything after, it's clearly affecting you."

"Are you asking me a question?"

"I'm trying to work through the problem out loud"—he rolls his eyes at my snide question—"so that we can figure it out."

He's being all mature again. Here I go, wishing he would just fight it out with me instead. Clearly, I have a problem.

"I don't know how to figure it out, Rylan," I say, my whole body tired all of a sudden. It's as if the weight I'm carrying is becoming heavier by the minute. "The only plan I have is to see it through when it comes up, because I don't know what's causing it, and I don't know how to combat it and all I know is that I'm tired. So very tired."

Even admitting that much takes a toll on me, but I'm trying. I feel like all I'm doing is trying. Rylan gives me one of his long stares, and then nods, as if ending a silent conversation with himself.

"We'll go into town," he announces, "the normal people way. Then, we'll look around, and see if we can figure out what's going on around here. And we'll get a place we can clean up and call Stella. She might have some information for us."

It's that quiet alpha voice that gets me. He's taking charge, but in the most natural way. This is the Rylan I can't resist. So I don't even bother trying. I simply nod and motion for him to lead the way.

CHAPTER 11

We take the roundabout way of getting into Williamsburg. Rylan and I shift, and then we race over to the nearest gas station on the outskirts of town. Our plan is to ask for a ride into town, except that we look intimidating even when we're smiling. Well, Rylan looks intimidating, and he hardly ever smiles, so I have to improvise. Plus, his shirt has that unpleasant rip on the side.

When a truck pulls up at the pump and a nice-looking grandfatherly type gets out, I know he's our way in. He's wearing a baseball cap, and the gray hairs stick out at the sides. But there are laugh lines on his weathered face, and he looks like someone who often has kids around him. His clothes look worn and comfortable and I'm not sure why, but he just seems like someone who won't question us asking for help. Maybe my perceptive powers are getting better. I step right into Rylan's personal space, slipping my hand into his and using the other to tuck the ripped part of the shirt into his waistband. His whole body goes rigid, glancing down at me as if I've lost my mind. I might've actually, but for some reason my mind immediately goes to that movie I watched with the witches and the words are on my lips before I had the chance to fully form them.

"A couple on their honeymoon is much more likely to entice sympathy," I whisper only loud enough for his ears, as I snuggle my body into his. There's a moment of stillness, but then he takes the hand I'm already holding and wraps it around my shoulders, so I end up in a tight embrace against his body, fitting there exactly right. I try very hard not to respond to the press of his side against mine, or just how completely at home I feel in the circle of his arms.

I glance up, looking from the strong lines of his jaw that currently carries a bit of a twitch to the angles of his nose and cheekbones, before I finally reach his eyes. He's looking down at me already, performing his own study at me being this close.

All at once, my mind goes back to that kiss and my long-buried desire for a repeat performance. Except this time, there're no games involved. Just him and me, this close, with our defenses lowered.

His gaze heats, as if he's thinking the exact same thing, and I can't tell if it's his body or mine that suddenly feels a million degrees. His heartbeat matches the erratic rhythm of mine and I have the feeling we could stay just like this for a while, which is why I tear my eyes away and focus on the man by the truck. We have to move now if we're to catch him.

"Come on," I say, nudging Rylan forward, annoyed that my voice comes out breathy. I don't miss the smug smirk he throws my way before he leads me toward the truck.

"Excuse me, sir?" I begin, now grateful for the breathlessness, because it'll help to sell the ruse. Because that's all it is—

it's not real. Of course, I have to remind myself of that, which is getting ridiculous.

"What can I help you kids with?" The man turns, giving us a quick once over before he greets us with a kind smile, and I answer it with my own.

"Might we bother you for a ride into town? We're doing a road trip for our honeymoon, and what do you know, our car broke down a ways back! We've been walking for a bit and the town can't be far, but—"

"I said I'd carry her all the way, but she's concerned for my wellbeing," Rylan adds, dropping a quick kiss to the top of my head that makes all of my coherent thoughts fly right out the window. I stare up at him as if I've never seen him before, my whole body tingling from the top of my head down to my toes at that simple contact.

"Can't have him hurt," I mumble, probably quiet enough that the man can't hear me, but it doesn't seem to matter. There's so much heat in Rylan's gaze, I think I'll melt right here, in the middle of a dingy gas station parking lot. His arm around my shoulders tightens just a tad, as if he wants to bring me even closer, and I find my free hand coming up to rest against his stomach. I can feel his muscles contract, and I have the sudden urge to run my hand up and down them.

"Oh, goodness me. Of course." The man's voice snaps me out of my trance. I turn to find him watching us with a twinkle in his eye. "Get in. I am always happy to help out a lovely couple." He grins at us, and I give him a grateful smile. Rylan tugs me even closer against him, and I use my arm on his stomach to wrap it more fully around his waist, settling into him as if I belong there.

"You two are the cutest," the man says again, motioning

for the truck. Rylan pulls the passenger door open for me, and I get in first, sliding to the middle of the bench seat. Rylan follows suit, folding himself in beside me. I scoot over to give him room, but his arm reaches out to wrap around my waist, pulling me tightly against him.

"We're supposed to be in love," he mumbles against my hair, sending pleasant shivers down my skin. That word sounds like the sweetest melody on his lips. I can't stop my body from responding, sinking into the crook of his arm. He lifts his arm to the back of the seat, but he reaches with the other, picking up my hand and threading my fingers with his.

I stare at the contact, our palms pressed together, his thumb making slow circles on my skin as my back rests against his front, and for the first time in ages, I feel settled. The moment the thought comes, I fight against it. We're not friends, we're not enemies. We're something entirely different and messed up, changed by years of pent-up hatred and betrayal. But the more I learn to trust him all over again, the more I can't deny that he balances me out in a way no one else ever has.

My sharp edges, sharpened by his, are made stronger and more useful, but less dangerous. Maybe I'm finally becoming someone who's not flying off the handle or fighting all the time. I'm becoming something else, and he's here with me every step of the way. It's no wonder I feel this wave of emotion toward him, even if I'm not ready for it.

THE MAN DROPS us off in front of the motel and won't take the money we offer him.

"You two just hold each other tightly, and that'll be enough of a payment for me." He grins, then waves and drives off. I have no idea what he saw in the two of us and I'm in no good emotional or mental space to process it right now anyway. Giving myself those ten minutes to relax against Rylan was a bad, bad idea. I am a mess and I need space. Immediately.

Rylan doesn't say anything, but he responds as if he can read exactly how I'm feeling. Which he probably can, because I'm too tired to hide things from him. He checks us into a room and leads me there, without a word. I barely even glance at the bed, before heading straight into the bathroom. A shower sounds like the perfect way to hide right now.

The moment I see myself in the mirror, I freeze. I look different. There's something about the way my skin glows, the way my hair shines with almost a purple tint at the ends. I blink my eyes, trying to chase away the hallucination. That's what it has to be, right? When I look again, my hair seems normal. I'm tired, my dress marred by dirt and dust, but it's my eyes that really capture my attention.

They seem more mature somehow, and yet full of the kind of emotion I always try to keep at bay. There's too much there, and I'm thankful for the thin door that separates Rylan and me because I don't know if I could face him right now.

I turn on the shower, strip, and wash my underwear, before I climb in. I turn the tap to nearly scorching, letting the water wash away all of these conflicting thoughts and emotions.

It's difficult, but I force myself to focus on our problem. Or maybe I should say our many problems. So far, the town hasn't shown itself to be anything other than what it is. But we only drove past a dozen buildings before we landed here, so maybe the next step should be exploring. There has to be a reason they're patrolling the woods with rifles. Clearly, I'm assuming things here, but what else would it be if there are people stationed around the entrance of the town. The fact that they used guns has to mean they're human, right? But who knows? I sure don't, considering I can't seem to get headway on any part of what needs to be done. If I was making a list, I would be really frustrated at the lack of checkmarks next to the bullet points. But I'm not going into those woods again until I talk to Stella. I'm hoping she has something helpful to say.

Begrudgingly, I will admit that Rylan's idea of coming into town to regroup was a good one. I, on the other hand, had the terrible idea of pretending we were a couple, because even that tiny amount of time is forever imprinted in my mind. And on my skin. No matter how hard I scrub, I can't scrub off the feeling of Rylan's fingers gently caressing mine.

Clearly, I have a problem.

Pretty sure I come to this exact realization daily.

The water cools, and my skin has turned pruny, but I still don't leave the shower. When I go out there, I'll have to face Rylan, and I'm simply not ready. I know—so mature of me.

But I also know I can't stay in here forever, so I finally turn off the tap. There's a robe on the door, and since I'm about to call Stella, I feel like I can get away with holding off putting on my dirty dress for a bit. Brushing through my hair with my hands, I pull on the robe, and finally step out of the room.

Rylan is nowhere in sight.

I check on the pack link, and he's around, he's just not in the room. He's also not in trouble. I should probably ask, but

I don't feel like it at the moment, so instead, I head for the phone.

Stella picks up on the first ring.

"Were you expecting my call?" I ask, when she says hello. Stella chuckles. I have no idea if her powers extend to any kind of premonition, because even though she says they don't, I'm not sure if I believe her. She anticipates way too well for that.

"Are you safe?" she asks, and now I'm thinking, doesn't she have premonition powers? Honestly, I don't get witches.

"Relatively," I reply, glancing around the small hotel room. "There's something off about this town. Williamsburg seems very similar to Holden. Except that someone is patrolling their woods with rifles and shooting at anything resembling a wolf. And the forest behind the town has a heavy magical protection."

Stella is silent for a moment, as if she's letting the information sink in. Then she sighs.

"That's what I was afraid of."

"Oh, so you knew this was a possibility?" Even though she can't see me, my eyes narrow with suspicion.

"No. Not specifically. I was simply afraid the towns would be taking matters into their own hands to fight off the Ancients, and they'll be going about it in the wrong way. I never thought Williamsburg would do this."

I didn't even think about the Ancient aspect. I guess now that they're just an ordinary part of our lives, they're not as predominant of a thought as when they first started waking up. But that would make sense. This area might not even be aware of the stuff going on with rabid wolves. They might simply be trying to keep their town safe from Ancients.

"Tell me about the magic." Stella's voice interrupts my thoughts. It's my turn to sigh.

"I wish I could tell you something other than it assaulted my senses to a point where all I felt was pain and then Rylan carried me out of there."

"You mean he wasn't affected?"

"No. Maybe he sensed something, but I can't tell if he was just sensing my distress." There's something in her voice. "Why is that important?"

"Because if it's only affecting you, then it's probably related to your True Alpha powers."

"Which we know nothing about," I say.

"Which we know nothing about," Stella echoes.

Glorious. This supposedly super helpful thing is becoming a completely useless power. A hindrance, really, at this point.

"Do you have anything for me that can help?" I ask and I already know the answer, before Stella even replies.

"No. None of the witches I know reside in Williamsburg any longer, which is a little concerning."

"Duly noted." I run a hand over my face, frustration seeping into every pore. "There is magic here, though. I can feel it." Which is yet another new development of my alpha powers that I also have no idea how to deal with.

"Yes, but I can't help you with that. If I was there, it would be different. The best I can tell you is to stay away from people. Keep the protection crystals on you at all times. They won't work to protect a space, since I need to cleanse them again, but they will help to muddle the waters if someone is looking for you. You still have your bracelet, right?" I glance down at it on my wrist. "That'll help too. I'll keep asking around, but—"

"Don't hold my breath. I got it."

I'm not really upset with Stella. It's more the whole situation. Also, it doesn't help that I'm exhausted.

"Get some rest, Trinity," Stella says, as if she can see the yawn I'm fighting, "and be careful. If the magic is affecting your True Alpha powers, my best guess is that either an Ancient is close by or someone who is messing with the Ancient's powers. Good news is that you're searching for that very thing, trying to see if someone can use Ancient powers and how. Bad news, things are more dangerous than you thought."

Which is exactly what I'm afraid of.

When we hang up the phone, I don't move from the bed. My limbs feel completely weighed down, so instead of fighting it, I tuck my feet under me and curl into my side. Rylan will be back any minute, and then we'll decide what to do next.

CHAPTER 12

I sleep with no dreams, which in itself is surprising. When I finally manage to pry my eyes open, I know Rylan has been back. And has gone again. I'm a little surprised I didn't wake up, but I guess my body needed to rest more than I thought.

There's a sandwich on the bedside table and a strip of red at my feet. I sit up quickly, looking down to see a dress. It's a new dress, my favorite shade of red, with a skater skirt, a square neckline, and quarter sleeves. It looks comfy, and when I reach for the fabric, it feels comfy as well.

I sit and stare at the dress as if it's one of the rabid wolf puzzles I'm trying to solve. Rylan must've gotten it for me. A change of clothes, because he knows how much I love to pamper myself and then put on a clean dress. My brain seems to have stopped computing. I take a deep breath and reach for the sandwich first.

While I eat it, I continue to stare at the dress. I'm not sure why it's getting to me so much, but it might be simply because my walls are already way down when it comes to Rylan and I have no idea what to do with that.

Once I've finished my food, I shake my head at myself and grab the dress. Stepping inside the bathroom, I can see that Rylan has been in here as well. He took a shower and probably changed before he left again. My underwear is still hanging where I left them, and my face flushes bright red to match the color of my dress as I think about Rylan being in here. It shouldn't matter, but now he knows the color of my undies, and that's bringing up all kinds of unwanted emotions.

My hair dried into a wavy mess while I slept, so I brush through it with my hands once more. I wash my face and rinse my mouth with mouthwash Rylan clearly left for me. I look slightly more rested, so I'll take it. Then, and only then, do I pull on my new clothes.

The fabric feels amazing against my skin, a comfortable t-shirt material that stretches over my body. The skirt reaches mid-thigh, and it's perfect. I'll be able to run and fight in this, no problem.

I hear the door to the main room open and take a deep breath. I have to face him; it's not like I can hide in here indefinitely. When I step out of the bathroom, Rylan is by the bed. He's definitely showered and changed. His black t-shirt and dark blue jeans appear tailor-made for him. I realize I'm letting my eyes peruse his body just as I notice he's doing the same to me. When our gaze meets, I see the satisfied sparkle in his eyes upon seeing me in the dress he picked out. He seems very satisfied with himself, and I'm fighting the blush threatening to give me away.

"Did you rest?" I ask, breaking the silence, because one of us has to. Rylan shakes his head.

"You needed sleep more than I did," he replies. I narrow my eyes.

"Did you sit outside the room like a guard dog?" He doesn't like that, but I feel much more comfortable pushing his buttons than trying to figure out how to deal with that heated look in his eyes.

"Something like that," he says, right as the door behind me opens.

When Ezra and Zach step inside the room, I know I shouldn't be surprised, but I am. I stare at both of them as if they're some other form of mythical creatures, sprung up from the bowels of underground.

"What are you doing here?" I ask, hands going to my hips as I glare at each of them.

"It's great to see you, too, Trinity," Ezra says, and then all three pairs of eyes swivel to him, because that is definitely a Zach comment. Ezra's face is completely stoic, but there's a slight twitch at the left corner of his lips that I don't miss.

"I called for reinforcements," Rylan answers. This time, I'm glaring at him.

"How?" I'm trying to think back. I didn't feel anything through the pack link, but I was out of it there for a while, so maybe—

"I used the phone," Rylan points to the contraption on the bedside table. He's trying not to laugh. What is with these boys!

"You thought it would be a good idea to not only go behind my back to bring them here, but to leave the pack unprotected and put them in more danger than they already were in?" My voice rises with each part of the question, until I force some air into my lungs and breathe. The alpha in me is just as agitated as I am, if not more. I already feel like I failed to protect Rylan, and now there's more of them. My vision tunnels for a second, as I shove my overactive imagination to the side before it bombards me with every possible horrible scenario.

"Hey," Rylan is in front of me in a flash, his head bent so he can look me in the eye without requiring me to raise my head. He's not touching me, but he's close enough that I can feel his body heat. "Talk to me."

There he goes again, messing with my head with those three simple words. I take another deep breath, doing my best to keep the panic at bay, and look up at him.

"Stella doesn't know anyone in the area and has practically no information regarding anything to do with that weird magical assault I experienced, so we have to do our own recon in town, and I have no way to predict what we're walking into, and I don't like this. Any of this. At all."

Apparently, word vomit is how I speak now. I hate walking into situations where I don't have any information. It feels like that's all I've been doing lately. I have no idea how to keep myself safe, let alone anyone else.

"I suck at this alpha thing," I mumble, but of course shifters with supernatural hearing hear me no problem. Both Ezra and Zach grunt, but it's Rylan who steps back into my space so that I now have to raise my head to look at him.

"You don't suck at being alpha. You've been alpha for less than a month with zero preparation. You'll make all kinds of mistakes, and you'll come back from them."

"How encouraging," I roll my eyes, but it does actually make me feel better.

"Rylan should know. He makes mistakes all the time," Zach quips. Now I'm trying not to smile, while Rylan growls a warning, glaring at the beta. Ezra shakes his head, and steps forward, his eyes on me.

"Trinity, you know there is no way we would have left unless I found the right wolves to watch over the pack. Matthew is in charge of the guards, and Finn is one of the village teachers, who also trains the pups in defense. Both have been in charge before and are fully aware of what's happening."

The more Ezra talks, the calmer I feel. Rylan gives Ezra a firm nod, before he ducks his head a little to catch my eye once more.

"Ezra and Zach are here because we need reinforcements. There's more going on here than we anticipated. I trust my wolves to have my back. And since you are their alpha, you can check on them any time. Do you feel any danger?" Rylan asks, ignoring Zach's chuckle. I pull on my pack link, searching for the wolves, and when I find them, they seem content. Maybe not happy in the way they would be if this mess wasn't present, but safe.

"See, nothing to worry about."

"When did you turn into such an optimist?" I grumble, raising an eyebrow.

"When I was no longer allowed to be the grump, since you've decided to take that mantle for yourself," Rylan replies, with no hesitation. I mock gasp and realize I feel better.

When I glance at the betas, Zach is grinning, and Ezra looks calmly ready for orders.

"Okay. I guess, let's do some recon or something. We still need to go into those woods, but first, we need to make sure we won't be ambushed when we do. This isn't a vacation, boys."

When Zach salutes me, I let my smile blossom.

* * *

WE LEAVE THE MOTEL BEHIND, keeping to the main street. I wasn't kidding when I told Stella Williamsburg reminds me of Holden. It's nearly the same setup, right down to the mountains in the distance, but maybe most of the towns around this area are. The streets are filled with planters and historic looking streetlamps, and there is a smell of freshly brewed coffee and bread in the air.

When we turn down a street and a sign comes into view, as well as a crowd of people, I nod toward them. The guys look and I say, "Seems like the perfect place, right?"

It's dark out, shadows dancing between the twinkle lights and streetlamps. But even at this distance, I can hear the music coming from the bar. The steady flow of people in and out is a sure sign that just like in Holden, this is probably the place to hang out at night. Rylan holds the door open for me and we walk in, instantly surrounded by more noise.

The place is much larger than Stella's. There's a ground floor, and a balcony on the upper floor, overlooking the dance area. The bar is on the opposite side of the room, against the wall, on a slightly lifted platform, so it provides the best vantage point.

People are laughing and arguing all around us, and with a simple glance at each other, we separate. Zach and Ezra are immediately surrounded by bodies. At least five people ask them to dance before they've taken three steps, and I can't help but smile. I also can't help but feel slightly proud, as if I'm the one who made them handsome. Maybe that's an alpha thing. Although I doubt Rylan feels the same.

When I turn my attention to Rylan, I don't feel the same sense of pride. I feel possessiveness. Two girls are vying for his attention currently, with a bunch more people right on the outskirts of his seat. He's leaning half against the bar, half out, watching the room. Or rather, watching me. I raise an eyebrow at him, just as one of the girls leans over to say something in his ear.

The desire to walk over and rip her pretty face into shreds for even getting that close to him is a bit overpowering, so I twist my body away and run right into someone.

"Easy there," the man's voice says, and I look up to find myself looking into eyes so dark brown they look nearly black. Nothing like Rylan's midnight blue. There's an easy smile on the guy's face, but it doesn't reach his eyes. He's watching me almost like he knows me, but I have never seen him before. He seems like he's in charge…of something. I can't tell if it's just my unease because of our proximity and his imploring gaze, or if I'm actually picking up a wave of danger from him, but it feels almost like he sought me out.

"My bad," I smile up at him, and he grins broader.

"New here?"

"Just passing through."

I don't move away from him, and he seems to like that. The noise of the bar rises above us again, and this time I notice it a little more. There's an unnatural pitch to it, almost like people are laughing in unison, but that doesn't make sense.

"How about I get you a drink and you tell me all about it?" The guy says and I don't miss the use of 'get' instead of 'buy.' He definitely has status here.

"I think I'll like that idea," I reply. The desire to turn and find Rylan is pressing on me, but I refuse to give in. I know he's watching me, because I can feel his gaze on me like a brand.

The guy leads me to the opposite side of the bar, the people parting for him like he's the king and it makes me more curious. There's also a sense of…something in the air. I can't really tell if it's my paranoia, or if there's truly something magical going on. I try to study my surroundings as we walk, but all I see are people. Everywhere. Probably too many for this space.

The guy settles against the wall, and I know that technique. He can see the whole bar from here, which is annoying because now my back is to the crowd…and I don't like that.

"I'm Paul," the guy says, leaning toward me a little, as if to be heard over the noise.

"Trinity," I reply, and he grins. He's cute, in that polished kind of way: neatly trimmed brown hair, a barely visible five o'clock shadow. His clothes are pressed, and he looks like he was wearing a suit jacket earlier, and has shed it now, for that effortless, after-work look.

Except he doesn't look like he would be someone who works at the office. His hands look like they've never done a day of work in his life. He looks like someone who would employ a bunch of goons to keep order because he's too clean to get his hands dirty.

"So what brings you to town, Trinity?" He takes a drink from the bartender and puts it next to me on the bar. I don't reach for it.

"Oh, you know"—I lean forward, resting my elbow on the bar, so I can look up at him from under my eyelashes—"looking for a bit of fun. And maybe somewhere to settle down for a bit."

"Is that right? What brought you to Williamsburg?" He's definitely interrogating me, in the most nonchalant way possible.

"A truck," I reply with a smile. He laughs, a little more loudly than I would expect, and that's when I know without a doubt that he's fishing for information. I guess if he is someone important in this town, then he wants to know the strangers who pass by. But also, he's studying me almost like I'm a piece of merchandise he would like to purchase. I can't really put my finger on it, but if I were betting, I'd say there's more to this conversation than meets the eye.

"That's an interesting tattoo, Trinity," Paul says, looking down at the white outline of the wolf on my wrist. I glance down as well, always forgetting that it's there and when I look up again, there's a different kind of a gleam in Paul's gaze. More direct somehow—just for a second, before it disappears again. Something is happening here, and I'm not exactly sure what. Now he looks almost…hungry. For what, I can't even begin to guess. A chill creeps up my spine the longer he's near me, my wolf just as uncomfortable as I am. The way he's staring at my wrist makes me think he knows what it means. Or, at least, guesses at its power. I've never seen anyone look at it like they recognize it.

"It was one of those 'on a whim' moments," I say, laughing as well, but even to my own ears, it sounds a little strained. That uncomfortable feeling intensifies, and I resist the urge to turn and look behind me. There's definitely something in the air here. A spell?

"Interesting whim."

"Now, Paul. You seem to be finding everything interesting about me." There, that sounds far more relaxed and flirtatious. He leans closer, ducking his head toward me and I fight my impulse to move away.

"That's because you're interesting."

Just then, something catches his attention over my shoulder, and his eyes harden for just a moment, before he looks back at me again.

"I have to take care of something real quick, but please don't leave. I would like to continue our...interesting conversation." He speaks with a sort of intensity in his voice that surprises me. I nod, with a little smile, and he seems satisfied. He gets off the barstool and heads back across the floor. I turn to watch, and when he reaches a door and pulls it open, I realize the magic thing isn't just in my head. The door itself is nothing special, but as I watch him slip inside, it looks like there's steam coming off it. I blink, trying to figure out if I'm hallucinating, but then it hits me almost like a breeze finally reaching me from the open door. There is definitely magic here, and it's pulsing off that door.

CHAPTER 13

Now that I know my instincts seem to be correct, I do another slow study of the room. There are way too many people crammed in here, which is a bit surprising. I thought humans were supposed to have capacity laws or something along those lines, but there's almost no air left in this room from all the bodies moving through the space.

Even the balcony upstairs is at full capacity with people dangerously pressed against the banister. When I search for my wolves, I find Ezra first, leaning against the wall to my right under the balcony, eyes focused on the crowd. He feels my gaze, and when his eyes shift to me, I notice the same kind of concern that's rushing through me. I nod a little, before I turn my attention to Zach.

He's on the balcony, near the left side, opposite of Ezra below. He's talking to a pretty girl, but I can tell his attention is on his surroundings as well. His shoulders are set in that rigid way that tells me he feels it too.

Finally, my eyes turn to Rylan. He's on the opposite side

of the bar, about four people around him vying for his attention, but his gaze is on me. I can always feel it, like a physical brand.

He catches my eyes with his heated ones, and I have a distinct feeling that it has more to do with me flirting with Paul than it does with whatever is going on in this room. I give myself half a second to enjoy that look, before I raise my eyebrow, almost baiting him. Even at this distance, I can hear his low growl. Which only makes me grin.

I don't want to use the pack link, just in case it alerts anyone to us in the way our presence hasn't. But I'm sure that's just wishful thinking, because clearly there's a lot going on here that we're not privy to, and whoever is in charge is plenty aware.

Motioning with my head to the other side of the room, I slip off the stool and head to the space below the balcony, near the stairs. Without having to look, I can feel the others moving toward my central location.

The bodies around me continue to grind and drink, and there's a sense of abandonment about the way they move that makes me think they're not quite in control of themselves. When one girl bumps into me, she turns with a laugh, her eyes glassy as they look through me. My brow furrows as I watch her. I turn to the next person, and I'm met with the same vacant look. There's a smile on their faces, and outwardly, they seem to be enjoying themselves. But they're not actually present. It's almost like they're in a trance.

When I reach the guys, they don't automatically talk. We stand mostly back-to-back, not really looking at each other, but also obviously together. I can feel the tension radiating off them like heat.

"Something is off about this place." Zach is the first to

speak, keeping his attention on the people around us. "Are they under a spell?"

I'm glad I'm not the only one who can tell something is off. If we were in a different circumstance, I would laugh at the fact that Zach's brain went to magic. I'm definitely rubbing off on them.

"They're under the influence of something. Maybe Trinity's new friend could shed some light on what's going on." I don't miss the bite in Rylan's words and I'm glad he's not looking at me because I grin. He's definitely jealous.

"I'd say I could get him to talk. Maybe in a more private setting—"

The growl rips out of Rylan before I can even finish the sentence, and I'm pretty sure even Ezra is trying not to laugh at this point.

"He disappeared into that room over there." I nod in the general direction. "Should I follow?"

This time, his growl is even more pronounced, and I can feel it vibrate against my back as he turns to face me. His body grazes mine as he twists, and I feel his hot breath on my neck.

"That would be very unwise." His words are barely above a whisper, spoken directly into my ear, and my mind immediately travels back to the last time he was possessive and the way his lips felt on mine. Almost like he can sense where my thoughts have taken me, he closes what little distance there is between us, putting himself directly against my back. His fingers circle my wrist, and I can feel the conflict within him. He doesn't know whether to pull me closer or to push me away. So I make the decision for him.

I lean against his back, bringing the arm he's holding across my stomach, tucking myself into him. The music gets louder, the thrashing of bodies more pronounced, and that's when I feel it. The pull of magic, like fog rising over fresh morning dew, dancing in the air and then whisked away in the direction of the door.

The crowd moves closer, closing in, as ramping up to the final event. Everything is shuffling around us, which allows me to notice a few men behaving differently. They're stationed around the room in a very precise manner and not by accident.

This is not a normal bar. We walked into an event that I would guess is a magical one. Which is not great considering I have no tools available to tell me what it could be or how to handle it. My mind goes to the worst-case scenario, but I push it away.

My back is still to Rylan, and I feel his body vibrating from my proximity and the music around us. I hold onto him like an anchor, as if he can keep in in place amidst the waves of people around us. The louder the people get, the more potent this fog of magic feels to me. It clouds my vision for a moment, and when I blink, it goes away. That's when a thought comes to mind.

"I think it is a spell," I say, keeping my voice lower than usual. "And I think whatever it is, it's feeding off the energy in this room."

It seems strange and not something I would've ever thought of, except that the witches have mentioned the siphoning of magic to me before. It can be done to a place or a person. Even as I think more about it, it makes sense. So many people, so much natural energy in one place—it makes me think of the rabid wolves, of the men we saw being pushed into that cave. Their essence is not quite there but not quite gone. If someone could find a way to bottle that up, there would be no stopping them. And now, there're four shifters in the middle of this bar, probably supplying even more energy than before. No wonder Paul made a beeline for me. He must know. Which means, this is a trap.

"We have a serious problem."

* * *

THE GUYS ARE THINKING. I would make a quip about them trying not to hurt themselves, but this is neither the time nor place for jokes. Glancing around, I can almost see the danger descending. The crush of people, the lack of oxygen, the bodies, bodies, bodies falling down, covered in blood, blood...

No. I shake my head, dispersing the images. Now is also not the time to give into panic and start imagining the most terrible outcome scenarios. No jokes and no panic, Trinity.

Except, no matter how hard I try to shake the images off, it's like they're photographs sent straight to my brain. I better not be developing some weird premonition powers alongside everything else, because enough is enough.

I can feel Rylan's gaze on me, even though I'm still pressed against him. It's like he can feel me spiraling, and he's getting even better at it now than he was when we were kids. No matter how much I try to hide things from him, he reads me like a book. There's no hiding from him.

Needing a bit of space, I drop my hand from his arm, and step away from his embrace. When I turn, he's still watching me, and not for the first time, I wonder what he sees. I think he's going to keep me captive with that gaze indefinitely when Ezra's voice breaks through my thoughts.

"We need to find a way to break them out of their trance,"

he says, his eyes doing that quick scan that they always do before looking at Rylan and then at me. "You're the expert in magic, is there a spell? Or..." He trails off because these shifters know absolutely nothing about how magic works, well, besides what they've learned from me.

"I'm not a witch," I reply, raising an eyebrow. It's lucky we have supernatural hearing because it's hard to hear over the noise of the music and voices. Stella's is the only bar I've ever been to but even on a day when it's packed, it's not like this. Whatever influence they're under, it's keeping them rooted in this room and it's keeping them loud.

"I think our best bet is to get in there," I cock my head to the right, and I know the boys can see the door over my shoulder. Since my newfound alpha powers can apparently read the magic pulsating from in there, we have to follow through. It's also the room Paul went into, and I know Rylan doesn't like that. But unless we can make it outside—which doesn't seem like an option because with a quick glance I see there are now people positioned at the only visible exit—we need to see if we can break through some other way. And that magic room seems the best option.

"There are too many of them," Zach comments, and I know this part as well, because it's hard to miss the large goons seemingly positioned everywhere. I don't understand the endgame here, but I'm definitely in a 'fight now, ask questions later' mode. I'm sure the boys agree.

"Could we fight our way through?" Ezra asks.

"We could," Rylan speaks up for the first time, his eyes on me, "but too many humans would be collateral damage. We can't risk that."

He's right. If we start an assault in the middle of the dance floor, many humans will be in the way. They don't look like they'd feel any of it, but that doesn't matter. Since Paul knows we're here, he might be prepared for that anyway. His little disappearing act is just too coincidental to be just that.

"What we need is a distraction."

I say the words out loud and all three look at me like I've spoken a different language.

"What? If we can draw enough of the goons' attention away, we can sneak through and see what's behind the door. But it can't be something that puts the innocents at risk."

Which means there aren't many options. Especially for three tall, gorgeous wolf shifters who are not equipped in the ways of human interaction. Zach, by far, has the most outrageous ideas.

"I could shift—"

"No!" The three of us nearly shout, and Zach raises his arms in surrender.

"It was only an idea."

"We're trying to keep people from knowing what we are," Rylan comments, narrowing his gaze on the beta. The guys start arguing that since the humans are under some magic anyway, maybe it won't be so bad. The majority of the world doesn't know about magic, and something like that could be explained away by drugs…which seems like the cover-up this town will have to use to explain all these people losing their minds in one place.

As the guys continue their argument, I slip away. They'll be here until the sun comes up, and we can't wait that long. So I do the only thing I can think of.

Snaking my way through the crowd I reach the bar, where the music is being played. Leaning forward, I put on my best smile, as the bartender comes over. He gives me an appreciative once over and it makes me love my red dress even more. It never fails to draw attention.

"How about you play something a little more…dance-worthy?" I say and his eyes flash conspiratorially.

"I have just the thing."

He moves to the stereo, pulling up an upbeat oldies melody. I grin. Just what I needed. Without hesitation, I pull myself onto the bar, crouching down so I can lift the bottom of the bartender's jaw up with one finger, snapping his mouth closed.

"Mind if I borrow your bar for a minute?" I ask, and he shakes his head, as if unable to speak. I stand to my full height, tugging the bottom of the skirt at the sides, as I launch into a dance.

The music fills my senses, the determination to see this through even if it's a bit terrifying. I've never danced in front of anyone before. Well, no. That's not true. One person *has* seen me dance.

As I turn, my eyes zero in on Rylan. His whole body has gone as rigid as a statue. Even without supernatural vision, there's no way I could miss the fire in his eyes. He watches me—not only with his eyes, but his whole being, it seems—as if I'm the only wonder of the world. The heat in his gaze fuels my boldness, and then, it's like I'm dancing only for him.

My hips sway, my arms going over my head as I lose myself to the beat and the rhythm of Rylan's heart. I can nearly hear it, even with all this noise and distance between us. Because no matter how much distance there is, we're always tethered together on some cosmic level. My skin is on fire as if surrounded by open flame, and for as long as I live, I will never get his look out of my eyes.

He sees me, fully and completely, for everything I am—and he's mesmerized.

I want nothing more than to jump down from this bar and rush into his arms. But that's not who we are, and that's not why we're here. It takes a second, but then I remember. Tearing my gaze away from Rylan is nearly physically painful, but as I turn, I see about half the goons have moved toward the bar, or are watching me. I do another spin and find Ezra near the door, with Zach blocking him from the rest of the room, and I'm glad to see that at least they remember why we're here. The beat of the music rises again, and the people nearest the bar start jumping to the beat with me. Ezra slips halfway inside the door and peeks inside, before catching my eyes and nodding. Then he and Zach are inside. I twirl again, jumping with the crowd.

The energy is addicting, and soon the rest of the room is shouting the words to the song. I want to lose myself in this moment—I want to lose myself in Rylan—but I keep my attention off him for as long as I can.

When the song finally ends, the people near the bar clap and I'm laughing at their enthusiasm. Rylan is suddenly there, reaching up to me, and when I let myself fall into him, I'm not even thinking. Simply reacting.

He catches me around the waist, and I twine my arms around his neck, as I stare into his eyes, a broad grin on my lips. I'm flushed, my hair is a mess, and I can't seem to catch my breath. Rylan doesn't set me down, but keeps me pinned against him, so we stay eye-to-eye. I can see the war he's having with himself, the array of emotions in his deep blue eyes, and I don't speak.

I want him to kiss me.

I just want him.

We haven't talked about our last kiss. We haven't talked about any of the new and rising emotions brewing between us. And we won't. Not now.

So I put my heart away, and the next grin I give him is a cocky one.

"Not bad, right?"

He sets me gently back to the floor, but he doesn't step away. His voice is low and hoarse when he does speak.

"Not bad at all."

CHAPTER 14

Clearly, we didn't break the trance, because people keep shouting with the music. But what we did—what I did—is kind of start a riot. People press up against the bar, trying to take my place on top of it. The bartender is shouting, and a throng of people slams against me, pulling me away from Rylan. But then his hand is on mine, his fingers wrapped securely around my own, and he pulls me away from the crowd.

Most of the goons are now trying to keep the people at bay, and the door is unguarded enough for me and Rylan to follow the betas. Zach and Ezra are inside what appears to be a small corridor.

"A lovely dance," Zach comments, wiggling his eyebrows. Which causes Rylan to growl in response. And that makes me grin.

"Thank you, Zach," I reply, giving him a big smile. Rylan —who's still holding my hand—tugs me a little closer to him. It feels like an automatic move, and I give myself a second to enjoy it, before I extract my hand and place both of mine on my hips.

"What have you got for us, boys?" I ask, looking between Zach and Ezra. The latter is the one who answers. I can't tell in the dim light, but I think he's looking a little amused.

"One door to the left and an exit straight out. Can't hear inside, which means it's cloaked. There are no guards here and since there's a mob happening outside, I'd say we have very little time to decide what we're doing."

I can hear the noise rise at our backs, not much protection from the small door that separates us.

"I say we leave"—I nod toward the exit door—"and regroup. There's way too much happening here for us to do anything. And if we step in there"—I nod to the door on our left—"I have a feeling we'll find ourselves in an even worse situation. We're basically walking around blind."

"Which seems to be us in every situation currently," Zach mumbles, and I don't disagree. But the guys don't argue, and Rylan doesn't offer an opinion, so we turn and head for the exit.

Right as we reach it, the door next to it begins to open, so I push Zach straight into Ezra and the exit, grabbing Rylan to yank him behind me. With our supernatural speed, we're out before the door swings fully open, and then we're running.

We're in an alley at the back of the bar and outside. The only thing we can hear at our backs is the music. The shouting has ceased. Or else, there's a magical barrier so the public isn't concerned. Either way, we don't stop until we reach the woods. And then we still don't stop.

I shift on the run, racing away from the town as fast as I can. The need to be away from there is overpowering. My skin feels dirty somehow. It's as if I'm covered in mud and I desperately need another shower.

It's about another fifteen minutes before we slow down. I shift, running my hands over my hair, head spinning.

"What was that?" Ezra asks from beside me. I turn to find all three of them shifted and watching me. The nervous energy is still running through me, head spinning with questions.

"We've clearly walked in on something magical," I say, my hands working automatically through the knots in my hair. "The whole place felt so…"

"Sleazy," Zach supplies, and I point at him.

"Yes! I couldn't tell if it was shifter senses or if it was something else, but there was clearly something going on. And then that door." I stop for a moment, letting my mind conjure it up in my head. There's no rational reason behind what I say next, but I say it anyway. "It was almost pulsating with magic."

"I felt it too." Rylan's words are soft, but my eyes fly up to meet his. He's watching me in that steady Rylan way of his, and for a moment, my mind flashes back to the bar and the dance and the way his gaze held me captive. His look heats, as if he's thinking the same thing. It takes all of my willpower to tear myself away.

"It was there," Ezra speaks up. When I glance at him, I know he's not missing the tension between Rylan and me, and he's giving us an out. I hold his gaze for an entirely different reason, and he inclines his head just a tad before he continues. "The energy inside the room was near staggering. It was heavy and full."

"Potent." Zach adds. So we're all on the same page, apparently. There was enough magic there for even them to feel it.

Considering they're never attuned to magic the same way I am, there had to be loads of it in the air. That says a lot.

"Have you ever sensed magic before?" I ask the wolves. And all three shake their heads.

"You know that feeling when it's super hot outside and you step out of the house and the air kind of hits you in the face?" Zach asks. "That's kind of how it felt."

It's definitely not how it feels to me, but maybe similar in a sense.

"The guy you were talking to," Ezra begins, and I feel—rather than see—Rylan move closer. "Did he say anything?"

"It's not really what he said, but how he said it. There was a sense of a cat and mouse game in every word. Now that I think about it, he knew who I was—or at least that I was a shifter—of that I am sure." I'm not exactly sure how I know that, but it feels very right. Maybe it was the way he singled me out or his fascination with my tattoo.

"Whatever is going on in that town, it's definitely not what we expected before coming here," Zach says.

"Correct," Rylan replies. "But the question remains, does this have anything to do with our mission?"

The four of us exchange a look, because it's what I've been thinking as well. Do we deal with this now or do we deal with this later? Or is it a direct influence on what we're trying to accomplish here? Once again, we have all these questions and are no closer to any answers.

My body buzzes from everything that's happened—the near miss of danger and that dance. But even more so, from feeling Rylan's eyes on me and his arm holding me close. I'm spinning in a whirlpool of emotion, and as I try to find my footing again, I can feel myself in danger of crashing.

Part of me wants to go back there, turn the music back

up, and lose myself in its rhythm. But I can't just hide away from my responsibilities. The three wolves in front of me are my responsibilities, and I will do whatever it takes to protect them. Which adds a ton of pressure on me, when I'm already at a breaking point.

Because that's what it feels like, right there—me, on the edge. And now they're looking at me for more direction and how do I not fail them? If I'm being honest, I'm terrified I can't handle the responsibility of always coming up with the answers. This stupid True Alpha power is useless. It was never in my mind to be a leader, and now it is my direct responsibility to make decisions that cause life and death outcomes. How's that for a life plot twist?

My brain is spiraling again, my own thoughts, coupled with the responsibilities of the alpha, and everything we have experienced so far are pushing at me from every side. I push air into my lungs, my wolf just in as much of a distress as I am. The sounds of the forest become too much, and it seems like I'm about to slip fully into a panic when Rylan steps in front of me, blocking it all off.

I look up at him, my breathing faster than it should be, and find comfort in his steady gaze. We might be at each other's throats most of the time—less now than before—but he still focuses me, pulling me out of my whirlwind before I can fully give into it. And he doesn't even say anything.

My wolf calms at his steady look, and then I follow suit. This ridiculous—and repetitive—loss of control is getting... dangerous. If I lose it like this with minimal triggers, then who's to say I won't do that when it's important. I've become unreliable, and I have no idea what to do about that.

"My personal opinion is to get to the forest behind the town," Rylan speaks up, as if nothing is the matter, and we're having a normal conversation. He's still blocking my view of the others, his gaze not leaving my eyes, but he's talking like everything is normal.

"We have reinforcements now. And since we weren't able to find any witches in the area, we're going to have to do it ourselves."

I understand what he's doing—he's bringing me back to myself—so I nod and pick up his train of thought. Much like I used to do when we were kids.

"You looked for witches?"

"After I called the guys."

I nod again, feeling a little more stable.

"So if we double back around, keeping a wide berth around the town, we can get back to the spot we found before. It's risky, considering how it affected me the last time, but there're four of us now. Ezra and Zach can watch your back if I can't."

That truly is my concern. If I'm so unreliable, if Rylan has to drop everything to help me in a middle of an assault, then everyone is in trouble. But with the betas here, we might actually stand a chance.

"The town will still be there once we've checked out the forest," Rylan comments and I know he's right. I simply want to do everything all at once. Which isn't smart. We came here to see if we can find the first shifter, or any sign of him, so we'll do that first. Then we'll figure out what's going on in Williamsburg and how we can help. I don't exactly like leaving all those unsuspecting humans to fend for themselves.

I meet Rylan's gaze and I know he feels the same. It's almost like he makes me a promise without saying a word, that we'll figure all of this out. I can't help but trust him. Look at me, making progress. Finally.

"What do you say, boys?" I ask, stepping around Rylan and facing them. "Want to travel into the unknown?"

"Thought you'd never ask." Zach grins, while Ezra nods.

Take two, here we go.

* * *

WE STOP in the area past Williamsburg, closer to Valley Springs, and far away from where my wolf lost it last time. We didn't sleep, deciding to travel through the evening and half the night before we finally reached the area. It's making me uncomfortable leaving things the way they are at Williamsburg, but there's nothing to be done about that now.

I'm sure the boys feel the same when I say that we are going to go back and figure it out. It's our—well, my—responsibility, and since I'm no longer running from that, here we are.

We don't have a plan; we're going by instinct at this point, which is actually incredibly frustrating. The boys are staying quiet, and I can't tell if it's because of what happened at the bar or if they're being extra cautious. I'm simply trying not to think about what happened at the bar...or look at Rylan for any length of time. My body is still fully aware of the way his eyes felt on me.

I'm not sorry I danced, and I'm not sorry I keep pushing him, but I do have to make a conscious decision not to show outwardly just how much he's affecting me, because neither one of us can handle that right now.

"So what is our next move?" Ezra, the voice of reason, speaks up. We shifted into our human forms as soon as we got close to the area, afraid to set off any kind of silent alarm if we approach as wolves. I look over at the beta, and his eyes are on me. Between him and Zach, Ezra would be the one to ask all the questions. Zach is more of the blind follower type. Although, I wouldn't say blind. He has incredible faith in Rylan not to steer him wrong. One day, I hope to instill that kind of a response where I'm concerned.

"What do you mean?" Rylan speaks up.

"I mean, do we just continue to creep through the woods at a snail's pace hoping to find this tree or—"

"That's exactly what we're going to do," I say, before Rylan can reply. "It's our best bet at this point."

Which is a sad narrative all in its own. There's a pause, then Zach speaks up.

"So we're not going to talk about what happened at the bar?"

The question immediately thrusts me back on top of that bar with Rylan's heated eyes on me. I concentrate entirely on Zach, refusing to look at the other alpha. I have a feeling he's doing the same.

"What is there to talk about?" Ezra asks.

"I've been thinking about it." Zach perks up, leaning forward on the log he's sitting on. Making a fire is too dangerous since we don't want to give away our position and we'll have to rest soon if we're to move at first light. But all of us carry too much energy inside right now.

"I think the town has a full-on mafia ring!" Zach continues. I don't miss the way his eyes sparkle with excitement.

"I think you've watched too many movies," Rylan says, but Zach is undeterred.

"Think about it. That club is obviously a front of some sort. But it's also like a people well!"

"A people well?" Now Ezra is looking at him like he's lost his mind. Which Zach ignores completely and keeps going.

"Yes. A people well of energy. The whole place was pulsing with it, right? So if you stuff all the people in there and find a way to bottle it up…or it could be like a people farm. They could simply be drugging and selling people!"

"We did think that was a possibility," I comment, and Zach grins. "Not the people farm thing," I hurry to add, as Zach rolls his eyes, "but the magic aspect. We were already thinking they were cooking something with magic."

"Exactly. So then you'd have to figure out what to do with that, right? And what better way than to sell it on the black market. There's got to be a black market for magical items, right?"

"Right," Ezra says.

"So, this dude—" Zach looks at me.

"Paul."

"This dude, Paul, is the ring leader. Or like the front man. He gets this magical setup, pumps people free of energy, and then sells it on the black market. It's probably why the woods are so heavily patrolled. Think about it. If your town was full of magical power, wouldn't you be extra careful on who you let in?"

That…actually makes a lot of sense.

"Trin and I caught a ride, and no one tried to stop us," Rylan points out, and I refuse to have an outward reaction to the nickname. He's only used it a few times since I've been back, and every time, it hits me with full force.

"But you were in your human form. I think that's why they shot at your wolf forms."

"Or maybe they're having a rabid wolf problem like we are and are just protecting the town," Ezra says.

"Okay, fine. It could be that too." Zach rolls his eyes, and I can't help but smile a little. How such different shifters become nearly brothers is beyond me. Zach is nearly bouncing in his seat.

"That dude looked super shady—we could all see it. I think his skin was like baby soft or something. And his clothes? Basically, suave like a mafia boss. They might even be in on the whole rabid wolves thing. I mean, if they're dabbling with magic, maybe they're selling magic…something to whoever is experimenting on the wolves!"

"Zach," I say, and his excited gaze turns to me. "You might actually be onto something."

Because it actually makes a lot of sense. We all felt it when we were in that bar. Zach grins at me, and I can't help but smile back at how proud he looks of himself. Even Ezra gives him an encouraging nod.

"But," I begin, hating to ruin his excitement, "that's a problem for another day. We find the tree first and, hopefully, some sign that may lead us to the first shifter, and then we go back and figure out if we can see what's happening in Williamsburg."

Zach's grin isn't diminished at all and he simply pumps his fist a little, like he won something. He's adorable. Not sure I can ever say that out loud. Calling a six foot four nineteen-year-old shifter adorable is probably not going to sit well with him.

Although, it is Zach. He'd probably love it, actually.

It's interesting how it's taken me no time at all to figure out their personalities again. Ezra, still the quiet proper one. Zach, the easygoing one and the first to throw a smile my way. And then there's Rylan.

I glance at him now, looking proud of Zach, while the

beta eats it up. They're friends, they're brothers, but Rylan is still their alpha. And having him proud is an accomplishment and a reward.

Now that I'm looking at Rylan, I can't seem to look away.

The memories of betrayal are still at the front of my mind, but now they're dimmed by the truth of the man he's become, staring right at me. The knowledge that those memories are probably not even true just adds to the intensity of what I'm feeling for him. Because like it or not, I'm feeling a lot. And I don't know what to do about that.

Once again, we're here.

"Let's rest now," I say, tearing my gaze away and focusing on the betas. "Tomorrow, we'll figure out our next step."

.

CHAPTER 15

If I said any of us actually rested, I would be lying. We're past Valley Springs now, farther away from Williamsburg, and while I feel slightly better putting the distance between us, I'm in no way feeling safe. My mind spent its time spinning with all the possibilities and all the horrible outcomes. The horrible outcomes are obviously winning. Having Rylan, Zach, and Ezra here is sending all of my thoughts into worst-case scenario mode. I may not be ready to admit it to them, but they're my pack now, and I take full responsibility for their wellbeing. And not only that, I actually like them. I don't want anything to happen to them.

Especially if it ends up being my fault.

Because that's the other side of this that I can't turn off. I'm in the middle of all of this. From my out-of-nowhere True Alpha power to being called back by the Oracle. Something in me is supposed to help everyone, but I have this sneaking suspicion that it's actually just causing more problems.

Okay, the suspicion isn't sneaking, because I do have a

tendency to jump first and wonder about the consequences later. I'm trying. I really am. But I don't feel like it'll be enough.

"So what's the plan?" Zach asks, as we all get up and dust off our clothes. We're hungry, but I haven't seen or sensed anything to hunt, so we'll have to hold off on that. They're all looking at me, even Rylan, waiting for me to make a decision. I honestly don't know how I'm feeling about Rylan being this agreeable. I know he said he wants to try, but it's weird not fighting with him. I'm more comfortable when we're at each other's throats.

"I don't know. What's the plan, Rylan?" I ask, raising my eyebrow at him. He knows exactly what I'm doing, if his little smirk is any indication.

"We have no choice but to keep moving inward," he says, no hesitation in his voice. Oh, to have that kind of confidence. "The intel we have about this place, besides all the weirdness we found in town, mostly relates to this forest. The area northeast of the mountains is the one that's completely veiled, and if we can find this tree that the witches...scried for, then we should have a starting point."

Rylan's calm deliverance of the facts actually does help with the perspective. We are on the right track; we just got sidetracked a little. Not that it could be helped. But now that we're back on the original path, it's time to start preparing myself for what we might find. Or not find. The first shifter is kind of our only lead in trying to figure out how the wolves are getting shifter powers stripped and losing their magic.

"I'm good with that." Zach shrugs and I can't help but throw a smile his way. He makes all of this feel so normal, he's so nonchalant about it. It's a nice balance to the tightly wound anxiety I'm feeling at all times.

"I don't think you ever said how we're going to find this tree," Ezra comments as we begin moving. Shifting would make this much easier, but I'm too nervous about setting off some magical alarms, so walking it is.

"Trinity will be able to tell," Rylan says, and I throw a glare his way.

"It's not that simple."

"Oh, it's not? I thought you were a magic detector. Isn't that what you did in the bar?" He turns just barely to give me one of his looks, and I roll my eyes.

"I didn't—" Except I can't finish that sentence, because I did. I was able to sense the magic behind the door, as well as its pulsating through the room. So as much as I don't like to admit it, Rylan is right. Which just puts extra pressure on me, but what else is new.

"So we're looking for a giant tree that will be glowing with magic. Seems easy enough." I glance back to see Zach shrugging again.

"It's not going to be glowing," I say. "I don't know what it'll be doing. The only thing I truly know is that it's a giant willow tree."

"Well, that's something," Ezra comments from his place on the other side of me. When I look closely, I see that they're spread out around me, almost in a protective detail. Rylan is on my right, and Ezra is on my left, with Zach bringing up the rear. The unconscious way they always seem to do this brings a smile to my face.

"What do you mean?" I ask Ezra. His eyes stay on our surroundings, but he answers without hesitation.

"I mean there are some three hundred and fifty species of

willows, but since we're looking for a giant tree, that narrows it down."

"I'm sorry, what?" I freeze in my tracks because that's definitely not a piece of information that I expected.

Ezra smirks a little, before he continues.

"Most people associate willows with the giant weeping willow trees, with branches that hang low, usually used in areas for oriental purposes. But there are actually shrubs and smaller varieties all over."

"So how do we know what to look for?" Zach asks.

"I'm going on assumption here, but I would say the magic would be potent for Trinity—something she can feel. Also, willows aren't native to this area, so even if it's not what we expect, it'll stand out. Bees might be helpful as well."

"Bees?" Zach is asking all the questions at this point because I'm struck dumb.

"Yes. Willow trees produce the nectar that bees use to make honey. So if there's a particular tree that's attracting bees at this time of the year, it'll most likely a willow."

I stop in my tracks, staring at Ezra like I've never seen him before. He stops as well, watching me back steadily. I'm honestly not sure why I'm surprised. Ezra has always been one to love books. I guess I just never realized exactly how much information he holds in that handsome head of his.

"Well, wow, Ezra. You were holding out on us," Zach says, coming up and clapping the other shifter on the back. Ezra pulls the Zach move with his shrugging, but I can see a little bit of a smile.

"Seriously, Ezra. That's amazing and incredibly useful," I say, and this time I don't have to guess how he's feeling because his ears turn a little red as he glances down. Such a simple compliment and he's blushing.

"I like to read."

"And we love that you do," I reply. Rylan hasn't come any closer, but he has stopped walking. When I glance over, I notice the proud look on his face. He loves his wolves. If I ever have to question anything about Rylan, it's not that.

"We really should've had this conversation earlier," I say, as I begin walking again, "but I guess it didn't make a difference until now. I am glad you're here. Both of you," I give Ezra and Zach another smile, and keep moving forward. The betas stare at me for a moment longer, as if I surprised them somehow, and maybe I have. I don't praise them nearly enough. I don't look at Rylan, but I can feel his smugness even from over here.

The mountains are nearly upon us. I can see them through the giant trees. We fall into silence as we walk, climbing over fallen branches and skirting around trees. The air grows thicker, the darkness descending as the mountains block whatever little light shone through the trees.

Our senses heighten almost automatically, as something shifts in the space around us. But none of us speak. As a pack, we're usually attuned to each other, but now with my alpha powers, I can tell the way the boys stand up just a little bit straighter, their bodies a bit more in control as they fill with alertness. We don't open up the pack link, just continue to move forward. I can't tell if we've been walking for minutes or hours, because every step is heavy somehow.

It's a different kind of oppression, not quite as bad as the last time Rylan had to carry me out. It feels more like treading water. When I glance over at the betas, I see that they're walking exactly as if they're moving against the waves.

And then, right as I think I can breathe a little easier, the forest darkens in a split second, as if someone turns off the lights.

"Trinity!" Rylan shouts. The light returns. And we're all still here. None of us have moved, and yet the forest around us has changed. It begins to darken again, and I motion the guys closer to me. They move as one, stopping so we're back-to-back, covering all the points of access around us. The light dims again, and then it doesn't come back.

* * *

WE STAND in complete darkness for what seems like hours. However, before I can come up with our next move, the light reappears. Everything around us has shifted somehow, almost like there was an earthquake and every tree and bush and blade of grass moved over a few inches, but wasn't standing exactly upright.

"What is happening?" I ask, looking around. We're still back-to-back, but I take a step forward so I can look at them as well. Rylan and the boys seem just as confused as I am. It's as if we've stepped into a completely different world.

The air around us feels otherworldly and everything is covered in a sort of soft glow, as if the leaves themselves carry light inside of them.

"We're still in the forest?" Zach asks. I can feel his worry through my alpha link, his wolf reaching for the surface. We are always so much calmer when our wolves are present, but now is not the time to shift. We have to be careful.

"We are," I reply, turning my attention to Rylan who has taken a step toward me. His protectiveness is on full display, his eyes flashing as he scans the area around me. I don't think he even notices it. But I can read him because my own urge to protect him rises.

"It feels similar to stepping into the Oracle's garden," Rylan says, glancing down at me, and I nod. My thoughts exactly. It's Ancient magic, that much is obvious, but I can't pinpoint the entrance point, not like I had with the Oracle. We didn't walk through a gate, at least, not one I could see.

This doesn't make any sense.

"What did you do there?" Ezra asks. He is still the calmest of the lot of us, and I often wonder just how much it would take to see him unsettled. Not that I actually want to find out. I feel like if I ever see him unsettled, it'll be the end of the world.

"We didn't do anything," I reply. "We simply followed the Oracle through the tree entrance."

"So did we just walk through an entrance without realizing it?"

"I don't think so," Rylan's words are sure. I glance at him again. He's studying our surroundings, and there's something in that gaze that makes me stand a little taller.

"What do you think?" I ask.

"I think," he begins slowly, turning his attention to me, "we were let in, and I think it's a—"

"Trap," I finish for him. His gaze latches onto mine, his body coiled tightly, and I can read the alpha in him. And my own answers in kind.

It's such a strange sensation, such a strange realization. We're so used to fighting, we never stop to think how both of our alphas can work in tandem. But that's precisely where my wolf is now. I can feel her rising to meet the challenge. I'm ready to work with Rylan; she's ready to walk with the alpha.

But that's the exact moment when I realize my vision is clouding over, and just before I plunge into the dream, my lips form one word.

"Rylan."

He's beside me immediately, reaching for me as I drop straight into the dream.

Everything gets brighter around me, just as fast as it dims. It's the same feeling of the world falling away and coming alive. The emotions hit me from every side, but then there's a sort of hole in the midst of it; I latch onto it with all my might. It's the first time I've ever seen a way out of this darkness, and I have an undeniable need to get to it.

The space itself fights me, as if I'm attached to it by threads of darkness and I have to rip each and every single one. I breathe through it the best I can, my forehead damp from perspiration, but I'm not about to give in. My muscles strain, but I keep pushing and pushing and pulling and then, I fall through, landing on all fours.

There's darkness here, too, but it's not as blinding as the one I left behind. It's like I stepped through a doorway into a better lit room. I can still feel the emotional assault at my back, but for the first time, I seem to be able to breathe. There's an area beyond my line of vision, and I squint to see better.

"Not bad," a voice speaks from the void, a barely visible outline of a man or creature steps into view—I can't tell. But the voice chases some of the assault away, so I don't hide from it. I push forward.

"Who are you?" It's difficult to form the words, but I do.

"The one you're seeking."

For some reason it surprises me that he (or she?) replies. I can't tell if the voice is even human, or if it's something else entirely. It also surprises me that the creature admits to who he is. I decide on he. I'm almost positive. I'm so used to these creatures playing games, I was almost expecting one instead of a straight answer.

"Who are you?" I try again.

"You're not asking the right questions."

And here we are with the games. Seriously, I spoke too soon. They do like their riddles and games.

"Fine, where am I?" Speaking is becoming slightly easier, and I manage to push myself to my knees.

"Still not the right question."

"But I would really like an answer." Now that I seem to be able to breathe again, my snark is back. The creature surprises me with a noise that sounds remarkably like a chuckle.

When he doesn't say or do anything else, I sigh.

"Fine. What questions should I be asking?"

The creature makes that noise again, and I honestly don't know how to take it. I've never met a magical Ancient creature, if that's what he is, and I've never expected him to laugh at me.

"Is this a trap?" I try again. He seems to like that question better.

"No, this is a test."

This time I groan. Of course, it is. Because if there's one thing these Ancient beings love, it's a test—nothing straightforward and everything in the most roundabout way possible.

"If this is a test, then I need to know the rules."

"Now that is a much better direction of inquiry."

Okay, the sarcasm is definitely not appreciated.

"The rules then?" I nudge, since the creature doesn't

continue. When he makes the noise this time, I'm one hundred percent sure it's a laugh. He seems determined to draw this out, and I have a feeling he wants to say something, but then decides against it. Time seems to drag and stand still at the same time as I wait for this creature to make a decision.

"There's much for you to discover, but now is not the time. The rules are simple, Trinity Whitewolf. Survive."

And then I'm thrown straight out of this vision dream and come back to myself screaming.

Rylan's arms are around me, cradling me on his lap as I'm on my back, my whole body shaking as he tries to keep me from thrashing.

"Trin, baby, focus on my voice, come back to me."

That's when I realize there are tears streaming down my face and I'm gasping for breath. Raising my eyes to meet Rylan's worried ones, I feel more tears pool because he looks so fierce and gentle at the same time. It makes my heart skip a beat.

"I'm back," I say. Rylan yanks me up against him, and I bury my face into his shoulder. He hoists me up into his lap, wrapping his strong arms around me, and just holds me.

His body shakes just as mine does, and I can feel his heart beating erratically against mine.

For some reason, I feel the need to soothe him, just like he always soothes me. I turn just slightly, so I can wrap my arms around his torso, and run my hand up and down his back. He shudders at my touch but doesn't do anything else.

We stay like that for a very long moment, and I don't even have to think about it. I just let myself be here, in this moment, soaking it in for what it is. The feeling of comfort, the feeling of home.

When both of our breaths seem to even out, a different type of awareness creeps in. My skin buzzes for all different reasons, and I force myself to pull back.

Rylan follows suit, inclining his head so he can meet my eye and then he says something that explains his intense response entirely.

"You were unreachable. For over an hour."

CHAPTER 16

I run my hand over my hair once I'm back on my feet, trying to soothe myself with such a normal concern as untangling my locks. Zach and Ezra are standing near Rylan now, and all three of them are watching me carefully.

When Rylan was holding me, my thoughts were only on him. I didn't even stop to think about Ezra and Zach. Now what does that say about me as alpha? Probably nothing good.

But the other side of this is the fact that I was in that dream vision for over an hour. How is that possible? It felt like mere minutes, and that felt like too much.

"Tell me what happened," I say, and it's Ezra who replies.

"Once you went into the dream, you started screaming, and then suddenly you weren't. It's like your whole body simply froze, you started crying, and then finally shaking, but no matter what Rylan did, he couldn't get through."

"Not even with the alpha command," Zach adds. And I would be lying if I say that I'm not a bit freaked out by that.

"It didn't feel that long to me," I say, pushing my hair behind my shoulders. "I got pulled into that same dream, and then something else was there. It's almost like it opened this door for me to walk through so I can talk to it, and I did."

"What was it?"

"Not what," I say, "but who. I think it was the creature we seek, but I'm not one hundred percent positive anymore. He said this wasn't a trap, but a test." I'm grateful there are no gaps in my memory this time. I'm getting very tired of visions I can't remember. So yay for progress?

"Because why wouldn't it be?" Zach grumbles. I have to agree.

"What kind of test?" Rylan asks, all business once more. The stoic alpha is back, as if those glimpses of his worry never peeked out.

"I wish I could tell you, but the only rule the creature shared with me is that I have to survive."

That one word weighs heavily in the space around us, because we all understand just how absolutely horrible this test may be. Quickly, I give them a rundown of everything else I remember, including how it felt to be in it. Once I'm finished, the boys look at me just about the same way I'm feeling. Confused.

"That's all I got for you," I say. "I don't know where to go from here."

"I think the only way to go is forward," Rylan says, his eyes never leaving my face, the whole time I've been talking. It's like he's afraid I'll fall into the weird dream trance again. Truth be told, I'm nervous about that as well because I have no idea what causes it or how to gain any control over it. It just happens in the most inopportune of times, and I have no choice but to see it through.

But what if it happens when we're in a middle of a fight? Then I become a liability. That's one more thing for me to worry about, and one I can't focus on right now, or I'll completely lose it and be good to no one.

"Forward?" Ezra asks while I'm having my internal freak-out. "As in, into this unknown forest full of who knows what?"

"Maybe you should go back," I say, looking at the betas in turn. "Back to the pack." I peek over at Rylan. "They need their alpha."

"No. Absolutely not."

"No."

"Nope."

All three answer at once, and I roll my eyes.

"What is the point of me being alpha if none of you listen to me?" I ask no one in particular. "There was nothing in his words that suggest it's a test for anyone but me. You weren't the one who was pulled into this weird dream vision thingy nor the ones given this random yet specific responsibility."

So eloquent, I know.

"I am not leaving you alone." Rylan's tone leaves no room for argument, but I'm going to argue anyway.

"And what happens when both of us can't get back to the pack? Who's going to watch over them then?"

"Ezra and Zach."

"Who are also here!" The panic is starting to creep in again at the thought of any of them hurt.

"Because we needed help. You agreed it was a good idea." Rylan's voice is calming, but it's not working. I make sure to glare at him extra hard.

"And now I need all of you safe, so I can concentrate on figuring this out and surviving!" My voice rises with each word, echoing around us with the last syllable. The wolves look at me with the same kind of a protectiveness that I feel within myself. We're about to argue until we're blue in the face, I can feel it.

"Can I order you back?" I ask, not particularly asking, since I do have the power. But still not feeling right just doing it without their permission.

"Please don't," Zach says, and my heart cracks a little at his tone. These are my wolves, I feel it in every part of my being. But I'm also theirs and it's about time I accept that.

I study all three, with their different personalities and quirks, and yet all determined to stand by my side through all of this. I can't bring myself to use the alpha command on them, not when Zach's soft plea is echoing in my mind. Taking a deep breath, I smooth my hands over my dress and sigh.

"Okay, I'm not ordering you back."

I just really hope that's not a mistake. Because I don't know if I can live with myself if anything happens to them.

WE CAMP for the night right where we are, since we have no idea which way to go. The forest is still that strange not-quite-fully-there presence, with the glow like leaves and the shadows dancing as if they're alive. There's no sense of danger in the air, not like before. It just feels like we're in an entirely new place—like we were expecting to walk into a familiar room, but ended up in a completely different house.

I'm still mulling over our predicament as we settle in for the night, and then as the shift changes happen. I know they don't want to leave me. I know I don't want them to leave, but I want them safe more than I want them here. It's not ideal, but I think that if I stay incredibly quiet and wait until they're asleep, I can leave while I'm on watch. Rylan is going to hate me for it, but what else is new. If he's safe, I can live with his hatred.

When it's my turn to take watch, it's the middle of the night. I've been lying awake while both Zach and Rylan stood watch, and now Rylan comes to wake me.

I turn to face him just as he reaches me, his eyes shining in the glow of the magical forest. There's an air of determination about him that screams alpha. His movements, his stance, even the way he breathes is all precise in a way that's inherently him. I can't help but stare before I catch myself. I'm sure he can tell I haven't been sleeping, but he doesn't say anything. He simply nods.

I move to stand while he settles near the tree I've been lying beside. Instead of lying flat on the ground, he sits with his back against the bark, his legs stretched out in front of him, and his arms crossed over his chest.

His eyes are on me.

It's almost like he can tell exactly what I'm thinking of doing. It's that manner of always anticipating each other's actions that made us so hard to find when we were kids. We didn't have to speak through the pack link, and our parents couldn't find us when we were determined to disappear. Now I'm finding this incredibly annoying.

Sending a glare his way, I move to the opposite side of the small camp. We didn't light a fire, because who knows how that would've reacted to the magic around us. We still haven't figured out food, and that's something that'll have to be priority tomorrow. Zach is sleeping to my left and Ezra is to my right. Rylan, of course, is right in front of me if I turn and look back into the camp. But I don't.

The awareness I feel any time I'm near him takes my breath away. I'd like to say that it's because we've been going through a million emotional changes. The whole concept of our memories being messed with has changed things for us. Even though we haven't been able to figure that part out, the who and the how, it still helps to know that our anonymity isn't as true as we've always thought it to be.

I have to forgive myself, and I have to forgive him, because both of us are in the wrong here, and it's not even truly our fault. I have no idea what to do with these realizations, only that I have to take them into consideration and go from there.

"Don't even think about it." Rylan's voice is barely even a breath of a whisper, but I can hear him clearly. As if he's spoken straight into my ear.

I don't turn around, ignoring him completely as I continue to stare into the forest. I want to be very nonchalant about this, I want to laugh it off, but he'll see through whatever tactic I may take. And I find that incredibly annoying.

"Trinity, I'm serious." His voice does things to me, and that is also ridiculously irritating. Goosebumps race down my spine as my mind conjures up other instances where he would be whispering in my ear.

"Trin."

This time, his voice is a growl and the way my body sits up, just a bit straighter has me folding my hands into a fist to keep them from fidgeting. It's like he can sense where my thoughts have taken me, and I can't tell if my name on his lips is a warning or something else entirely. This is the only way I can never anticipate him and I'm not sure what to do about that.

When I hear him move, I still don't turn. I'm not sure why I even thought he would just leave it alone. That's definitely not Rylan. We have that in common.

I feel him settle beside me, and only then do I finally glance his way. His knees are bent, arms resting on top of them, as he mirrors my staring into the forest. I know he knows I'm looking at him, but he doesn't meet my gaze, so I give myself a moment to study him.

He looks tired—as if the weight of the world is on his shoulders. And I suppose it is. The laugh lines around his eyes seem to have become a scowl. He's always been serious—it's one of the qualities I adored about him actually. There's no one who could take life seriously the way Rylan could, and it was such a him thing that I loved it.

Now, his intensity is even more pronounced in the way he carries himself—in every word he says. I wonder, not for the first time, if things might have been different back then. If I had stayed and helped him when he became the alpha, would he smile more often? Or was he always destined to be the protector of everyone?

I know that even if I stayed, he would've tried to carry it all. But I would've pushed him to let me help. I would've pushed him until he let me. Because that kind of a responsibility chips away at you until there's nothing left. And Rylan? He deserves the best the world has to offer. Not this.

Which is why I know I need to leave. I need to take this fight away from him and finish it so he can be there to take care of the pack. I haven't been around for years; he'll be fine without me. He's been fine for all this time.

"I know what you're thinking and don't." Rylan breaks the

silence, still keeping his voice low. I can't tell if Zach and Ezra are awake and are just really good at pretending or if they're too exhausted and trusting us to make sure they stay safe so they can rest. Either way, I also keep my voice low as I reply,

"You have no idea what I'm thinking."

Rylan makes a gruff noise, clearly disagreeing. But technically, I'm right. Even if he can guess, I doubt his thoughts would take him where mine have taken me.

"I know that you're itching to disappear into that forest so we would be forced to return to the pack and leave you alone in this."

Okay, so he definitely figured that part out. I kind of want to punch him a little. Instead, I sigh.

"Rylan, we both know it's the best way. The pack needs their alpha. We can't both be rushing into danger headfirst, thinking we'll always be okay."

I feel like we keep having this argument over and over. He won't let me go alone, and I don't actually want to go alone, but I know I should.

"No one can take care of the pack the way you can," I continue, because for once he's not arguing—he's actually listening. "We have no idea what these tests are going to be. And if both of us…" I don't want to say it but I know I have to. "If both of us die, what will happen to the pack?"

I know my words are getting to him, because that responsibility is instilled in him and cannot be turned off. But there's also something in the way that he holds his hands in front of him, gripping the fingers together that makes me think he's keeping himself from physically responding.

"I wish you would stop doing that," he finally replies. That's not what I was expecting.

"What are you—"

"Keep putting yourself in needlessly dangerous situations as though you don't matter to anyone." He's not looking at me, but his words pierce me just like his gaze usually does.

"Rylan—"

"No, there's nothing to argue about. I get that you have this whole mission that's been thrust on you, but I called you back. I did that. So we're in this together. Better get used to that."

He doesn't wait for a response, but motions for me to go back to where I was lying.

"I'll take the rest of the watch. You need to rest."

"So do you." I manage, but then he turns his eyes on me. They're so full of emotion, it nearly takes my breath away.

"Please, Trin."

It's the nickname that gets me. He's used it a few times since I've been back and every time, it gets to me. I want to question why he came and woke me for the watch in the first place. I want to argue that he's probably more tired than I am. But I don't. I give this to him. With a nod, I stand and head back near the others.

My heart is filled with a million emotions and I don't know what to do with any of them. I glance at Rylan's back, at the determined set of his shoulders, and lie back down. Here in the darkness of the night, I can let myself feel everything I'm feeling, if only for a moment.

But one thing I know, I'm not leaving.

CHAPTER 17

RYLAN

The fact that she would even contemplate leaving is making my whole body tense. The urge to grab her and chain her to me is nearly overwhelming. Not that I need a chain. I'm already attached to her, and I can't even pinpoint when that happened. But it has, and she's a part of me.

My mind flashes with snapshots of her. Fiercely fighting off the wolves, her hair and dress in constant movement around her. Holding her hand in the truck, breathing her in when she was pressed up against me. The way she looked dancing on that bar, as if she was dancing just for me. The protective way she looks at me when she thinks I don't notice. She's the perfect balance to everything I am.

The bad memories from our childhood are still there—the betrayal I felt, the pain—but I don't take them into consideration anymore. Somewhere, days prior, maybe in that cave or when I carried her through the forest, I forgot everything but who she is now. Just the fierce alpha who is determined to protect her pack.

She might not have said so out loud, but I can see it every time she looks at Ezra or Zach. Anytime her eyes flash with the same protectiveness I feel toward them.

My wolves.

Dude if you're going to be angsty over there, can you at least shut off the link so we can sleep? Zach says, and I nearly jump. I thought they were asleep.

We were. Ezra sighs. *But then you started processing your emotions and woke us up.*

I turn just slightly to glance at Trinity, but she actually seems to be sleeping. Good. Finally.

Come on, Rylan. We get it. You've got it bad.

Zach's whine may be dramatic, but I don't miss the undercurrent of happiness in it.

She was going to leave, I say, turning back to the forest. *She was going to leave us behind and sneak away.*

Of course she was. This comes from Ezra. *Because she and you are two peas in a pod, and this is exactly what you would've done.*

Did you just say two peas in a pod? Zach's voice sounds near outraged. *Who are you?*

Ezra ignores him as usual, and I can't help but chuckle. It was the right call to bring them in. I feel better having them here, even though the pack is without them. And without me.

You're worried. Ezra isn't asking, and I grunt in response.

I am. I've tried reaching the pack but can't. I assume it's because of whatever magic this place carries, but it's making me and my wolf very antsy.

Understandable. But you know the pack can take care of each other. We always do.

I know that. Of course, I do, or I wouldn't be here right now. I have absolute trust in every single member, and I know they will do whatever needs to be done to make sure they're safe. But the responsibility for them is still there, and I hate that I can't be in two places at once.

Don't do that, Zach says. When I'm this riled up he can read my emotions as easily as I can read theirs. *You are doing what needs to be done. This mission, this quest—whatever we're calling it—it's to help all shifters. That includes our pack. You can either keep them safe now or help make them safe forever.*

When did you become the voice of reason? I ask, and Ezra chuckles. It's true. Ezra is the one who usually shares the wisdom when it comes to the three of us.

I'm a growing boy. I have gotten in touch with my emotions, and it's making me very wise.

You're an idiot, Ezra says, and I grin. Just talking to them has calmed me down some. Between spiraling about the pack and about Trinity, I really have become quite the head case. Not that I could help but be anything but when it comes to her. She's—

Please, for the love of all that's good in the world, can we not listen to you pine for her in the middle of the night? Zach asks, and I send a bunch of annoyed emotions his way, which simply makes him chuckle.

I'm shutting this down now, I say.

Can you shut down your emotional turmoil too? Because we can feel it even when the link is off. Ezra's comment makes me pause in surprise. I guess I am feeling more than I think I'm feeling.

Shut up and go to sleep, I grumble and then shut off the link to their laughter. What a bunch of schoolgirls. Giggling at my expense.

But also, they clearly approve. Not that I'm surprised, but it does make me very happy. I can feel how much they care about her too. I have no idea what tomorrow will bring or what these tests entail, but I do believe that I have reached the part where I've forgiven Trinity. Maybe, I have even started to forgive myself.

* * *

TRINITY

The memory hits me like a leaf dropping from the tall tree, gently yet noticeably. It was such a long day, a few years ago, after Jay and I finished sparring. My hair was tangled, my muscles stronger. We were sitting on a log, taking a drink of water.

"Your mind wasn't present today," Jay commented, pulling my attention to him. His eyes were already studying me, and I'm sure, as always, he saw more than I wanted him to. Since the day he appointed himself my big brother, he could read me like no one else could. Of course, he noticed.

"You know what today is."

"I do."

It was the anniversary of my exile. The day my best friend kicked me out of my own pack. Four years, and it still hurt as if it had happened yesterday.

"I think we need to talk about it," Jay said, but I was already shaking my head.

"We really don't."

"Trinity, you can't keep running from this."

I stood, pacing the small clearing, ready to shift and race off into the woods. But Jay would just try this again later, so I stayed. A part of me knew this was coming.

"I'm not running from anything," I replied, pointing to myself, "Clearly."

Jay only shook his head, narrowing his gaze. "You need to forgive him."

At that, everything inside of me stopped. He couldn't actually be serious. I couldn't forgive the alpha, not after he threw me away like garbage. Not after he didn't even listen to what I had to say. Anger and grief rose up in me like a wave, and I struggled to get the next words out.

"I will never forgive him."

Because if I did that, he would win, wouldn't he? He hasn't earned his forgiveness. He made the worst decision in my life, and there was nothing I could do to stop him. And now, I had to forgive him?

"You think that you should only forgive if the other party has earned that right," Jay's quiet words reached past my internal struggle, and I turned my attention to him. He stayed sitting, but he was leaning toward me, holding me in place with his words.

"Isn't that how forgiveness works?" I whispered.

"We forgive to give ourselves the freedom, as much as let go of the other person." Jay stood then, walking over to stand in front of me. "He may never ask for your forgiveness—he may never say he's sorry—but should you still carry the bitterness and hatred for him within your heart? No. You forgive to heal yourself. The other part? That's up to him."

"But if I forgive"—I couldn't even say the word out loud without choking up—"if I give him that pardon, that makes it okay."

"Forgiving someone doesn't mean you're approving of the other person's actions." Jay's voice filled with even more tenderness...if *that was possible. He was looking at me like he wanted to protect me from every evil thought that has ever crossed my mind. My whole body felt like it was going to explode from all these emotions I kept bottling up inside of me.*

"Forgiving someone frees you from the burden you carry. Trinity, you don't remember much of what happened, but you remember the pain. And it has fueled you for all of these years. But eventually, it will burn you out. When all that's left of you are ashes, there is no rebuilding after that. You have to put out the fire before it gets that far."

Tears threatened to overtake me, but I pushed them back. I didn't want to break in front of Jay. I couldn't allow myself even that small sign of weakness. But for the first time that day I realized that maybe letting people in isn't weakness. Maybe forgiving isn't giving up, but a way to rebuild who you are. Jay took me in his arms then, holding me close, and I clung to him as I tried to calm my heart. The pain I carried inside of me for so long was a dark and empty hole that I kept filling.

I tried after that to let go—to forgive. But I never quite learned how.

Opening my eyes, I stare up at the star-filled sky. I didn't understand what Jay meant back then. But now, spending all this time with Rylan, I think I've finally reached that breaking point. Maybe I didn't even realize it, but I think I have forgiven Rylan. As an alpha now, I understand the tough decision he's had to make a lot better. I can see the sacrifices laid out in front of us, and if I was in his shoes back then, I can't say that I wouldn't have done the same.

We now know that not everything in our memories is true. There's still a veil of fog over exactly what happened, but I know I played a crucial role. And so did he. Maybe if I learn to forgive him, I'll learn to forgive myself as well.

Jefferson told me once that we are not defined by our past, we simply carry it with us as a reminder of what was but not who we need to be. Every day, we choose who we need to be.

"You okay?" Rylan's voice breaks through my thoughts, and I turn my head to find his eyes on mine across the small distance between us. Without moving, I hold his gaze, and he holds mine. I see the moment he realizes something is different, but he doesn't ask, and I don't offer an explanation. I might eventually, when we're both ready to talk and figure out where we stand.

After a moment's hesitation, I get up and walk over to sit beside him. He turns, and I put out my hands, palms up. He seems to realize exactly what I'm doing, so he turns and places his hands over mine and we're now sitting facing each other. His skin feels heavenly against mine, the way no one else's ever has.

"How do we do this?" he asks.

"Stella said to be open and remember. When the time is right." It didn't quite work the last time we tried it, but we have to keep doing so if we're ever going to figure out this mystery.

Rylan looks at me, cocking his head to the side. "Why do you feel that the time is right?"

Good question. Maybe it's simply because I feel like I'm finally on the path to forgive myself and him. Maybe it's simply because I want to be able to have my friend back. To laugh and cry with him, the way I did when we were kids.

My mind drifts back automatically, to the first time we held hands. I was seven, only starting to realize that we were different in a way my mom and dad were different.

"Do you remember how you punched me the first time

we held hands?" Rylan asks and I lift my eyes to find him studying me. Somehow, we're on the same page.

"I'm pretty sure I didn't punch you."

"You most certainly did. You told me that if I ever did something as dumb as that again, you'd rearrange my pretty face until even my own father wouldn't recognize me."

"I would never say such a thing!" I keep my voice low, but the smile blossoms across my lips at the memory. I did punch him, right in the stomach. And then I walked away, flexing my hand. Not because it hurt but because it felt unusual to have Rylan be so gentle with me. I couldn't stop thinking about his fingers entwined with mine for days after.

"Mm-hmm, sure. You called me pretty, though. And the punched me in the stomach. I remember that."

"Also, didn't happen." I roll my eyes. "I'm a lady. I would never hit you."

"Trin, you beat everyone up. Reacting on impulse. I had to step in more than once to bail you out."

We grin at each other, our hands still clasped but I don't feel any magic creeping in. Well, none of Stella's magic at least, just the way that Rylan has always affected me.

"I don't think this spell is going to work," I whisper, afraid to break this small comradeship we've created.

"For this memory, we didn't seem to need it."

The intensity in his gaze sends a shiver over my skin. His thumb rubs the skin of my hand, lulling me into a sense of comfort that I've always attributed to Rylan. The same sense that was ripped away from me when I had to leave.

But he's right. The spell didn't come again, but we still remembered something that we shared. A bond, unlike any other, and one that we're slowly rebuilding. It scares me, but maybe for the first time, it also doesn't.

CHAPTER 18

Ezra takes his shift, and no one bothers to wake me up, because the boys apparently have decided that I need rest. I want to call them out on it, but I can't help the way my heart fills at the thought of them taking care of me. The more time I spend with them, the more I can feel my edges softening. And for the first time, I'm okay with that.

I always thought that if I ever came back to the pack, even before I was summoned, I could only ever allow myself to be shut down—cut off, with walls as high as the redwood trees. But that's not the case, and as much as I won't admit it out loud, I'm glad.

"Does it feel like we're walking in circles?" Zach speaks up after we've been hiking through the woods for at least an hour. Maybe it's been five. Time here seems to be different, but I can't exactly put my finger on how. A sense of déjà vu hits me with Zach's question, and I glance over at Rylan, who seems to be thinking the same thing as me.

"When we went to see the Oracle, we had the same sense

of disorientation," Rylan says, "it felt like we were walking in circles."

"So what you're saying is we are"—Zach sighs—"and that it's magical. Peachy."

I glance over at Ezra. He has that pensive look on his face that tells me he's in the midst of figuring something out.

But I never get a chance to ask.

The wave of pain hits me out of nowhere, like a bird that just flew straight into a window. It's much more powerful than before and I drop to my knees, my hands digging into dirt as a scream is ripped out of me. My vision tunnels like it always does, but this time it doesn't pull me all the way in.

And that's when I realize I'm not the only one screaming.

It takes all of my concentration just to force air into my lungs. But then a wave of protectiveness over my wolves overrides that enough that I am able to turn my head to the side to find the three of them in the exact same position. Zach is flat on his face, trying to push himself up, but it's as if something is pushing him straight into the dirt. Ezra's body twitches, like he's getting kicked repeatedly.

And Rylan—

His face is full of pain and determination as he crawls to me, each move a painstaking choice that hurts him.

I try to move toward him, but I can't make my body obey. But then, I feel his hand on me as he reaches out, and I grasp his fingers like a lifeline.

I can feel Rylan trying to communicate through the pack link. But I hear nothing. There's only pain, blinding, excruciating, nausea-inducing. This isn't the first time magic has assaulted me in this way—maybe not at this intensity—but I should have better ways of coping with it. I should. I have to.

It's not just me who's being assaulted here. It's my wolves as well.

I refuse to let this—whatever it may be—win. My wolf is whining, the pain somehow doubled as if she and I are feeling it separately, even as we feel it together. She's barely contained, but I have no idea what would happen if I were to shift right now. So I do the only thing I can think of. I focus entirely on my wolf and her agony, and I soothe her.

She whimpers in that way that makes my heart hurt, but she responds to the calming intention. It takes a long tense moment but then we're back to being one, no longer two separate beings, and I can take a full breath for the first time in who knows how long.

I concentrate on keeping her calm, which calms me and pushes the pain to a manageable level, if only barely. Rylan twitches beside me, and I pull myself toward him as much as I can. Squeezing his hand, I hold his gaze, breathing deeply. His eyes latch onto mine, and I'm held entirely captive by the vulnerability there.

Reaching out with my other hand, I get closer, until I'm grasping his forearms and he's holding me near my elbows, our foreheads touching. We breathe together, and while I can't get the words past my lips, it's like he can tell what I'm doing. It's almost like my wolf is soothing his now.

He calms gradually and so do I, and then suddenly, I can think clearly. I can't tell if it's been minutes or hours; my body is simply exhausted. I meet Rylan's eyes again as I pull back, and he nods, before tugging me to a kneeling position, keeping one of my hands in his. I don't pull away. Together, we turn and look for the betas, who have stopped screaming at some point.

That's when I realize they're gone.

"Rylan?" His name is barely a whisper as panic hits me all over again. They were just here and now they're not. Because I'm still holding Rylan's hand, I can feel his body go rigid.

"Ezra! Zach!" he shouts. He tries again, this time through the pack link. I try to search for them, looking for a connection, but they're completely cut off from us.

"Rylan, I can't reach them," I say, my heart expanding with the onslaught of panic. Before this, I never wanted the alpha responsibility. But now, any time one of my wolves is in trouble, I can't imagine not having it. I need to be their alpha as much as they need an alpha.

"I can't either. I don't—"

Suddenly, the space around us dims abruptly as if someone turned off the lights once again. Rylan squeezes my hand tighter, and we turn as one, staying back-to-back as we study our surroundings. I can feel the danger reaching out to us through the shadows, but I can't tell what it is or if there's actually something there. The alpha in me is going insane, needing to find the betas, making it really difficult to concentrate on anything else.

"This is a test," Rylan says, and I grunt in response. I figured as much, but now I'm worried and annoyed. Is this about to be my constant state of being? It feels like it.

"We stay together, and we move through…whatever this is," I say, keeping my voice low.

"I vote for not shifting."

"I agree."

I love it when Rylan and I are on the same page.

* * *

RYLAN KEEPS his fingers laced through mine as we begin to move. It's the most natural thing. I keep my pack link open, searching for my wolves, but there's nothing. Only complete silence. Plus, even with my supernatural eyesight, I can barely see the trees around us. I have no idea how we're going to find them, only that we have to.

I glance at Rylan, at the set of his shoulders and the tiny twitching of his jaw as he stubbornly tries to see past the unnatural darkness. We nearly walk into a tree, stopping in time only because we smell the bark. The tree itself blends right in with the surroundings. Rylan goes left and I go right, but then he tugs me with him and I pivot, coming right into his side.

"Good idea," I comment, breaking the silence. "If I lose you here, I'll never find you again."

"You will," is Rylan's gruff response.

"Is that right? Will you stalk me to the ends of the earth?" Maybe if I can tease him, maybe if we can find some kind of normalcy, my heart will stop trying to beat out of my chest. Rylan is quiet for a long moment, and I don't think he's going to reply, but then I feel a slight pressure on my hand, as if he's reassuring himself that I'm still here, before he says,

"Magic or no magic, Trinity, I will always find you."

There's promise in that last statement, and I let it wash over my whole being. I don't know what to say to him—I don't know if there's anything to say. So I do the only thing I can think of and step closer, tucking myself against his side. The sense of comfort our nearness brings does something to me, and I know it has the same effect on him. Together, we're better, we're stronger. That's a fact.

"Do you hear that?" Rylan's whisper breaks through my thoughts. We've been walking in silence for what feels like half a day, with no trace of the betas. Not being able to fully rely on our shifter senses, we've taken turns holding our arms out in front of us to guide us through the forest. But there's been no sound...at all. Just a stale kind of silence.

I strain, trying to pinpoint what Rylan has picked up. We stop walking so I can concentrate. At first, I only hear the silence of the forest, but then, a faint scratching sound.

"Is it them?"

"Or something coming to grab us next."

What a cheery thought.

Time to stop wandering through the forest and face this head on. It's not ideal, but we need to see what's causing the sound, since it's our only lead.

How do you want to play this? I ask through the pack link. Rylan gives my hand a quick squeeze. I know what he wants to do, and it's the same thing I would want, but it's not something either one of us are keen on right now.

Tag team, he replies, which means we'll have to separate. It's our best bet if we're going to sneak up on whatever is out there. Whether it's a trap or something else, we can't be caught together. I don't want to let go of his hand, but I have to.

We don't know what we're walking into, I point out.

When has that ever stopped us?

Good point. Doesn't mean I like it. This forest gives me the creeps and that scratching sound is that of nightmares. What if we get lost?

Trin. I glance up to find Rylan watching me. *I'll always find you.*

I can't help but trust those words exactly as they are. I squeeze his hand in response and then we take off in the direction of the noise, both of us keeping one arm in front of us as we weave around the trees. He keeps my hand in his until we reach a spot of almost light, shining through the trees. The noise is definitely coming from that area.

Clearly a trap, and a smart one, because if my betas are there, I'm obviously walking right in. Exhaustion weighs my body down, but determination fuels my every step. I have no idea how long we've been at this—it seems like it's been days—but we're closer than ever. I feel it.

Rylan tugs at my hand, meeting my eye for a moment and then after another squeeze, we head in opposite directions. The noise grows louder as we move toward it, and I can barely hear Rylan's footsteps on the damp ground straight to my left. I pump my arms, keeping up with his pace purely on sound. When he makes a sharp right, I make a sharp left.

In two steps, we're near the sound, and then my feet stop automatically at the nearly blinding sight after all the darkness. The clearing is lit with that otherworldly glow, the scratching noise so much louder here. My eyes snag on the branches, and I forget to breathe for a moment.

Birds—giant vultures—cover the branches of the trees around the perimeter of the clearing. Except there's something wrong with them. Their flesh hangs off their bones, and there's a rotten smell coming off them that's very similar to the smell the rabid wolves put out.

But what makes my heart drop is seeing Ezra and Zach in the middle of the tiny clearing, completely passed out. I can't even tell if they're breathing. I can barely make out Rylan on the other side of the clearing, his eyes on his betas.

Ezra, Zach. I nudge them through the pack link, but there's nothing. Well, at least from them. The birds seem to hear me, even though I'm not speaking out loud. They shift in their seats, the branches shaking under their weight.

Rylan's eyes catch on mine. I know what he's thinking. They can't actually hear me using the pack link, can they? They only thing I can think of is that they're reacting to the magic in me, the same way the rabid wolves seem to. Although, these creatures are definitely a different magical breed.

Either way, this makes things more difficult. We can't come up with a plan if we can't talk through it. Not that there's much to talk through. I'm about to alpha command Ezra and Zach to wake up, and Rylan and I will race straight into the clearing, surrounded by monster birds. As if they can hear my thoughts, the grating of their claws against the bark becomes louder. I meet Rylan's eyes once again, and I nod. I forget that we don't actually have to talk through anything when he can anticipate my responses so well.

He springs into action immediately, racing into the clearing as I alpha command.

Ezra! Zach! Get up! Now!

The sound seems to echo all around us, and the birds go wild. They swoop down, dive bombing directly onto the betas' prone forms, but Rylan and I are already there. We shift at the same time, swiping at the birds with our own claws, batting them away. Blood sprays all around us like rain, as the birds continue their onslaught, not even slowing down.

Now, Ezra! Get up, Zach! I shout once more through the alpha command, and this time, they stir. My heart thumps in my chest at seeing them alive, right before I grab a bird with my teeth and fling it into a few others.

I jump near Zach, butting my head into his body, making him groan in response.

Shift! I alpha command. *Move!*

Zach's eyes focus on mine and then round in surprise. He pushes himself up just as he shifts, and I see that Rylan has reached Ezra as well. The birds and blood continue to rain down on us. I try to keep the worst of it off Zach as he orients himself. I butt at his side again, and then push off my back paws to yank another bird out of the air and slam it down to the ground beside us. Zach stares in horror, but that seems to shake him out of his sluggish state. I push him in the direction of the others, and race after them as we head for the trees.

The boys are moving slower than I would like, but we have to keep going. The birds fly after us, but end up slamming into the trees, as if they can't see well enough to fly around them. I dare a quick glance behind and keep pushing forward. I don't want to take any chances.

My eyes shift between the direction I'm running and the boys. The darkness descends on us once more, but it's not blanketing us as it was before, almost like we passed whatever test that was and get a little bit of a reward now.

I don't understand how anything that happened back there could have been a test. A trap? Yes. But a test?

Did that creature truly think that I wouldn't run headfirst into an assault to save my pack? If that's what he thinks of me, then he would never actually help us. But maybe this is the proof that he needed. I will absolutely do whatever it takes to save my wolves, even if it means putting myself in danger.

We close ranks almost automatically, as we're afraid the darkness will descend again and we'll lose sight of each other, but we don't speak. I have too many questions and not enough answers. And I'm getting really sick of that.

CHAPTER 19

When I feel like we have lost the birds altogether, I slow down and shift back. Turning toward the boys, I spring forward to catch Ezra as he stumbles. He drops his arm across my shoulders as I prop him up. Zach and Rylan both reach for him, but I keep a tight hold.

"What is it?" I ask, looking up at him. He looks pale, his typically neat hair in disarray.

"I don't...I don't know. My head feels heavy, like I can't think straight." When he meets my eyes, the glassy look in them makes me extra concerned.

"Here." Rylan motions to a spot against the tree. I deposit Ezra carefully, staying right by his side as he leans back and closes his eyes.

"We need food and water," I say, noting Ezra's pale complexion and beads of perspiration on his temple. Glancing up, I register the same anomalies on Zach's skin. Reaching out a hand, I pull him down beside me. He doesn't hesitate to plop himself next to me. Leaving Ezra for a moment, I run my hand over Zach's face, checking for any cuts or bruises. He feels cool to the touch, but sweaty.

When I crouch down in front of Ezra and run the same assessment, I find similar results. Rylan hasn't moved a muscle, his rigid stance looming over his two nearly unconscious wolves. I stand up, moving into his line of vision. His eyes continue to jump from one beta to the other, fierce protectiveness etched in every line of his face. He doesn't even register me standing in front of him.

Carefully, I place my hands on either side of his face, and he jerks at the gentle touch, his eyes finally moving to meet mine. I can see it now, how he's experiencing a sense of hopelessness. It's the same thing that I'm feeling, because we're in uncharted territory here, with little to go on.

"Hey, breathe with me." He doesn't move at first, but then I feel his body shudder with a breath, and he inhales. Much like when our wolves were assaulted, I hold onto him, as he holds onto me, which brings us both to a more solid ground. After a few breaths, he nods his head, and I drop my hands to my sides.

I miss the feel of him instantly.

Instead of dwelling on that, I turn toward the betas. Their eyes are open and on us, but even as Zach tries to smirk, I can see that it's costing him to stay upright. Do I let them sleep, or do we push forward? I have no idea, and I don't think Rylan does either. Any decision we make here may be the wrong one. That's what's so terrifying.

"The pain came first," Ezra speaks up, his voice a whisper, but his eyes are on me. I'm starting to shake my head, letting him know that this can wait, but he beats me to it. "You need to know."

Rylan takes a step forward and crouches next to his beta.

"Then what?" he asks.

"It was much like you described, Trinity," Ezra continues, taking another deep breath, a bead of sweat running down into the collar of his shirt. "My wolf panicked in a way I've never...never experienced before. I felt disoriented and then—"

"The wolf was gone," Zach picks up when Ezra trails off. "He was just gone, and I couldn't reach him, and then, a blinding pain at the back of my head like someone hit me."

"Then, we woke up in the clearing while you were beating up the weird looking birds." Ezra finishes.

"So there was nothing in between?" Rylan asks. "You have no idea how you got there?"

"Just...darkness," Zach says, running a hand over his face as he sighs.

"Darkness in the worst sense," Ezra adds, his head falling back. They really don't look good, and I feel entirely too helpless staring at them. Rylan stands and gives me a look that I'm sure mirrors my own.

"But you feel your wolf just fine now, right?" I ask. Zach manages a nod, and I exhale. At least, there's that. I can feel the shifter magic on them, the same kind of magic I carry within myself. But is that why we couldn't reach them? Because something—or someone—was blocking their wolf?

I kneel beside the boys, checking them over again, but they're still cold to the touch. Ezra leans into my hand for just a moment and his carefully placed masks slips when he looks at me. In that split second, I can see past his always proper exterior and to the part of him that missed me. I blink my eyes to keep them from filling up.

"How about you lie down?" I say, pressing on Ezra's shoulders gently. "Can you shift?"

He nods his head, and then he shifts, curling up into himself immediately. I move to Zach next. He grips my hand when I reach him and shifts before I can say anything else. They look like they've been drained of all energy. Maybe even drained of some of their magic. Something is going on in these woods, and I'm not sure I have any power to stop it.

"We need to find water," I say, standing and turning to face Rylan. The look in his eyes is different this time and turned entirely on me. My whole body heats, and I swallow hard, pushing the physical response down. It takes everything in me not to step into his arms and demand that he promises that everything will be okay, that my wolves will be okay. I tear my gaze away, glancing down at their sleeping forms.

"We can't leave them alone," Rylan replies.

"And we can't separate because we have no idea if we'll find our way back." I finish what he doesn't say, because we're both thinking it. This whole forest is one big trap, and we're in the midst of it.

I want to punch something. I want to scream into the air. What's the point of me having all these True Alpha powers if I can't do anything with them? Have I asked this question before? Probably. Will I ask it again? I have a feeling—a million more times. A user manual would be nice.

My eyes search the forest around us, trying to find an answer within the shadows. The darkness hasn't descended fully, but the dimness is there. Pushing at the edges.

"Rylan, did you see that?" I jerk to attention as a streak of light catches my eye. Rylan is by my side immediately, following the direction I'm pointing, but whatever I saw is gone.

"What did you see?" he asks, and the fact that he doesn't

question if I did or didn't see something is elevating. We've definitely come a long way in a short time. But I guess that's what happens when you're forced to trust each other.

"I have no idea. I can't—" I don't want to admit it out loud, but it's definitely happening more often than not. He should be aware.

"Trin, what is it?"

"I think I'm seeing things, Rylan," I say, keeping my voice low and my attention on the forest. I can't look at him. This is almost an admission of weakness, and we don't admit weakness. Especially not to each other. But we're trying.

"Explain."

"I don't know how to explain," I say honestly, my eyes still on the forest. "It's kind of like that door in the bar. Sometimes, it feels like I can see the magic."

"We expected that, with the powers." Rylan nods to the tattoo on my arm. I glance down at it, always forgetting that it's there, because it feels like it's always been there.

"But sometimes it's not the magic. Sometimes I just feel like I see someone. Or something." Which is not something I want to admit even to myself.

"Like right now?"

"Yes, maybe. I honestly don't know, and it's very frustrating. Just like everything else right now."

I have the sudden urge to lean over and hug Rylan, so I lace my fingers together in front of me instead and turn back to the betas. We'll let them rest, keep watch, and, hopefully, in a few hours, find some water and food. And then, get the heck out of this stupid magic-infused forest.

* * *

The boys sleep for a long time. But I guess since there's no way to keep time, I don't know specifically. It just feels like a long time. The forest doesn't get darker, but it also doesn't get lighter, so all I have to go on is Rylan waking me up to stand watch. He does it three times, as do I.

My head is heavy, and my stomach is very hungry. The thirst is what's getting to us, and we can't even chew on leaves because the leaves here are just as dead as everything else. I mean, they look alive, but once you touch them, they crumble. No idea what that's about.

When the boys finally wake, I check their eyes. They seem much clearer than before. I breathe a little easier.

"Let's find you some water, shall we?" I ask, offering Zach a hand up, which he takes gratefully.

This was hours ago. It feels like we've been walking for days. There's a certain sense of foreboding around us, hanging low in the trees like fruit weighing the branches down, it grazes over our shoulders as we walk. We look like we've been through a battle.

I can't tell what time it is or how long we've been here, because everything seems different. It's almost like we're in between places, in the same forest we started in, yet, not quite the same. Everything is muted and loud at the same time.

When I glance over at the boys, their shoulders are pulled back, chins raised in determination. However, they look like they're ready to collapse, and the only thing that's keeping them upright is sheer stubbornness.

I open my mouth to speak, but then stop. Rylan's eyes are immediately on me.

"Do you hear that?" I ask as my senses pick up a noise.

The guys have already stopped, but now they turn their faces to the sky, trying to pinpoint the sound I'm picking up.

I have to say, this is the part of being with my pack that never gets old. Just how absolutely attuned we are to each other.

Rylan glances at me, giving me the tiniest nod. He and I are attuned more than anyone I've ever heard of.

"Water," he says, and the four of us turn as one toward the sound.

It's another trek—I can't tell if it's been five minutes or ten—but then the sound becomes incredibly clear. We push through the trees, and there, in the midst of this dying forest, is a stream of the clearest water I've ever seen.

The guys move forward immediately, but I grab their shirts, yanking them back.

"You can't just be rushing in," I say, as they look at me bewildered. "Everything here is a test."

"It's water, Trinity," Zach whines, letting me see a bit of his despair. "We need water."

"We also need to be careful." I reach up and squeeze his forearm in comfort. "Let me check it out."

I can see Rylan moving forward already, his face set in determination, but I just shake my head at him. I close my eyes for a moment—I'm not sure what I'm looking for, but I'm hoping for some inner magical strength. Having all these powers and no idea what they actually do is quite frustrating. But I'm just going to keep trying whatever feels right and see where we end up.

Right now, it feels right to center myself and then expand my senses, to see if I can notice any danger. Granted, it's what I already do with my shifter senses, but it feels like more somehow. Or maybe I'm just dehydrated and hallucinating good ideas.

It's very helpful that my powers are tied into my shifter being, because at least my instincts are still intact.

When nothing jumps out at me immediately, I motion for my betas to move back and step out of the trees toward the water. Moving slowly, I turn a full three sixty, but I can't see very far into the trees, and I don't sense anything that screams danger—no monster birds in the trees, at least.

Still, I keep the boys at bay, as I stand near the water, letting my senses adjust. Nothing seems to happen, and when I finally feel satisfied enough, I bend down to try the water. It tastes normal, so I motion for the others to join me.

Rylan is beside me in a moment, his growl barely restrained in his chest.

"You're being reckless," he says, as the betas drop down to their knees to drink the water.

"I think that was the most levelheaded I've been, actually," I reply, raising an eyebrow. He doesn't like that, but he can't argue. My impulses are often the thing that get us in trouble, so he can't complain when I go carefully.

"You should've let me go."

Okay, apparently, he can complain, but I will argue. I turn to him, giving him my full attention.

"And what? It would've been so much better for you? Why? Because you're a guy?"

At this point, are we arguing for arguments sake? Possibly. But that's what he gets for questioning me.

"This has nothing to do with that," Rylan snaps, his eyes flashing. "But what if you walked into this clearing, and there were more vultures waiting to attack?"

"And what? I would've fought them off, and you would've had my back." I don't understand his issue.

"You're not expendable, Trin." He sighs, suddenly looking fifty percent more tired, which is saying something considering he looked one hundred percent tired before. But his words hit me right in the heart, because if I'm not expendable, that means—

"Neither are you," I say, my voice firm. He looks over my shoulder, as if he doesn't want to argue the point because I'm already wrong, so I grab his shirt and yank his attention to me. His eyes flash again as I pull the material down until his face leans over mine.

"Don't for a moment entertain the idea that you are expendable in any way." I make sure my words are clear, as I look directly into his eyes.

I can tell he wants to argue. It's almost like a reflex. And that makes me angry.

I'm not better than any of them. We can't move forward if he thinks that he can just sacrifice himself willy-nilly. Maybe I haven't even admitted it to myself the way I should, but we're a team. We have to work as a team.

"You're the True Alpha," Rylan says, his eyes still on me. "I'm just—"

"You're not just anything," I snap, my anger rising. "You're alpha and, according to the pack, a pretty good one. So stop this pointless argument, and get some water."

I take a step back, dropping my hand to my side, because being this close to him is affecting me as usual. He stares at me for another moment, then nods.

"So you think I'm pretty."

The laugh that bursts out of me heals my soul. Rylan gives me a small smile, very proud of himself. And that's when I remember that we're not alone. I turn to find Ezra and Zach watching quietly, the way they always do. It must be very confusing for their loyalties, to figure out who to answer to when the wolf inside of them is torn between two alphas. However, when Zach grins at me, I think maybe it's not all that hard, and they're just here for Rylan and me to figure out whatever in the world we're doing and get on with it.

"Well, don't just stand there." I motion to the water. "Drink. We'll camp near here."

We can all use the rest, but we can't stay by the water. If there are any more predators in these woods, and I'm basically one hundred percent sure there are, they'll come to the water eventually. I'm surprised we haven't seen any lately, but I'm sure it's just the magic creature playing more games —maybe testing our resilience. Either way, we'll be close enough to the water if need be, but far enough to get some rest. Because we desperately need it.

I want to shift to drink, but I don't. Getting down to my knees, I look into the water, taking stock of just how dirty I look.

My hair is a wild mess of knots. It's going to take some time to untangle it. My skin is marred by dirt and a bit of blood. I cup my hand in the water, taking a little sip, then splash some of it on my face and scrub. Pulling the bracelet off, I place it beside me, and scrub at my wrists all the way up my arms. I don't even want to know what my dress looks like at this point.

Glancing over at the boys, I see they're also washing up a little. The water has a soothing effect against my skin, so I dip my hands in again, letting it splash over my face and arms.

A noise reaches my ears, but this time, it's not the trickle of the water. I lean back over, to look into the stream, staring at my mostly clean face.

There's something...a song of sorts coming from the water. Is it the sound the stream makes running over the rocks? The gentle lulling of the water rushing over the smooth pebbles makes a melody of sorts. I want to hear it better. I want to move closer. Pushing the hair out of my face I lean even farther out.

I could climb right into it and never leave. I want it all around me.

Before I know what I'm doing, I'm diving into the water headfirst.

* * *

RYLAN

THE SONG GROWS LOUDER by the second. Everything we've experienced so far fades into memory as I focus on the sound.

My belly is full of water and feels almost like I ate a full meal. My skin is buzzing with the cold, as the water I used to wash off the dirt cools against it. But I don't notice any of it. Just the song.

If I close my eyes, I think I can picture Trinity and myself dancing to it. The moment I think of dancing, my mind travels back to Trinity on top of that bar, completely absorbed by the music...and by my eyes on her.

My heart speeds up, its beat filling my senses for a moment. The dull thudding covers the song coming from the stream for a moment. It's like my senses snap into alignment.

It's the exact moment Trinity goes in the water.

My body moves before I realize what I'm doing, racing over to where she's disappeared.

"Trinity!" I scream, but there's no response. The water is only a shallow stream, and yet she's completely gone.

Ezra and Zach are suddenly beside me, grabbing me around my waist and hauling me back.

"What are you doing?" I thrash against their arms, desperate to go after Trinity.

"It's a siren's pool! Rylan, snap out of it. It's a siren's pool."

Ezra is shouting into my ear, trying to break past my frantic need to get to Trinity.

I push against Zach, and then a fist slams right into my face, sending me reeling. I growl, twisting my attention to Ezra, but his steady look focuses me. My cheek stings where he punched me, but it's enough to dull the sound. It's enough for me to focus.

I move farther from the water, even though I want to go forward. I need to get to her.

"A siren's pool," I say, looking at Zach and Ezra. They're standing between me and the water, blocking the view, creating a wall.

"If you go in, you won't come out," Zach says, as I stare past him to the water.

I can't remember much about siren pools; I've never had to encounter one. But I know they're portals to cages kept by the magical creatures who feed off the panic and pain of their captives. There aren't many on our side of the world, but in areas near the water, they're a danger.

"I have to get to her."

"We need a plan first," Ezra says, keeping his gaze on me. This is why I called them in the first place. They've always been able to draw rational thoughts from my mind the way no one else has. And Trinity, she makes me feel irrational. She makes me lose all sense of control.

"Ezra..." I'm not sure what I'm trying to say, but my whole body buzzes with the need to be in that water. To save her.

I have to save her.

I reach for her through the pack link, but there's nothing. *Trinity!* Nothing but silence.

"Rylan, focus." Ezra nearly barks as Zach moves closer. They're creating a human barricade between me and the river and my need to go after her.

I force my attention to my beta, because Ezra is the scholar. He's the one who will know what to do. I try to breathe through my panic, my wolf nearly inconsolable as he pushes me to act.

"I have to go after her. Tell me how I can come back."

When I finally give myself the time to look at Ezra, I see just how hard he's fighting to stay in control. Zach is a stone wall beside him, but the despair on his face is evident. They're fighting the effects of the pool, but they also want to save her as much as I do. She's their alpha, but she's also become their friend. The way she took care of them earlier is forever imprinted on my mind.

"You need an anchor. Something you can come back to," Ezra says, but the only anchor I can think of is the woman in that water.

"What kind of an anchor?" I manage, through grinding teeth. Ezra reaches out and yanks on Zach's shirt, when the other starts moving toward the water.

"Something tangible, something you can hold."

There's nothing in my pockets, nothing I can think of that'll tether me to this world. Not when she's in the other.

Ezra and Zach push me back some more, probably for their sake as much as mine.

My eyes search all around me, but I can't think of anything. It's getting physically impossible to stay still, the need to go—

That's when I see it. Right near the bank.

"There." I point. The guys turn, their eyes finding the same thing I see. Trinity's bracelet. It must've fallen off when she jumped in. Who knows how, but it doesn't matter. I push past my betas, but they grab me once more.

"We'll have to move into the forest," Ezra says, yanking me to attention. "You'll be on your own. We can't help you. This one is on you."

I meet his eyes briefly, and I find a rare show of emotion there. He's worried for me and for Trinity.

"I'll come back, and I'll bring her back."

Zach squeezes my shoulder once, as Ezra nods, and then I'm racing for the bank and the bracelet. I have barely any mind left to grab it, pulling it on my own wrist, before I dive into the water, giving over to the song. My whole mind is filled with Trinity, and I don't even notice the all-encompassing cold…or the fact that this tiny creek is a hundred feet deep all of a sudden. I don't think of anything at all, but push myself farther down into the depths, following the song. I let it guide me, give it the freedom to pull me in. Because if I let it pull me in, it'll lead me to her.

CHAPTER 20

TRINITY

Everything blurs...my head doesn't feel attached to my shoulders.

My wolf whimpers, a sound so heartbreaking it makes me want to cry.

Wait, I'm already crying.

Everything is wet...or is it just the tears?

I can't tell the top from the bottom.

I can't see past the distorted wall of water around me.

Is it water? Where am I?

I am so cold.

So, so cold.

Rylan.

Where is he? Is he safe?

My wolf cries for a lot of different reasons now. I try to push myself up, but all I can do is lie on my side, watching the water dance to a rhythm only it can hear. Nothing makes sense. But everything feels like the end.

The end of me.

The end of possibilities.

The misery hits me like a wave, and I gasp, tears pouring out of my eyes.

Pain, so much pain.

And regrets. So many regrets.

My biggest one was always Rylan.

* * *

RYLAN

My lungs are starting to burn, and my body is going numb from the cold, when something streaks past me. I twist in the water, trying to catch whatever it is, but it's too fast even for my vision to track. The movement does disorient me, and when I turn back, I'm trying to figure out which way to go when I suddenly recoil.

A figure comes right out of the murky water, moving toward me slowly. Even from the minimal pictures of sirens that I've seen, this one looks like something is wrong with it. The hair sprays out around her like a fan, blending into the darkness of the water. Her skin is dark as well, but more of a dark gray than anything. Or maybe green. But it's her eyes that fascinate me.

They're sharp slits on her face, with no pupils that I can see. It's like someone took a knife and simply made two precise cuts, leaving the rest of the face intact. The area where the nose should sit has two breathing holes, and her lips look like normal lips...almost. I know she's watching me, even though I can't understand how she can see me. There are also patches on her skin, like something was once attached to it, but then ripped away.

I don't dare move and am treading water to stay in one place as she circles me. I may be the predator on land, but she is the predator in these waters. I can feel her song growing louder, almost like a caress against my skin. Even as she continues to circle me, I focus all of my attention on the bracelet on my wrist and the girl to whom it belongs. Her face becomes clear in my mind's eye, and I fight the urge to smile.

The song sounds sharper immediately, and I look at the siren as she rears back. She doesn't like that, almost as if she can see my thoughts. The siren gets right back in my face, hissing in a way that covers my already-cold body with goosebumps. If I don't move fast, I'll drown. Even though I can hold my breath longer, it doesn't make me immune to the pressure of the water and the magic.

The siren is back to watching me, as if she's trying to read my mind. I have no plan here, and I have no idea what I'm supposed to be doing. All I know is that I'm running out of time and so is Trinity.

I can't fight this creature—I can't even talk to her. She won't stop watching me, not moving closer, but not moving away. Almost as if she's waiting for me to simply drown. I have to do something, because I have to get to Trinity.

I have to—

Suddenly, I am being pulled backward through the water, and the next thing I know, I hit solid ground. Gasping for breath, I push myself up on all fours, trying to reorient myself. Ezra and Zach are beside me in a flash, and the scream that rips out of me shatters the quiet around us.

"Rylan, what happened?" Zach tries to pull me up, but I yank my arm back, frustration fueling my every cell.

"I don't know! One second, I was staring at the siren, the next I was being spit out here!"

The anger and panic are settling in, and I push myself to stand, heading for the water once more, but when I reach it, there's no water, just a dried-out spot where the stream once was.

My heart drops in my chest, and my body shakes as I jump into the dried-out area. Not even a drop of moisture is left. I'm shaking, and I can't tell if it's from the cold or from the fact that I lost her. Trinity is completely gone, and I couldn't do anything about it.

"Rylan, snap out of it!" Ezra is in my face, but I don't care. This is not very alpha of me, but I want to scream and tear my way into the ground, if only it would get me to Trinity.

"I couldn't get to her. I couldn't—"

Maybe I'm going numb from shock. Or maybe I have lost my mind. I feel like I have lost my heart.

"We have to find a way back," I say, looking up to meet Ezra's crestfallen face. No, he can't look at me like that. He can't be feeling these emotions, not when I need him to compartmentalize. He's the best at that out of all of us. I need him to help me keep it together.

"Don't look at me like that," I snap, pushing away from him and jumping back out of the dried-up creek. Zach looks like a lost puppy, and I have the urge to slap him to get him out of it. "Stop it, both of you. We're going to fix this. I'm going to fix this."

"How?" Ezra follows me out of the creek, coming to stand beside me.

"Magic," I reply immediately. Because that's the cause of

all of this in the first place. So it better fix it. "We need magic. And I know where we can find some."

"Rylan, what if she's—"

"She's not!" I say, cutting off Zach before he can utter aloud my biggest fear. I stalk right up to Ezra, getting in his face, "They keep their prey captive, right? Tell me how this works."

"Yes, captive," Ezra says, his mask of determination falling into place.

"Then we have time. Not a lot, but enough."

It has to be enough. I turn away from Ezra, staring into the forest for the first time. Something has changed. I spin around again, staring at the creak and then at the trees. And then I look up and see the clouds.

"We're not in the magic forest anymore," I say, realization dawning on me. "It spit us back out all the way to the forest we started in."

The guys do their own assessment of our surroundings before their eyes settle back on me. I shift without preamble, finding my bearings. The betas don't question, but follow suit, and I can feel them move behind me as I take off back toward the town.

We need magic, so magic we will get.

CHAPTER 21

RYLAN

I don't care what kind of alarms we're setting off; I'm not shifting back or slowing down until we reach the town. Even the sound of gunshots don't slow us down, as we weave in and out of the trees. We don't speak the whole way back, my mind filled with images of Trinity in pain. It's like I can't shut off that worst-case scenario in my head, and I need to get my head on straight if I'm going to be of any help to her.

Once we're within the city limits, we shift and head straight for the bar. It looks less impressive in the daytime, almost like it had a dazzling spell over it, but now it's simply a building with a sign. A man is stationed outside the front doors—one of those big goons, as Trinity would call them. He gives us a look that would make a normal person cower and steps in front of me when I try to move past him.

"The bar is closed," he says, putting an arm out across the door. The need to break his arm increases.

"We're here to see Paul," Ezra says from over my shoulder. The goon barely spares him a glance, before he looks at me again.

"Like I said, the bar is closed."

"How about you open it up?" I ask, giving him a smile. Well, it's more of threat than anything, and he visibly recoils.

"I would move out of his way," Zach says over my other shoulder. I grin wider. The goon shakes himself but doesn't move.

"No."

"Okay. I guess we'll have to do it ourselves," I say, taking a step forward. The goon reaches for me, but he's no match for my reflexes. I twist his arm behind his back, kick in his knees, and bring him straight to the ground.

"I did ask nicely," I say, before I toss him down. He slams against the ground, wind knocked out, but he's not that hurt. He'll be up in no time.

I get back up, yanking the door open and stepping inside. The bar is nearly empty, much like Stella's is during the day. A few of the well-dressed security guards are inside, some of them familiar faces from the night we were here, and they all stand when we walk in the door.

"We're not here to fight," I announce, raising my arms up in the air. "We need to speak to Paul. We'll make it worth his while."

I have no idea what I'm offering, but I know he's got magic, and that's what I need right now. I don't have time to take my time. I have to move first and figure everything else out later.

The guys don't seem to like my offer and move toward us, like they're prepared to fight, but then Paul steps up to the edge of the balcony and looks down at us.

"I remember you." His voice carries, and his security stops moving immediately. He gives my betas a quick scan before his eyes settle back on me. "You were with Trinity."

I don't like her name on his lips. The growl that leaves me is involuntary, and it makes Paul grin.

"Come on up, shifter. Clearly, you have something to say."

He motions for one of his men to move aside, and then I lead the way to the top of the stairs, Zach and Ezra close behind me. With a quick glance at them, I don't have to explain myself. They know how to read me, so they stay at the top of the stairs, watching my back, and the only exit, as I head to where Paul is now sitting on one of the chairs near the railing. Only one other goon is up here, but he's near the wall across the way, so we're as alone as we could ever be, giving us a sense of privacy. I wonder what it is he expects I'll say.

"Sit, sit. Where is the *lovely* Trinity?" Paul asks, and then proceeds to chuckle at whatever he sees on my face. "I had a feeling, but I wasn't sure."

"I don't know what you mean."

"I'm not sure if you're lying to me, or to yourself." Paul cocks his head to the side, narrowing his eyes slightly. I'm not intimidated by him in the least, but I don't like the way he's picking up on things—it definitely makes me feel uncomfortable.

"Trinity is in trouble." I decide a direct approach is probably best and will ignore these weird comments he's making.

"What kind of trouble?"

This is where it gets tricky. I can't exactly tell him we've been looking for the first shifter, but maybe I can give him just enough truth to make it count.

"We got caught in a magical forest of sorts on the

outskirts of the city." Paul jerks just enough to know that I have his attention. "There was a trap. We got separated, and Trinity was taken."

"Taken where?"

"The siren's pool."

Paul's eyes flash at that, then quickly narrow.

"There are no siren pools in my forest." I don't miss the way he says 'my.' I lean back, crossing my arms in front of me, a picture of nonchalance.

"Well, I guess you don't know your forest as well as you think you do. There is a siren pool there, I can lead you to it. Except—"

"Except?"

"I can't reach it without a lot of magic."

"Ah, and this is where I come in." This guy is smart—I have to give him that much. He's figuring things out before I even say them. It's almost like he's been in this situation before. It's my turn to narrow my eyes.

"You're not surprised," I say, leaning forward across the table. "You know there's magic in those woods. Can you reach it?"

Paul doesn't answer right away, but I see his jaw twitch, if just barely. He's trying to figure out just how much to tell me. It's not like he trusts me, which is fine. I don't trust him even a little bit, but he's my only option, unless I can make the Hawthorne witches appear out of thin air.

"I can tell you what I know, but what's in it for me?"

And there it is, the businessman. I saw the sleaziness all over him when he first approached Trinity. I immediately knew he approached her on purpose, even though it looked like a run in. The calculating look never leaves his eyes. This is where I have to figure out what will make him help me, something that is worth more to him than what I need.

What can I offer a man that deals in magic? There's only one thing I can think of.

"Me," I say finally, "You get me."

* * *

TRINITY

My body no longer feels like my own. The cold has seeped into every part of me, my wolf shivering right alongside the rest of me. She's weak, weaker than I expect her to be. But then again, I don't know what to expect or where it is I am.

Pain. There's so much pain.

Clarity comes in bursts.

I know I'm in some kind of a cage because there are walls of water around me. I know I was pulled underwater. I know that whatever is out there is enjoying my agony.

I don't know if Rylan and the boys are okay. I hope they are. If this is another one of these tests, it doesn't seem to involve them, so I hold onto the hope that they made it out.

I've been crying nearly nonstop, my body shriveling in on itself. I can't stop it, even though I want to. This place brings up every terrible image, every horrible feeling I've ever felt... and multiplies it tenfold.

I push myself from my back to my side, curling into myself just as a movement beyond the watery barrier catches my attention. I can't make out the shape—it moves too fast, and then it's gone. Maybe I'm hallucinating. Maybe I'm simply dying.

And I never got to tell Rylan how sorry I am.

. . .

Everything around me seems to move, or maybe I'm the one moving. Images shift in front of my eyes, and I can't tell what's real and what's a memory. Looking around, I find myself in my home forest, the trees as familiar as the fingers on my human hands.

The pack has been in a constant state of worry for days. Our alpha and my parents left for the council four days ago, and no one has spoken to them since. I'm concerned, of course, but I trust in my parents ability to take care of each other. However, Rylan has been especially distressed, but he doesn't like me 'acting like a girl' and caring for him. His words, obviously. He's such a guy sometimes. My annoyance with him overrides my worry for a moment and I wonder if I can get away with simply going over to him and beating him up, just to get him to show some emotion, besides the stupid stoic mask he's wearing. He acts like he knows something I don't, but he won't tell me what it is. Ezra and Zach are his constant shadows as usual, and even Zach won't say anything to me. I stopped being a little kid years ago, but they still treat me like one.

A noise catches my attention, and I turn, scanning the trees. I felt like staying in my human form today, and I've been aimlessly walking around the woods in my newest red dress, just to calm myself. But now, I know there's something here with me.

I'm far enough from the village that it shouldn't be anyone I know. But that is also concerning, because no one ever comes out this way. They shouldn't be able to find the village, even if they're looking for it. So maybe, it is one of my pack. Except, I can't sense anyone I know.

I'm trying to figure out if I should run or hide when a man steps into view. For a moment, my brain registers that I've never seen him before, but then suddenly, I feel like I do know him.

"Hello, Trinity."

His voice is...familiar. His presence...calming. I don't feel the need to run anymore, and instead, I take a step forward.

"Hello," I find myself saying.

"You have grown since the last time I saw you." The man continues, but doesn't move. I've come closer, almost like I can't help myself.

"We know each other?"

"Of course. Your father and I are old friends. We used to travel together on council missions."

I scrunch my face as I try to think through what he's telling me. I remember my father being sent away on council's errands. He's always been very high up in their circle of trust. And Rylan's dad has always had full faith in Dad.

"You father sent me, Trinity." My eyes snap back to the stranger. "The pack may be in serious danger and with your parents and the alpha gone, they need someone to help."

"You're here to help us?"

"Of course, I am, Trinity. How else would I have found you?"

But he didn't find the village, he found me and I—he pulled out a pressed flower from his pocket.

"Your mother said you gave this to her?"

I did, right before she left. So she could take a reminder of home with her on her travels.

I walk forward to look at the flower, smile up at the stranger, and then lead him to the village as if it's the most natural thing in the world.

Images flash before my eyes. *Chaos at the village. Screams of the pack fighting off an assault from people pouring in from all directions. Rylan holding a man's body to him and crying like I've never seen him cry before. Me being pulled away and ushered down into the caves. Shifters huddling together, their faces full of shock.*

Rylan taking his place as the alpha, reading off the list of my sins as I stood before the pack. The pain in his voice and in his eyes. I was terrified and angry about what was happening to me.

I thought I was bringing help, and I brought our demise. I thought that we could figure it out together, but he wouldn't even look at me. My best friend was gone and in his place stood a cold and calculating alpha.

The council would come to reinforce the magical protection of the village but that meant I had to be gone. And when Rylan exiled me, he made sure I'd never be able to find my way home.

I shake so violently with sobs, I'm making myself dry heave. But I can't stop. Not the images of the past, not the new knowledge I gleam from them. Someone played us from the very beginning. We were nothing but pawns. How did the man come to find me? Why did he have my mother's flower? Was I really so easily manipulated that I was the best choice? Even though I didn't bring an outsider to the village on purpose, it doesn't take away the truth that I was the reason the pack was in danger in the first place. I couldn't see past the manipulation, I couldn't see past my own pain. I couldn't see how it broke Rylan's heart to let me go, because all I felt was betrayal.

Maybe it's better if I die down here. I hope Rylan doesn't try to save me. I deserve what I got.

CHAPTER 22

RYLAN

Ezra slams me into the wall, pinning me with his forearm.

"Are you out of your freaking mind?" He growls right into my face. Zach is right beside him, ready to pull us apart if it comes to that, although he looks just as angry as Ezra. We all know I can take them both, but I don't fight.

"It's what needs to be done," I say, looking straight into Ezra's eyes. He holds my stare for a long moment, before he lets me go and stalks away to the other side of the room.

We're in a motel room down the street from the bar, the same motel Trinity and I cleaned up at. Paul set us up with a room, considering I'll be staying a while. When I told Paul he can have my services as a shifter, the betas nearly dragged me out of there by my shirt. They nearly launched into it there, but my being their alpha prevented it, I'm sure. Now we're alone, and they are not happy.

"You and Trinity both have the worst cases of self-sacrificing idiocy I've ever heard of," Zach says nonchalantly, and Ezra and I turn to him in shock. He shrugs, but doesn't take it back. Not that he should. He's not wrong.

"What happened to taking care of the pack? You're the alpha," Ezra turns back to me, as I straighten up and adjust my shirt. There's a small dent in the plaster now; I hope Paul has to pay for it.

"I have you to take care of them," I reply.

"You're out of your mind." Ezra sits on the bed, rubbing his hands over his face. He's always been the levelheaded one out of the three of us, but I also think it seems that way because he's the best at guarding his emotions. I've never doubted that he has a great many emotions. Only now, I'm pushing him to his limits.

"If this is what needs to be done, then that's what I'll do," I reply simply, because it really is that simple for me. Every moment that she's gone and I'm here feels like an eternity.

"Rylan, we all care about her," Zach says, taking a step forward, "but pledging yourself to the mafia boss of Williamsburg is the dumbest decision you could've made."

"Okay, so do you have a better idea?"

"The witches," Zach replies immediately. "Trinity trusts them. They can help."

"They're too far away," I sigh, because of course I had thought of this. "We need help now. Ezra, tell me I'm wrong. We don't know how long the sirens keep their prey. We don't have the luxury of time."

"What about the luxury of an alpha?" Zach asks, "Can we have one of those?"

"You can have two, when I get Trinity back." I grin, even though I'm not feeling even an ounce of happiness. I can't be fighting them while I'm fighting everyone else. I need my brothers by my side.

"You know we have your back," Ezra says, like he can read my mind, "and we want her back too. We all love her." Ezra raises an eyebrow as he meets my eye.

"I don't—"

"Stop lying to us," Zach interrupts before I can come up with an argument. "We have eyes, you know."

"You should keep them to yourself," is my very eloquent response.

"*You* should keep them to yourself," Zach replies, chuckling. Even Ezra's lips pull into a small smirk. I guess if they can still laugh at my expense, then we'll be okay.

"Paul will be here any minute," I say, getting back to business. "I need you to head back to the pack. No. No arguments," I raise my hand, even as Ezra stands. "You want to fight me on this? If it makes you feel better, take your best shot, but I'm not changing my mind. I rather not alpha command you."

Ezra studies me for a long moment, a touch of sympathy on his face.

"You haven't been able to reach her through the link?"

"No."

The total silence on her end is making me feel caged. My wolf is just as agitated as I am, which makes me feel everything twice as strongly. I have no idea what I've gotten myself into with Paul, but I will always do whatever needs to be done to protect my own. And Trinity? She's at the top of that list.

"Get to Stella and update her on everything. I tried calling her and there hasn't been a response. She knows about you two, you can...trust her."

"We'll have her update the witches, too, they'll want to know, even if they can't do anything about it," Zach says. I don't rebel at the idea immediately.

"Whatever is in these woods..." I trail off, trying to put into words the array of thoughts running through my mind. "It could be the first shifter, but it also could be something else. We have no way of knowing for sure, but it's more powerful than we thought either way. The witches will want to know."

The guys nod, because I think they feel it too. Maybe the creature was testing us, like it told Trinity, but I think it was also playing with us, for its own amusement. Whatever it was, it felt like it was amusing itself after all these centuries. The tests had no actual meaning, except for putting us—Trinity—through a lot. Even if we did find this creature, I doubt it would be helpful. But that's a problem for another day.

"You're going back into those woods with no one to watch your back," Ezra says, bringing my attention back to him.

"It's more important for me to have someone watch over the pack," I reply honestly, because at this point, I have no idea where all of this will take me. And the pack is a constant worry in the back of my mind—the need to protect them what fueled this mad dash across the forests in the first place. Zach and Ezra were here to bring me that moment of clarity, but now, it's up to me. Me and Trinity.

"Finish your food." I motion to the rolling cart. None of us felt good about eating, but we need the energy. They have a long way to go and I have—well, I have no idea what I have to do, but it feels like I'm waiting for the lightning strike at any minute. Ezra seems like he's about to say something else just as a knock sounds at the door. It opens before I can reach it, and Paul walks in.

"We need to get moving," he says, looking from me to my betas. They're standing at my back, ready to attack, and I know Paul doesn't miss a thing. I have so many questions about his operation, but that'll have to wait.

I turn back to the betas, looking them each in the eye. They're my brothers, through and through. I would've never made it this far without them. But now, I need to do what is required of me. All on my own.

Take care of each other, I say. The guys nod.

Bring our girl back. Zach replies, and I give him a smile. I intend to do just that.

* * *

WALKING AWAY from my betas takes a lot out of me. Part of me wonders if I should've seen them to the edge of town, but they keep in contact until they're beyond the town boundaries.

We're good, Rylan, Zach says just as Paul and I leave the town behind and step into the woods. *We're heading home.*

Satisfied that they're out and as safe as can be, I focus on the man walking beside me. He really can't be more than a few years older than I am. His button up shirt, dark jeans, and expensive looking shoes are a contradiction, just like the rest of him.

"How long have you been in charge here?" I ask, risking the question. Walking around with no information won't be good for any of us. Trinity is going to be so mad at my impulse decision. But first, I need her to be okay so she can be mad.

Paul glances over at me, that mask of amusement back on his face. The cocky gleam in his eye, mouth slightly turned up at the side, as if he's listening to some private joke. It's the same air of confidence that I saw it when he was talking to Trinity, and I liked it even less then.

"A few years," is all I get from him. Great, he's going to be one of those. Trinity would be so much better at this. I don't know how to converse with humans.

"And what exactly are you in charge of?"

Paul chuckles at that, and I'm finding it hard to hide my annoyance.

"This town needs protection. I provide it."

"By leeching magic and life essence off unsuspecting people." Okay, maybe I have absolutely no diplomacy left in me. But Paul just chuckles again.

"You're a smart one. Or maybe it's Trinity who figured it out. She seems very in tune with the magic."

I barely restrain my growl, but Paul doesn't miss a thing—not that he seems concerned at all. He only brought one of his goons with him, and the man is walking behind us. I study Paul again, trying to see if he carries any kind of magic of his own, but he seems like a regular man. Not that I can sense magic, but I can at least tell he's not a shifter. If I watch someone long enough, I can see the subtle tells of the animal underneath the human dressing. But Paul just seems—weak. He wouldn't be able to run through the forest the way I can…or catch prey. My wolf huffs at that thought, almost like he's laughing. And Trinity didn't feel anything off about him when she met him, just the magic in the place, so does that mean he's not a witch? I seriously don't understand any of it.

"What do they need protection from?" I try to keep us on

subject, because I truly would like some answers. He looks over at me again, as if deciding how much to tell me.

"I'm sure you're not ignorant to the way our world works. Magic is no longer the secret it once was. People pay to see the unbelievable and the unattainable. I provide a service, minuscule spells and enchantments to give someone a high and experience the other side of the veil, so to speak."

"And in return?"

"In return, they come to my bar." He doesn't miss my look and chuckles again, which I find nerve grating. "Don't look at me like that, shifter. I don't take anything they don't freely give."

"Even humans?"

"Everyone carries a bit of magic in them, even humans. It fills my well, and in turn, I provide this town with protection from what's out here."

Zach is never going to let us live it down that he was correct in his outrageous mafia idea—but then I realize what Paul just said, and I nearly stop in my tracks. He knows something is in these woods, something that's not quite right.

"What is in these woods?" I ask, my voice leaving no room for argument. I think Paul can tell, because for the first time, he seems a little more cautious around me.

"I don't know," he lifts his hands before I can argue. "I don't. It may be an Ancient. It might be something else. I've never seen it with my own eyes. But I know the kind of creatures that come out at night."

"That's why you patrol the woods."

"Yes. We've had attacks by rabid wolves, but there was also a tourist last year who was lulled into these trees and was never seen again. I'm just doing my part."

"Oh, so you're the good guy, huh?" I nearly spit the words out, because even sarcastically they don't sit right.

"I never claim to be anything," Paul replies, which is telling. He's only here for himself. If push comes to shove, he'll trip me right over a cliff. He's not out here to help me or Trinity. He's only here to help himself.

"Where do I come in?" I know I need to ask this question, even though it won't make a difference one way or the other…not when it comes to getting Trinity.

"There are a lot of powerful people in the area who would love my setup." Paul doesn't hesitate with his response. "I need all the protection I can get, especially from an alpha."

That jerks me to attention. I never told him I was an alpha.

"Don't look at me like that, either," Paul says, pointing at my face. "I didn't get where I am by being unobservant. Plus, you have enough magic on you to light up a city. Only alphas carry that much."

I'm about to ask him how he can sense magic, but I doubt that's something he'll be willing to share. It seems like one of those secrets one would carry close to the chest. But I do ask him something else.

"How did you come to power?" He raises his eyebrows at me, as if he's surprised by the question. He was most likely expecting me to ask about the magic.

"That's a story for another time," he replies, and I would argue, except that we're getting closer to the area with the creek. I still have no idea how he's going to help me, but he said that if I take him there, he would. I also still don't trust him, but I have no choice at the moment.

We're a lot closer to town than I thought we were when we were traveling through the forest. It was like we were walking in circles for days. But now, we've only been walking for an hour and the clearing is visible up ahead. We grow quiet as we get closer, the guy following us falling even farther behind. I don't question it. It doesn't matter anyway.

When we stop near the edge of the clearing, Paul looks at me. I'm not sure what he's asking, but I scan the immediate area, looking for any signs of danger. Or really, anything. The forest is uncharacteristically quiet. Considering Paul was just talking about creatures coming out of here, I'm a little surprised we haven't seen any on this side of the forest—only in that weird half dead place. Maybe the Ancient knows we're up to something.

I step out into the clearing first, my senses heightened, but there's nothing. I walk over to the dried-out creek, looking down as if it's going to provide me with answers. When I see nothing but dirt, I turn back to Paul. He takes that as a signal, walking over to stand beside me.

"This is the deep pool?"

"I wouldn't question magic," I snap. We're wasting time. She's down there—or somewhere—where I can't reach her. It doesn't matter what he sees or doesn't see. He said he can help, so he'd better help. Or I will have to do what I've wanted to do this whole time.

"I get it. You want your girl back," he comments, before jumping into the creek. He doesn't give me a chance to contradict him either. Not that I would. He motions for me to follow him, so I do. "Are you ready?"

"For what, exactly?"

"To make some magic, of course."

And then he pulls out a knife and cuts across his palm.

CHAPTER 23

TRINITY

I can't quite think through the pain anymore. Not even a little bit. There's just pure agony in every cell of my body. My wolf is weak, barely hanging on, and I'll go next. I know it. I can feel it.

The edges of my consciousness grow dimmer and dimmer. I've seen the creature's form pass by the wall of water that surrounds me, but I no longer care to find out what it is. Everything I've done, every mistake I've made has led me here.

I'm getting what I deserve.

"Is that any way for an alpha to think?"

The voice sounds from behind me, and I turn, finding myself in the forest near the large boulder once more. I don't remember falling asleep or stepping into a vision. One moment I was dying in the dark underwater cavern, and the next I'm here.

The giant white wolf steps out from beyond the trees, the ever-

present breeze ruffling her glowing white fur. She glides instead of walking, keeping her eyes on mine. From her question, I expect to see disappointment in her gaze, but all I see is a cool assessment. As if she's actually expecting an answer. I give her the best one I have.

"I'm not an alpha," I say, shrugging a little. "I've only ever played one because of what I've been told."

She doesn't respond immediately but continues watching me steadily.

"You are telling me, honestly, that you do not feel the pull of the call? The wolves in your care do not feel like your own?"

I open my mouth to respond, but of course, I can't. Because if I say no, I'm lying. I do feel the pull, I called them mine. They are mine.

But it still doesn't change the fact that I feel like a fraud.

No matter how much I think of them as my wolves, it's a calling that stands to be unexpected. Something I never thought I would be a part of and something that I am incredibly unqualified for.

I am not enough, and that's the truth.

"It doesn't matter what I feel," *I say, meeting her gaze once more.* "I can't protect them. I can't seem to do anything right. Why did I come back? Why were these powers given to me if I can't actually use them to make a change?"

That's the part that scares me the most—failing. But not for my sake, for the sake of those under my care.

The pack. Ezra. Zach. Rylan.

Rylan is so much better off without me. He was right to exile me. He was right to protect the pack from me.

"You are lying once more."

My eyes fly up to the wolf, shock plainly displayed on my face.
"No, I'm not."

"You are, but you are lying to yourself, and that is the most *dangerous lie of all."* The wolf makes a slow progression around me, circling as if she's looking for a different way in. The argument sits right at the tip of my lips, but for some reason I can't make myself say it. Because she's right. It doesn't feel true.

"Tell me, Trinity Whitewolf, what kind of a being are you?"

The wolf stops behind me, and I turn to face her, as she waits for me to figure out whatever it is I've forgotten.

"I don't understand."

This time, there's a shred of sympathy in the wolf's voice, but only barely. She's not here to coddle me, but she will push.

The way Rylan always pushes me.

The way my parents did. The way Jay and Jefferson did. I am the result of the people in my life who never gave up on me. For a moment there, in my despair, I had forgotten who it was that they raised.

"I am a fighter," I say, holding the wolf's gaze steady. Now that tastes exactly right on my lips.

"I'm a fighter," I say again, my voice stronger and my doubts a little quieter. Not gone, just diminished by the sound of my own voice, my own determination. The wolf inside of me stirs, as if she's getting her footing back as well.

"Where am I?" I ask, trying to push the fog of fear from my mind and focus on the one truth I've spoken. I'm a fighter. I don't give up. I can figure this out.

"In a siren's pool." The wolf's response is surprising because she's so good at talking in riddles. But then maybe, right now, she sees that I need all the hand holding I can get.

"A siren's pool..." My mind tries to work out what I know about sirens, which isn't a lot. But—

"They feed on pain, agony...torture."

All those self-doubt moments magnified to a point where they're all I am. No wonder, I'm throwing myself the worst pity party. The *siren doesn't have to put these things in my mind; they're already there.*

"All you are feeling," the white wolf says, "are your own feelings, except the siren magnifies them to a point where you cannot control them like you normally would."

"So how do I get out of this?"

Because now that the white wolf has broken through the strange fog of despair, I can see that I need to get out. I can't just lie down and die.

"By accepting who you are, Trinity Whitewolf."

Oh great, we're back to the non-answers. My wolf makes a tiny noise, just as confused as I am, but she's stirring. I hold onto that. The agony tries to push its way back in, but now that I've been distracted from it, it's easier to keep it at bay and approach it almost like an outsider.

"This forest—these tests—they weren't real, were they?" I ask, leveling the white wolf with a look. *If she could raise an eyebrow at me, I feel like she would.*

"They were, but not for the reasons you seek."

Once again, clear as mud. I suppose it doesn't matter if I can't break out of this cage. I can feel the dream vision fading already, as if it's done the work it was meant to.

"I'm alpha," I say to the white wolf, conviction coloring my voice. "I'm a True Alpha."

The white wolf fades slowly, almost becoming the mist herself. But there's a smile in her eyes that I don't miss. And then a voice calls my name.

I twist around, searching for the source, before I look straight up. A tear appears in the sky above me, and then I realize it's not the sky, but the top of the water cage I've been lying in.

That voice...I know that voice.

It sends a million pleasant shivers across my body, and my wolf goes crazy. I reach my hand up, toward the weird tear in the cage, and then everything goes black.

* * *

RYLAN

THE BLINDING LIGHT DISSIPATES, and I move before I even realize I'm doing it. Dropping to my knees, I reach for Trinity, pulling her right out of the ground and into my arms. She looks completely out of it. Her skin is cracked and bluish in color, as if she's been down there for weeks instead of days. She feels small and fragile in my arms.

My palm is covered in blood where Paul cut it for his ritual, so I use the back of my hand to push the hair out of her face. Her lips are cracked and her cheeks slightly sunken in, but when she opens her eyes, they're the same beautiful brown that I know. It takes her a moment to focus on me, and then she smiles.

"You found me."

The words are barely past her lips before she passes out. I stand, cradling her against me and turn to Paul. He's wrapped a bandage around his hand, his eyes on us. I step out of the circle he made with our blood, walking past him and out of the dried-up creek. I have no idea what kind of ritual that was, but it was no magic I've ever seen before, and it's left a bad taste in my mouth.

All I want now is to get Trinity away from here and away from him.

She's back, I say, and Ezra and Zach answer immediately.
You got her?

She's okay?

I glance down at the fractured shell of the girl, and my heart thuds as I realize how close I've come to losing her.

She's not okay, but she will be. I'll make sure of it.

That's enough for them, because they trust me. I shut off the link and focus on Trinity. Her body feels tiny in comparison to mine, even though she's strong. She's going to hate that I carried her, but she'll deal.

She's always been stubborn about accepting help.

Memories of the village attack flash before my eyes as I step over branches and rocks, holding her close against me. When I saw her that day, right after my father returned, I thought that it was a sign that everything would be okay. Two of my favorite people were together—I had expected him to be gone for much longer—and I was so happy I could barely contain myself.

But then the assault came. A stranger finding the village and leading other people in with him, bringing doom upon all of us. A man stabbing my father, right before my eyes. I remember rushing to him, holding him in my lap and screaming. And Trinity in the middle of it all. She was the one who brought the stranger in. They walked in together and even seemed to know each other, although he wasn't one of ours, and he wasn't a wolf. There were magic and protocols in place to protect us. And somehow, Trinity broke through the magic and led that man right in.

This is the truth that I've lived with for six years. But looking down at her now, I know that even if my memory was the truth, I would've forgiven her. We had such a close friendship, and that pull I've always felt toward her has only intensified since she returned.

I'm not exactly sure when I decided to forgive her,

regardless of the truth. Maybe it was the moment I thought she was gone forever. Or maybe I've been working on it all these years, and the anger I've carried toward her was only there to protect me from feeling the pain.

Trinity makes a little noise, turning into me. Without thinking, I drop a kiss to the top of her head.

I can hear Paul and his bodyguard walking behind me, but I pay them no mind. Without a backward glance, I carry Trinity straight into town and the motel room.

The moment we step out of the woods, I feel slightly better. There's definitely something wrong in there, but now is not the time to figure it out. All of my attention is focused on taking care of the girl in my arms.

CHAPTER 24

TRINITY

The first thing I see when I open my eyes is Rylan. He's standing with his back to me, looking out the window. Even though I can't see his face, I'm sure it's set in determination, the same way I can see his shoulders are carrying the weight of the world.

The setting sun plays with the color of his skin and hair, and I give myself a moment to simply study him unabashed. He has always been the most handsome man and wolf I have ever seen, but there's also a quiet strength in him, a fierce protectiveness that makes all of my being hum in awareness.

I must make some sort of a noise because he turns suddenly, catching my eye. My breath catches at the intense emotion displayed there, before he pulls it back.

"You're awake."

"I am."

This is going well. I'm so happy we're stating the obvious. Placing my hands on either side of my body, I try to push myself up, but I don't get far before Rylan is there. I glance up, my face mere inches from his, as he leans closer, grabs a pillow, and puts it behind my back. There's a moment of stillness, as he stays right inside my personal space, and then, he seems to shake himself and move back.

"I have water and some bread for you." He leans back and picks up the plate and cup from the bedside table. Without a word, I take the cup first, sipping carefully, then drinking the whole thing. Rylan throws me a quick half-smile as he takes the cup and stands to refill it while I munch on the bread. My stomach turns over a few times, making me nauseated, before it settles again.

"How long?" I ask.

"Two days."

That makes me freeze, with the bread halfway to my mouth. Two days? It felt like weeks. Very long and excruciating weeks. I suppose when you're being drained of your life force, everything seems longer.

I glance down at myself as I finish the bread, my cheeks growing hot at the complete disarray that I am. My dress is in tatters, my skin dirty and broken. I swing my legs over just as Rylan returns with water.

"What are you doing?"

"I need a shower," I say, sliding to a sitting position. Even that small move makes my head feel heavy. For someone who's been passed out for several days, I'm much more tired than I would have anticipated.

"You can barely sit up," Rylan says, placing the water into my hands. "Drink."

I want to call him out on his bossiness, but I don't. Instead, I sip the water until it's gone. When he takes the glass from me, I grab his hand, turning it over to look at a gash on his palm. It's clearly a fresh cut, even though it's begun to heal.

"What happened?" I glance up at Rylan to find his full attention on our hands. I realize I'm holding his in the palm of my hand, while my other one traces the cut. My skin tingles where it touches his, and even without the supernatural hearing, I can hear the hitch in his breath. My eyes move up to his wrist and the amethyst bracelet resting there. The one I made with the witches. For a second, I want to ask about it, but then he'll just give it back, and I like seeing it there, so I keep my eyes on the cut.

"It's nothing," Rylan pulls his hand back, before stepping a bit closer. "Let's get you to the bathroom."

"What? No arguments?" I fully expected one. He takes hold of my elbows, pulling me to a standing position slowly. Once again, we're barely inches apart, and I can't hide the way his proximity is making my body heat.

"I figure I'd give you a pass so you can save your strength so you don't keel over in the shower."

"Oh, someone's been using his thinking skills."

"I thought you'd be proud."

I raise my head at that, narrowing my eyes at his amused look.

"It's not as much fun when you play along," I say.

"I know," he replies.

He turns me toward the bathroom, and I take two steps before my knees begin to tremble. With a growl, Rylan steps closer, sweeping me right into his arms. He stalks over to the bathroom, depositing me carefully on the closed lid of the toilet before I can even protest.

I watch as he leans into the shower and turns on the faucet, tweaking it until a bit of steam starts to rise. Then, he turns to me, as if deciding his next move. I know what he's thinking. My body heats at the thought as well, so I'm the first one to speak.

"I'll shout if I need help."

He opens his mouth to protest, but snaps it shut and heads out of the bathroom. Of course, not before he grabs a towel off the rack and places it right next to me. And then he's gone.

I stare at the closed door, wondering what this attitude is all about. The way he looked at me, the feel of his arms around me, the care… I push all of it away as I stare at the shower. It's going to take all of my strength to undress and get in there, but I'm determined. I can't ask Rylan for help with this.

The progress is slow. I am much weaker than I anticipated, but the moment I step under that spray, I feel my muscles relax. Some of the tension seeps away as I let the water wash over me.

With my eyes closed, I let the water beat down on me. Images of the water creature and of the cage hit me all of a sudden, and I force my eyes open immediately. I don't need that. I have to push all of those thoughts and emotions down. I already broke down once when I was in the depths—I don't need to do it again.

"Trin?"

The voice is barely a whisper on the other side of the bathroom door, but I hear it. He's probably leaning against it, and the concern in his voice is evident.

"I'm almost getting out," I manage, as I grab some shampoo and conditioner and lather it into my hair. Lifting my arms for that long takes the wind out of my sails. Once I rinse the shampoo and conditioner combination out, I can't even tell if I've gotten all of it. I'm ready to lie down.

A knock sounds on the door just as I wrap the towel around me. I realize I don't even have a change of clothes. I lean against the counter as I move to the door but stop for a moment to study my reflection.

I look like I've been in a battle and have come out a deflated balloon. That's the best representation of how I'm feeling internally and looking externally. I need food and rest, I know that. But it doesn't stop the array of emotions as I stare at myself. My hair is so knotted, it's just one more representation of how wrong everything has become. Nothing has gone according to plan.

Pushing all those thoughts of self-doubt away, I yank the bathroom door open a little too hard.

"Trin?"

"I don't have a change of clothes," I say, trying to keep the sudden tears at bay. My emotional state is just as damaged as my physical one. Rylan moves toward me immediately.

"Here." I glance down to see him holding one of his shirts. I reach for it, but even that causes my arms to shake. Rylan notices immediately. He steps right up to me, invading my personal space as he raises the shirt.

"Ready?"

I nod because what else can I do? Rylan tugs the shirt over my head, his movements the most precise and gentle I have ever seen them. Once my head is free, he takes one of my arms, and loops it through the sleeve. Then he does it again on the other side. Tugging the shirt down until it's near my knees, I reach over the top and unknot my towel, letting it drop.

Rylan's eyes don't leave my face and I think he's going to

pick me up again, but instead he motions toward the bed with his arm. I sink on the edge of it, some of the water from my hair dripping down.

The little puddle it makes on the bed makes me want to cry. All sense of pride forgotten, I raise my eyes.

"Rylan."

My voice comes out uncharacteristically high pitched, and he's beside me in a moment, a towel in his hands. I stare at him in wonder, my eyes glistening with unshed tears, and I see something shatter in him. The cold exterior I'm so used to is cracked open, and his gaze is so caring. It makes me want to cry that much more.

"Turn a little," Rylan says, his voice gentle. I tear my gaze away, letting him have access to my hair. "I'll have to untangle it."

I nod. I'm still holding back tears. I have no idea what to say or do. Rylan settles behind me once more, and the way he squeezes the water out of my hair makes me want to weep.

"Do you remember when I was seven or so and you were barely four and you kept following me around everywhere?"

His question and the nonchalant way he delivers it throws me for a loop. I turn to stare at him as if he's lost his mind, and he's wearing a very pleased expression on his face.

"Me?"

"Yes. Admit it, you followed me around."

"I did not!" I say, appalled, even as my skin heats at the memory.

"You did too," Rylan chuckles, "And your hair was even longer than it is now. You were always getting leaves and twigs stuck in it because you left it down."

My brain latches onto the fuzzy memory, remembering how annoyed Rylan was. But also, how attentive. Always making sure I didn't clumsily fall off a cliff when I was in my human form. I'm not sure why he's bringing it up now, but his voice is soothing nonetheless.

"It was a big deal to you back then, being able to keep up with all the pups"—Rylan chuckles, and I feel a gentle tug on my head as he picks up a comb and begins to untangle the locks—"but you wouldn't give up your dresses or your long hair even when they put you at a disadvantage. You were always tripping over your skirts."

"The dresses were always too long," I whisper, turning my head to the side to give Rylan better access.

"You've solved that problem as an adult," Rylan chuckles.

"That I did," I manage, a small smile on my face. Rylan works slowly and meticulously, lulling me back into comfort. I think he's done reminiscing, but then he speaks up again.

"I asked your mom if she would teach me to braid hair," he says. I turn again to see his face. I didn't know about this part. He looks a bit sheepish, and then he places his hands on my shoulders and turns me back around.

"You didn't." I whisper.

"I did," he replies, his voice sending pleasant shivers to the back of my head. "Come on, move up."

He helps me get situated at the head of the bed before he moves to stand behind me.

"May I—" he stops, and I can't help looking over my shoulder at him. He looks so unsure of himself that it makes me want to reach out and comfort him.

"Rylan?"

My voice jerks him back, and he shrugs. "May I braid your hair?"

At first, I don't think I hear him correctly, but he doesn't waver and all I can do is nod. Turning away, I sit up straighter, offering him my back. It takes a few seconds, but then his hands are back in my hair, and I instantly calm.

The gentle tugs and pulls of the hair lull me into relaxing even more. Rylan doesn't speak, but I think, if I looked at him now, I'd see that same gleam of determination on his focused face. He's being so incredibly gentle, as if he's afraid that if he tugs on the hair a little too hard, I'll unravel.

But I don't. I simply sit and wait, giving my body time to rest. I think he could play with my hair for years, and I would never get tired of it.

When the tugging finally stops, I look over my shoulder to find his attention still on my hair. Slowly, I pull the braid over my shoulder and find a perfect tail with a tiny rubber band at the end. I glance up at Rylan, and he gives me another one of his boyish smirks.

"It was the best I could find."

"It looks perfect."

I think I'm about to cry for real and I don't want to do that, so I manage a quick thank you and then I sink down into the covers and close my eyes. But I don't fall asleep right away. First, I imprint in my memory just how proud of himself Rylan looked after braiding my hair.

I SLEEP off and on for days. It seems so unbelievable that such a small time could cause so much damage. But it did. My wolf and I have done our best to recover, but we're still weak. At least, we no longer look like we're going to keel over at any moment, so that's progress.

Rylan has been in and out every day. He doesn't tell me

where he goes, but he always comes back with food around the time I wake up. This morning, I was finally strong enough to check in with the pack through the link. To say that Zach and Ezra were pleased to hear from me is an understatement—even Ezra, who was the first to reply when I reached out. I could feel just how pleased he was, even despite the distance. Zach was his typical overexcited self, and I already miss both of them not being near.

I also tried calling Stella but there was no response. The boys did check on her and have given her an update, so at least I know she's up to speed. She'll let the Hawthornes know as well. I'm ready to be up and doing something. I feel like this whole trip has been a colossal waste of time, and it's hard not to blame myself.

When I hear Rylan down the hall, I don't move from my position by the window. I've been staring at the forest beyond the tops of the houses for an hour. Something is definitely in that forest, but it can't be the first shifter unless he's a complete and total jerk...which is very possible, considering he's been around a long time.

Still, I can't help feeling responsible for taking the guys into the forest, for being the one who led them into whatever game the magical creature was playing. I hear the lock click, and I feel Rylan enter the room even before I hear him. He places a bag on the table but doesn't speak immediately. When I turn, I find his eyes on me, and for a second, his emotion is unguarded.

My breath catches, and I can't think of any of the things I wanted to say to him as I simply stare back. He looks tired, more tired than I've ever seen him. He's been letting me sleep, but I have no idea what he does at night. I don't think he sleeps.

His eyes do a slow perusal of me, starting at the tips of my toes all the way to the top of my hair. I have no idea what I look like to him, hair messy from sleep, his shirt the only piece of clothing on me. Maybe for the first time ever, I feel self-conscious just standing in front of him, so I'm the first to move.

"Where have you been?" I ask, stepping away from the window and walking over to sit on the bed with my back propped against the headboard. He watches me settle in, then grabs the bag and takes it over to me.

"I brought dinner."

I roll my eyes. He always just answers like this or a similar non answer.

"I don't know why you have to be so secretive about your whereabouts. If you found yourself a girlfriend, just say so."

I'm joking, but it leaves a bad taste in my mouth. I'm positive if he tells me he met someone, I will hunt her down and punch her in the face. After I did the same to him. Not sure what this madness is I'm feeling, but I refuse to look up at him as I reach for my food.

When he doesn't respond, I have a sinking feeling in my chest and force myself to look at him. But what I see surprises me. He looks almost nervous, standing at the foot of the bed.

"What?"

"I got you, umm, some stuff."

Rylan produces another bag from behind his back, placing it in front of me. I peak inside, immediately reaching for the red fabric. Pulling it out, I see that it's not just fabric, it's lace.

The floral lace is a deep red, creating a rough but soft texture over the material. The top of the dress has a V-neck and spaghetti straps and is form fitting, while the skirt is cut in an A-line style and free flowing. It's a bit shorter in the front than in the back. It also looks a bit more formal than the dresses I usually wear, and it's gorgeous.

My eyes moist over, but I blink the wetness away before I look up at Rylan. He's gauging my reaction, and when our gaze meets, he gives me a very self-satisfied look, which makes me roll my eyes. We're back to our typical behaviors.

"Thank you," I say, because I can't not thank him. But there's more stuff in the bag, so I dive back in, pulling out shampoo and conditioner that smell like coconut, a proper brush versus the comb I've been using, new chucks since mine are basically falling apart, and a pair of underwear. They're red, just like the dress.

This time, I can't hide the blush that creeps over my skin, and I stuff everything back into the bag. Except there's one more thing in there. I pull it out, in complete shock.

"You got me a graphic novel?" My voice comes out small as I flip through the pages, my vision blurring as I stare at the art.

"They're your favorite, but I didn't know which one you didn't have so—"

"It's perfect, thank you."

I clear my throat and smile up at Rylan. He looks like I've given him the greatest compliment, and I have the urge to hug the graphic novel to my chest, but instead I put it on the bedside table.

"You've covered all the bases."

"You know I like to be very thorough."

His voice is low as he says it, as if he needs to clear his throat a few times. The way his eyes heat sends all kinds of pleasant tingles down my body, and now I'm the one actually clearing my throat.

"You didn't spend all day looking for a dress for me. Are you going to tell me where you go every day?"

Whatever atmosphere was present in the room before, it shifts immediately. He's definitely hiding something, and I don't like it. Especially since I've already decided we need to be on the same page if we're going to get anywhere with this.

"Rylan, don't make me ask twice."

"It's not important right now. You recovering is what's important."

He takes the bag from the bed and places it in the bathroom. When he moves past me, I grab his arm and pull him on the bed in front of me.

"Trinity."

"You know I get all hot and bothered when you use that tone of voice."

I smirk and see his lips twitch in response. He doesn't take the bait though, which worries me. "Tell me about this."

My hand is still on his arm, and I trace a vein down to his wrist, then run my finger carefully over the almost-healed-over cut on his palm. It should've been healed over completely, but it's slightly raised at the edges, and if seems like it can't fuse together properly. His hand twitches under the contact, but he doesn't move away. Instead, he watches my fingers like he's mesmerized, while I watch him. I can see him working through whatever it is he needs to say to me.

"It was a blood spell," he finally says. That is absolutely the last thing I expected to hear. He doesn't meet my eyes but stares down at our hands instead. His fingers curl just slightly, so he can graze them against mine.

"Rylan "—I take a deep breath—"what did you do?"

He looks up then, holding my gaze in his, as I force myself to remain calm. His eyes have always been the most expressive of his emotions, and now the dark blue is near midnight in its intensity.

"What I had to do to get you back."

His words wash over me, and the past me, the one who carried all the hate for him in my heart, would've pulled back and demanded answers. But for some reason, I don't want to do that. I curl my hand over his instead, as his thumb makes small circles over my skin.

"Tell me," I say, keeping my eyes steady on his.

He inhales deeply, before he speaks.

"I made a deal with Paul. His help for my services." I open my mouth to ask questions, but snap it shut. My blood feels like it's been replaced with ice water. "He said he had a ritual that would create a tear between the realms. He used his blood and mine to create a circle, and then he chanted in a language I don't understand. I didn't think it'd work, but then there was blinding light, and you were there."

"Are you being vague about this on purpose? What aren't you telling me?"

I'm not sure he's going to answer, but he surprises me.

"I felt a pull, a tug in my body. Like it was attached to the ritual. I can't explain it," he stops, taking another long inhale before letting it out. "But it doesn't matter. You're back, and now—"

"Now what? You're his personal guard dog?"

"Trinity."

"What do you want me to say? How could you do something so stupid?"

I rip my hand away, standing so I can pace. I don't know enough about this type of magic to comment, but I know one bit of information, one of the first things I learned from the witches. Blood magic is not good magic.

"I did what I had to do."

"You should've let me rot in there!" I nearly shout, twisting on him. The panic I feel has nothing to do with me and everything to do with whatever deal Rylan made. Because if Rylan was somehow involved in a blood pact…I—

He's suddenly in front of me, his hands on either side of my face, starting straight into my soul.

"I did what I had to do, and I would do it all over again. We'll deal with the consequences."

"How?" I wrap my hands around his wrists, holding him in place as he lowers his forehead to mine.

"Together."

It's exactly the right thing to say, which makes me angry all over. The need to fight rises inside of me, but it's not Rylan I want to hit. Even though he could use a lesson or two. I step out of Rylan's embrace and walk around him toward the bathroom.

"What are you doing?"

"I have a visit to make," I throw over my shoulder, as I shut the door. Paul is about to get an earful from me.

CHAPTER 25

Putting on my red dress feels like putting on armor. Rylan's eyes do a very appreciative scan of me when I step out of the bathroom, but I'm too mad to linger. My body doesn't have the same problem and neither does my wolf. She's more than happy to explore just what all these new and exciting feelings that are building between Rylan and me. Pushing all of that aside the best I can, I simply walk to the door, Rylan on my heels.

"I don't think—"

"That's the problem, isn't it. You didn't think. You probably bound yourself into some magical contract, and now, I have to be the one to save you." My voice stays low as we walk out of the motel, but I'm sure Rylan doesn't need me to yell to tell just how angry I am. He takes my wrist, bringing me beside him, as he lowers his head to my ear.

"Don't treat me like I'm some pup." His words send goosebumps down my arm, as his breath ruffles my hair. "I knew exactly what I was doing."

"Well, then you're just gullible." I turn my face up to look at him, and he doesn't move away. His own anger is close to the surface, and I can see the alpha in his eyes.

"Watch it, Trinity."

"Or what? You'll throw me over one knee and spank me?"

"No, you'd like that too much."

He drops my arm suddenly, moving away, and I'm left gaping at his back as he continues walking. We're so hot and cold, it throws me for a ride. But every time he pushes right back, I can't help but want more. And that's a dangerous place to be.

Giving my body a stern talking to and telling it to chill, I hurry after him. We reach the bar in no time, and since it's not quite five in the evening, it's still pretty empty. The goons are stationed outside, but they step inside to let Rylan and me in. That, in itself, tells me a lot.

Rylan leads me up the stairs and to the top of the balcony, where Paul waits.

"Ah, Trinity. It's good to see you up and about." He stands, reaching out a hand to me, but something in my face must stop me because he retreats it immediately. "Yes, well. Have a seat."

He sits back down, and Rylan pulls out a chair for me, before dragging another chair over and sitting right next to me. Paul's eyes go from me to Rylan, a knowing smile on his face.

"I would be curious to hear what you remember from the siren's pool."

It honestly makes me glad that he's not pretending at civility. He goes straight to business, which works fine for me.

"Is that why you helped Rylan? You wanted inside information?"

Paul's expression doesn't change much, but I see the tiny bit of respect in his eyes. He clearly likes the direct approach.

"Partially. We've been studying the forest for a while now, trying to figure out exactly what kind of creatures are hiding right under the surface. Without you, we would've never known there was a siren's pool right here in Williamsburg."

"That's important to you? A siren's pool."

"It's a great source of magic." Paul smiles, just as the bartender from the last time we were here comes over and places drinks in front of us. Neither Rylan nor I reach for ours, and Paul doesn't miss a thing.

"Don't glare at me like that, Trinity. You'll get wrinkles. Your boy toy here made a deal. The use of my magic for my use of him. It's all fair and square."

"I highly doubt anything you do is as simple as that." I lean forward a little, narrowing my eyes. "What do you want with him?"

I feel a sudden pressure on my thigh as Rylan's hand drops there and squeezes. It doesn't take a genius to know he doesn't like being discussed like he's not here, but I need answers. And Paul seems to be inclined to share some of them with me. I place my hand over Rylan's on my thigh and squeeze back, a little harder. I remove my hand, but he doesn't move his and I can't exactly comment on it as I wait for Paul to reply.

"Rylan is valuable."

"No duh," I snap before I roll my shoulders back, trying to keep my cool. "I would appreciate it if you didn't insult me by talking around the subject. What are the terms?"

"I do enjoy a straightforward woman." Paul smirks, then takes a sip of his drink. "Okay, I'll play."

He places the glass on the table and leans forward, his

eyes entirely on me. Rylan's grip on my thigh tightens, but I don't break eye contact.

"I'm sure you are aware that our world is filled with Ancient magic that was not accessible for a long time. Generations of my family have tried to access that power, and now, it's up for grabs. I am one of many magic dealers in the area, only a small portion of a much larger organization. The magic and human worlds are merging, and we have to find a happy medium."

"And by that, you mean something that would benefit you."

"But of course." He's completely unbothered by the accusation. "I protect this town, and in turn, this town provides for me. Rylan is simply a part of that now."

"For how long?" This man is getting on my last nerve with his half answers.

"Oh, I don't think that's a fair question. I did him a great service."

I slap my hand on the table, bringing the goons on the outskirts closer.

"How long?" I ask again, completely unbothered by the show of force. Rylan's grip on my thigh tightens once more, as if he's reminding me of where we are. But I'm not concerned. I could take these guys, and he knows it.

"Until the magic I used for the ritual is replenished."

For some reason I thought he'd say indefinitely, so the fact that there's an end date makes me feel instantly better. And somehow worse. Rylan is a complete statue next to me, and I place my hand over his automatically. I can feel a slight tremor against his skin, which makes all kinds of alarms go off in my head. Is this not the way the deal was presented to Rylan? There has to be a catch here, there's always a catch.

"Does this pact involve any lamb sacrifices, or do you just run around naked in the moonlight?" I'm watching Paul closely enough that I see the flash of annoyance there. It makes me want to grin. "I mean if you're into the whole naked under the moonlight, then by all means. But I would need a heads up—"

"It was a simple blood pact, his blood mixed with mine with an incantation and Rylan got what he needed out of it." Paul is a picture of control, but I'm clearly wasting his time with my absurd imagery, and I'm happy to see that under all that suave air he is still a man—who just gave me more information on the deal than he had intended to.

My heart is thudding too loudly in my chest as his words settle and the worry takes over. Blood pacts invoke a dangerous kind of magic—a level above a simple blood ritual. I will have to ask the witches, but they'll need specifics. I need to get Rylan out of this, somehow.

"How do you plan on replenishing your magic?" I ask, trying to stay on track and not let my mind run away with things.

"Ah," Paul stands suddenly, pushing back the seats. "Why don't you come to the bar tonight and see for yourself?"

He doesn't wait for a response, simply walks off toward the stairs. Finally, I turn to face Rylan, dropping his hand as he shakes his head. I can see that he's angry at me. Or maybe he's angry with himself.

"What are you doing, Trinity?" he asks, as Paul heads down the stairs. The desire to punch something is rising. This is a mess. I have to fix it.

"Going to a party, apparently."

I stand then, brushing his hand from my thigh, and head for the stairs as well. This whole place gives me the creeps.

* * *

THE BAR IS LOUDER than before, if that's at all possible. I absolutely hate it here, but a deal is a deal. I can't exactly be mad at Rylan, when I would've done the same thing, but I hate that he's indebted to this snake of a man because of me. I thought he was a snake then; I think it way more now.

We're near the bar at the front of the room, Rylan plastered to my side like he's afraid I'm going to disappear again. I won't lie when I say I'm not complaining. His heat at my back and the possessive way he keeps his hand on my hip is making my insides all kinds of happy.

"How does he do it?" I ask, keeping my voice low, but knowing that Rylan can hear me and understands what I'm asking.

"I don't know. I think it's a talisman of sorts or some conduit. He didn't share, and I didn't see anything on him when he did the ritual. But I was a bit distracted."

By me, of course.

"Did you ever find out what's in that room?"

The door we broke through earlier is still giving off the same magical signature as before.

"No, he hasn't brought me in there."

Rylan told me that the only thing he does for Paul is run errands. He goes around town with Paul and stands outside while the mob boss conducts his business inside. Because Paul has some magic on him, he clearly protects himself from the shifter's hearing, and Rylan has no idea what goes on behind the closed doors.

"I don't like this, Rylan."

"That makes two of us." He squeezes my hip briefly, as if reassuring himself I'm still here. He's been doing that a lot actually. Reaching for me, needing me close. Not that I'm complaining. I don't want to admit this even to myself, but I nearly crave his touch at this point, and that's a scary place to have arrived at. For both of us.

"He's here." Rylan's voice pulls me from my thoughts, and I watch Paul step into the bar from the outside, making his way through the crowd. He did this the last time we were here as well, when he singled me out. As I watch him now, it feels like he's being very particular about who he stops to talk to.

"Is he casing the people?" I ask and Rylan moves me even closer to him, pulling me into his chest and resting his arm across my abdomen. Automatically, I place my arms over his, holding onto him just like he holds me.

"I think that's exactly what he's doing."

We have absolutely no information about anything that goes on here. It's hard not to be frustrated. We came here to find any kind of lead on the first shifter, in the hope that it would teach us how to protect our packs—or, at least, point us to the next step—but we've just come away with more magical chaos. Paul was right about one thing: this world has changed, and we have to adapt before we're left behind.

Just then, Paul's eyes find mine, and I feel Rylan's body tense. I think there's a very big chance that Paul is going to get ripped limb from limb one of these days, and Rylan is going to be the one to do it—not that it isn't exactly what he deserves.

I expect Paul to approach us, but he doesn't. Instead, he continues to make his rounds, stopping every so often to speak to someone. He does a round of the whole room, including the upstairs.

Because I've been watching so carefully, I can see the

change in the people the longer they spend within these walls. They're acting like they're high on drugs, losing their inhibitions and themselves to the music. From our vantage point, I see the door with the magical pulses open just a crack. A man steps out. He finds Paul in the crowd and nods his head. Immediately, Paul disentangles himself from the person he's been talking to and heads for the door...much like he did when he met me.

"Do we follow?" Rylan asks, his breath sending goosebumps down my neck.

"Absolutely," I reply, straightening. I don't go far before Rylan captures my hand in his.

"Stay close."

The protective thing is definitely one of my favorite aspects of Rylan's character. Even when we both know I can take care of myself.

I can tell something is happening in the room, just like last time, but I don't know what it is. We reach the door but are stopped by two of the goons before we can open it.

"Is there a problem, gentleman?" I ask, giving them a brilliant smile.

"No one is allowed in."

"Oh, well, Paul definitely doesn't mean us." I move forward, but the man doesn't budge.

"He does."

He stares me down, thinking he can intimidate me, but I'm more wound up than I realized because I don't even pause before striking him right in the jugular. He gasps, and I knee him in the groin, while Rylan takes care of the other one. More are moving in, but we're already through the door.

The hallway looks exactly the same as it did when we

were there before, and I march straight to the door at the end near the exit.

"Trinity, wait."

"We don't have that option, Rylan," I reply as I turn the knob. The door opens into another hallway, this one much more dimly lit. There are two doors at the end, opposite each other. After Rylan steps through, the door shuts behind him. We turn back to consider our options, but suddenly, light floods the small hallway. I glance over to the now open door and find one of Paul's goons at a doorway.

"You might as well come in." Paul's voice carries through the open door.

Rylan and I have no choice, so we step into the room. The goon shuts the second door behind us.

It takes me a moment to register what I'm seeing. We're in a large open space, much larger than the area behind the bar suggests. The building is definitely not this big from the outside, and yet this room exists. Maybe the outside of the building is spelled as well?

We're standing in a room with floor-to-ceiling bookshelves lining one whole wall to our left. The opposite wall is filled with dozens of items—anything from pieces of old armor to masquerade masks and metallic arrows. There's a desk at the far end of the room and a sofa and chairs near the bookshelves. There are no other decorations.

But the part that really surprises me is the magic. It's so potent in here, it hits me like a punch in the stomach. I stumble a little under the pressure. Rylan wraps his arm around my waist to keep me steady. Not that it matters. Paul has been watching me like a hawk, and he saw my reaction.

"You really are a powerful magical being," he says, standing up from the desk and walking closer. "I should be used to myths being an actual reality, but I'm never quite ready for it anyway."

"What is that supposed to mean?" I ask, keeping myself as rigid as possible.

"It means that when I was told a True Alpha was coming to town, I didn't believe it. For this to work, I had to be sure. But let's be honest, I didn't have to do much. Just a little parlor magic, and you were rushing in headfirst."

Rylan's growl vibrates against me, and I can tell he's barely restraining himself. I reach down and grip the outside of his thigh, holding him in place, centering him with my touch.

"If you're going to brag, might as well do it without all the stupid riddles." I raise an eyebrow, and he laughs.

"It's that kind of attitude that got you into trouble in the first place, Trinity," Paul says, pointing a finger at me. "It's why it was so easy to test you."

The self-satisfied smile on his face puts it all into place.

"It was you. You were the creature in my vision. But how?" It shouldn't have been possible. He's not an Ancient, he's not—unless whatever blood magic he uses let him do this is Ancient magic. I have no idea how that would be possible for a man like him, or what it would entail for a human to possess that kind of power. This is about the time that it would be beneficial to have more witch information.

"I'm more powerful than you know. And I'm about to get another boost." He motions for his guys, and suddenly, I'm being ripped from Rylan and a needle stuck in my neck. My eyes find his, and I see that they stuck him with a needle as well. He's already passed out. My heart thuds in fear at what that might mean. They snuck up on both of us, while Paul distracted us. I can't believe I was dumb enough to fall for it.

My vision tunnels immediately, my wolf subdued and whining. I stumble to my knees, looking up at Paul as he walks over to me.

"Thank you for your service, Trinity," he says, right before I pass out.

CHAPTER 26

When I open my eyes next, I'm in a room that is very similar to the one we were just in, except this one is bare. Crown molding lines the top of the room, but it looks like gold with intricate designs etched into it. At the very corner, opposite the only door, is a tiny hole, which I assume is a camera. I have no idea what's going on, but as I turn, I see Rylan slumped in a heap on the floor and I scoot over to him as fast as I can.

"Rylan?" I take his head into my hands, moving my palms over his forehead and cheeks. He feels hot, but not overly so. I continue my perusal, touching his arms, torso, and moving down to his legs.

"Are you feeling me up?"

His groggy voice fills me with relief, and I throw myself on top of him, hugging him tightly. One of his arms comes around me, holding me close as I breathe him in.

"Hey, we're okay," he mumbles into my hair as he sits up, taking me with him. I pull back, just enough to see his face, checking him over again.

"I don't think we are, Rylan."

I motion to the room and the camera. We're not bound, but it feels too easy to just be able to walk out the door. Especially since we're being monitored.

"Shall we try?" Rylan asks anyway. I nod. We have to try. He stands, taking me with him, and we walk over to the door. It doesn't budge. We hit our shoulders against it a few times, but still nothing.

This definitely doesn't look good for us.

"What is he, Rylan? A witch? An Ancient?"

"I don't think he's magical at all, Trin," Rylan replies, leading me away from the door and under the camera. "I think he's just a very ambitious man who found himself a few spell books."

"It can't be that simple."

"But wouldn't it be nice if it was?"

Right as he says it, he stumbles, and I catch him, holding him against the wall. I feel it too, a weird type of a weakness running through my body. My limbs tingling as if they've fallen asleep, becoming intense in waves.

"Are we in trouble, Trin?"

"I think we are," I reply honestly, because there's no use sugarcoating it now. Maybe if I made better decisions, or if I wasn't as impulsive, then maybe—

"Don't do that." Rylan's words break through the start of my panic, and he rubs his thumb over my furrowed brow, as if trying to smooth it out. I glance up at him as he rights himself, regaining his footing, and I step back.

"Do what?"

"Blame yourself. I can see it happening. I'm familiar with how it looks."

My heart squeezes at the confession, and I want to hug

him again. I've been wanting to do that a lot anyway, but never given myself the space to process what that means for me. What that means for us.

He's always been a part of me, my best friend growing up. But now, he's so much more, and it's hard to deny it, even to myself.

He's watching me now like he knows what I'm thinking, so I turn away, running my hand along the wall to see if I can find some kind of gap or break.

"I didn't say things then, but I need to say them now," Rylan says from behind me and I pause but don't turn. His voice catches in that way it always does when he's about to open up, and I'm afraid of what he'll say, but I'm also desperate to hear it.

"Rylan, if you—"

"Please, Trin. Just for once, just let me get this out."

I couldn't stop him if I tried, and I don't want to. I turn slowly and meet his intense gaze. Any moment, our captors might walk in here, and it'll be the end. And then none of our history, none of this stupid unclear prophecy or petty differences will make any difference. I want to hear what he has to say, because I have things to say as well.

"You told me once that respect is earned, and I will admit it now—you have earned that from me," Rylan begins. I can't do anything but stand there and watch him. "But it doesn't end there. Everything about our lives—well, you've been there, you've seen it all." He takes a deep breath, before capturing my eyes with his and continuing. "If things were different, I would tell you just how alive you make me feel. How everything matters all of a sudden, and I'm no longer simply going through the motions. I was right below the surface, but when you returned, I could finally keep my head above water. I would tell you this—if things were different."

I don't want this. I don't want him to talk about this only as something to regret. I need to hear what he's keeping inside. So of course, I do the one thing I'm good at. I push his buttons.

"Don't be a coward now, Rylan," I say, cocking my head to the side as his eyes flash. "If you have something to say, say it. Does it matter if things are different? Or do you just—"

"You're mine." His words are quiet, but they seem to echo off the empty walls as my breath catches in my throat. He steps right into my personal space, so I'm forced to look up at him. "And I am yours. Not because of some mystical bond or supernatural prophecy. But because you are the missing piece of me. Don't argue." He hurries to add when I open my mouth.

"But I will argue."

"True," Rylan chuckles, "that's one of the reasons I—"

"Don't." I stop him, because it's the same words I want to say to him but won't. "Don't say that. Don't give them ammunition to use against you."

"It's too late for that."

And then he crushes my lips with his.

The kiss is hungry, full of all the pent-up emotions we've been carrying inside of ourselves. This is nothing like the kiss at the bar, nothing like the small touches or longing looks. This is a raging forest fire, burning everything in its path.

I can't get close enough, even as Rylan wraps his arms around my back, pulling me off the floor and against him. My legs wrap around his middle as I pour every part of me into this kiss. He holds me like I'm the most precious commodity and yet, the most unbreakable metal. That contradiction of gentle and rough is the perfect representation of our whole relationship.

He's just as hungry for me as I am for him. I'm drowning in him, and I want more. My hands tangle in his hair, pulling and tugging as a growl rises from deep in his throat. One of his hands travels to my lower back, gripping me there, while the other moves to the bottom of my neck and then up into my hair. The gentle tug positions my head for better access, and Rylan plunges straight in.

I want to live off the taste of him. I want to breathe him in for the rest of my life. If we could, we'd stay like this forever, but we both know this is not the time to explore just how well we fit together. So I'm the first to pull back. He moves with me, capturing my lips in a quick kiss, before setting me down. But then I'm the one who follows him when he pulls back, grabbing one more hungry kiss before I step back.

"Our timing is always impeccable," I say, and he grins. Before I can say anything else, a high-pitched wail sounds all around us, and I drop straight down to my knees, hands over my ears.

"What is that?" I scream, but I don't think Rylan can hear me. He reaches for me at the same time as I reach for him, just as the door opens and people pour in. The noise is disorienting and weakening, but they don't seem affected. They walk right up to me wriggling on the floor and pick me up. I try to fight, but the noise has rendered me useless. I think I open my mouth to scream for Rylan, but nothing comes out as they carry me out of the room.

*　*　*

I'm strapped to a table, the straps running across my wrists, my ankles, and my middle. A contraption is placed over the top of my head, putting pressure on my temples. I try to shift, but I can't. The high-pitched wail hasn't ended, and it's weakening in every way that matters for a shifter, almost like it's been made especially for us. I manage to turn my head to the right and find Rylan in a similar predicament.

We're on what appear to be surgical tables. There are bright lights overhead and equipment around us. Just as suddenly as the noise started, it dissipates, and I can breathe again.

"What do you want from us?" Rylan snaps, recovering a tad bit faster than me. The people move around us, and I realize I can't see their faces because they're wearing full body suits. This is definitely a medical facility.

No one answers Rylan, and no matter how much I try to fight against the restraints, they don't budge.

"Trinity, are you okay?"

"Yes, I'm a big fan of the accessories I'm currently sporting. You think we should get some for the house?"

I think Rylan half chuckles, half hiccups over my inappropriately timed sarcasm, but it is who I am. I can't help it. Another person leans over me. I see a needle just before it's stuck in the vein on my arm. They don't seem to care if they hurt us or not. It does hurt, but I don't react outwardly. Wriggling is getting me nowhere either. These restraints are tight and reinforced with something that even my shifter strength can't break through.

People continue to move around us, not one of them speaking a word. Another needle is stuck in me, and I'm about to demand more answers when Rylan screams.

I twist my head to see him better, and he's writhing as

much as he can against the restraints, his back nearly coming off the table. They're taking his blood. But they're also replacing it with something else.

"Rylan!" My voice can barely be heard over his screams. I'm fighting with everything I have, and it's just not enough. I feel my own blood being drained, and something is pushed into my veins, but I ignore it. My whole attention is on Rylan.

Rylan, can you hear me? He shows no outward response that he does, but I keep talking anyway. *Stay strong, Rylan. Do you hear me? There's a conversation we still need to have. You're not getting away with kissing me and then running away.*

You...kissed...me...back...

It's barely there, but I'll take it.

Did I? You're going to have to prove it. You hear me? I expect proof.

And how...do...I...do that...

You'll think of something. Maybe we can spar for the truth.

He's stopped screaming, but I can see that whatever is happening is still hurting him. He's trying to fight against it. He's trying to stay conscious. We both know if he passes out now he might not wake up.

I wouldn't...want to...embarrass...you...

It's only embarrassing if I lose, and I never lose.

He might've chuckled if he could have. But this isn't funny at all. Because I'm not winning right now, am I. This definitely feels like a loss. Someone pricks me with a needle again, and I growl at them, yanking on my restrains.

"It's not affecting her," a distorted voice says, and second person comes to stand near my arm. "I've done three doses and nothing."

"Hmm. Her blood didn't react to the initial testing either. Something must be off."

"Maybe if we up the dosage. Or do a full transfusion. Hers is the stronger one, we must make it work."

I have no idea what they're talking about or how they got my blood—until it dawns on me. When I recklessly snuck into the compound, one of the guards stuck me with a needle. In fact, they had the same deafening noise, maybe slightly less of a higher pitch, but similar. They must've been perfecting it.

Rylan, I think we're at the compound. The one we found near Holden. It's where they kept the shifters and humans they experimented on.

That's...great...

I have to find a way out of here. Rylan is clearly being affected by whatever they put in him. Since I haven't been affected, I need to use that to my advantage, but how? I need powers. I need this stupid True Alpha prophecy to do something for me instead of simply complicating my life.

I'm a fighter! I should be able to fight my way out of this. I need more information.

Hold on, Rylan. I'm going to save us.

I don't think he hears me, but it doesn't matter. I make the promise to myself.

Think, Trinity. Think.

There has to be something I can do. My wolf is ready to be unleashed on all of these people, but I can't even break the restraints to do that. It would be very helpful to have a chat with the white wolf and see if she can offer some pointers.

Wait. Maybe I *can* have a talk with her. Technically, she always finds me, but I've never tried to find her before. No time like the present.

I'm right here, Rylan. I'm not going anywhere.

I close my eyes and take a deep breath. This has to work. It has to. Rylan is whimpering now, and a tear slips past my closed lids at the sound. I have to save him. I have to.

It's hard to focus while my heart is breaking for him, but I try my best. Curling my fingers into a fist, I squeeze hard, trying to find some kind of an anchor point. Rylan mentioned using my bracelet as something to ground him when I was in the siren's pool. I never did ask for the bracelet back. There are many things I could technically focus on but the only thing that fills my mind is Rylan.

So I use that, and I plunge into my mind, searching for the white wolf. My body grows hot and tense, and I'm almost physically pushed out but I force myself to dive back in. I have no idea how long I try, until finally, I'm pulled backward and into a dream vision.

"*Congratulations, Trinity. You are learning,*" the white wolf says as I step into the forest.

"It would've been helpful to know I can do this," I snap, and the wolf nearly laughs.

"*It is part of the journey.*"

"I don't care about your journey right now. Tell me, is there anything that I can do to break the restraints currently holding me down? A spell? A power that I've yet to discover that you won't tell me about?" I have absolutely no patience for these games, and I think she can tell.

"*You have everything you need, Trinity.*"

"No! Don't give me that crap!" I yell, my heart hammering in my chest. Every second I'm here in this weird place, Rylan is back there, dying. "I don't need your half answers and the 'you'll find yourself' non-instructions. The man I love is currently strapped to a table with his blood being siphoned out. This isn't the time for games."

The white wolf doesn't speak immediately, watching me in that patient way that always makes me want to hurl a boulder at her face. Clearly, I'm itching for a fight. It always makes me feel like I'm actually doing something. And right now, it feels like I'm doing nothing at all.

"There is no easy solution for this, Trinity," The wolf finally says. My heart drops. She's not going to help. "I cannot provide you with the answers you seek because only you know what powers you possess."

"How does that make any sense?"

The clear sympathy on the wolf's face makes me want to scream.

"Every True Alpha is born and chosen, but also made so by their own choices. Your powers will develop with time as you learn more about who you are and what you are capable of. There have been alphas with magical powers, some carried the power to move the wind, some could talk to other shifters through the link. Your power lies within you."

Finally, some kind of information. I should be happy, but in fact, I'm the opposite. I can't help Rylan if I can't figure out what my powers are. And that's not going to happen overnight. I can't even save the only man—

I realize what I said out loud, the one word that I didn't allow myself to think about all this time.

Love.

I love Rylan. A part of me has always loved him. Sure, this is a different type of a love, but even as a kid, I knew he was...mine. Just like he said.

Mine. I protect what's mine.

Without a second thought, I pull myself out of the vision.

The room around me has emptied of people, the lights dimmer than I remember. I have no idea how long I was gone, even though it felt like minutes. Turning, I see Rylan passed out on the bed beside me, tubes still stuck in his arms. Looking at him lying there breaks my heart all over again. I wish for fire magic or lightning to come down and strike the restraints so I could get us out. But there's nothing.

Nothing but me and the man I love, his life slowly being drained out of him.

A sudden burning sensation fills my arm and I gasp, trying to see what's happening. The burning continues and I bite my lip, trying to keep the noise to myself. The pain is hard and fast, as if I've stuck my whole right arm in a fire and held it there. But just as suddenly as it comes, it's gone.

Sweat covers my brow, and I want to find a way to see what's happened when I realize I can lift my arm. The restraint falls away from it and I stare at the white tattoo that's no longer just a howling wolf. The tattoo has grown, a few intricate vines curling from the bottom of the wolf and around my arm. It's at least twice the size it was before, and it's shining in a gentle glow.

My arm is free, and that's all that matters. I'll figure out what the changes to the tattoo mean later. I reach up and pull apart the contraption on my head, then I unfasten the belt around my middle. I proceed to undo the other arm before I'm finally able to sit up.

I do feel lightheaded. They took a bunch of blood, but I think I can manage through that, because I have to. I reach over and grab one of the scalpels. Slicing through my leg restraints is a lot faster than trying to unfasten them. Then I'm moving to Rylan.

It takes some time to pull the needles out of his veins, and

I find gauze to wrap around the nasty holes. They clearly didn't care if they ruined his skin. Next, I slice the restraints.

"Rylan, I need you to wake up now. I can try and carry you out, but it'll be a lot faster if we could go together. Rylan?"

He doesn't move at all, has no outward reaction. I have to move fast. They could be back any minute, especially if they're monitoring the room on video.

Rylan? I try through the pack link and still nothing. There's only one option left. I'm using my alpha voice.

Rylan! Get up now! We have to go!

At first, nothing, but then I see him stir. I place my hands on his shoulders and shake him a little.

"Come on, focus on me."

His eyes find mine, and they're not as clear as I would like them to be. But he's awake, and he's trying to sit up. I grab some of the cotton balls from the table and stuff them into his ears and then mine. It probably won't get rid of the noise completely, but it doesn't hurt to try.

I place his hand across my shoulders and help him slide off the table. If we can shift, we can probably get out of here faster. We head for the door, with Rylan leaning heavily on me. I'm about to offer the suggestion when the door opens and security walks in.

"Sorry," I say, as I drop from under Rylan. He drops on all fours, barely catching himself as I jump into a full-scale offensive.

CHAPTER 27

I'm acting on pure adrenaline as I round kick the guard into the others coming behind him. Sliding across the floor, I slam the scalpel I took into another guard's foot. He screams as I jump to my feet.

Rylan is upright, barely fighting off one of the guys; I can tell he's weak. I block an incoming punch, dodge a kick, and then twist around to deliver a kick of my own to the back of the knees. The guy stumbles, and I punch him in the head. I reach Rylan just as he knocks out his attacker.

Yanking their security cards off them, I wrap my arm around Rylan's middle and lead him out of the room. We're in a long, well-lit hallway that reminds me of a hospital but creepier.

"Which way?" I ask out loud, trying to find the direction with my shifter senses, but everything seems muted here.

"Left?" Rylan offers, and I take it. We move as quickly as we can, and we stay in human form because I need to open doors. I hear the siren turning on again, the same wail we heard earlier, but the cotton balls seem to diminish the sound enough that we keep moving. I know it won't last, but this is all we've got.

After the fourth door, we're outside. It's pitch black out here, but I can smell the familiar forest. We're definitely in the compound. Voices and footsteps sound all around us as I lead us to the gate. Dropping my arms from around Rylan, I step up to the scanner and try a keycard. When it doesn't work, I move to the next one.

"Trin! Duck!" Rylan's voice sounds behind me, and I drop down just as a bullet whizzes past me. Two more cards, come on. I try the next one and bingo, the door opens.

"Rylan! Shift! We need to go!" I'm already halfway through the gate, motioning for Rylan to go, but he's not budging.

"I can't."

Two words. Time seems to stop. I race back over to where he stands completely hopeless.

"What? What do you mean?"

"I can't shift, Trin. I can't…feel him at all."

When his eyes meet mine, there's pain there. Pain and panic. His body shakes, sweat collecting at his temples. He gasps, as if he can't take a full inhale.

I grab his face between my hands, turning him to look at me, "Breathe, Rylan. Breathe."

He inhales as I lower my forehead to his. My alpha powers unfurl, and I try to feel his wolf, but there's nothing. My own wolf starts to panic, but I calm her the best I can, as I take Rylan's hand and pull him after me.

Another bullet hits the ground next to us, and I see the gate closing.

"Come on!" I run toward it, almost dragging Rylan

behind me. Then I push him through first. Glancing behind me, I see people gaining on us, so I turn, kicking the panel off the wall. I fit through the gate just before it shuts. Taking Rylan's hand, we start to move toward the trees, even as the gate behind us shudders with the impact of multiple people hitting it to try to force it open.

A spotlight makes circles around us, and any moment now, another shot will ring out and hit us. I can almost picture it in my mind's eye. Rylan stumbles but stays upright as I push him into the trees. We can't run. We won't outrun them, not like this. We can climb a tree, but if they have shifters, they will find us. There isn't much—

"The cave," Rylan says. "Take us toward the cave."

"You're not serious." The cave where they dropped off the rabid, experimented-on wolves?

"They won't expect it. And the scent will confuse anyone looking for us," Rylan stumbles against the tree, breathing heavily.

"Are you hit anywhere?" I'm beside him in a flash, and he shakes his head.

"Go, Trinity. Hide."

I pull back as if I've been slapped.

"Excuse me?"

"Go. You need to go."

"I'm not leaving you, you idiot. Come on."

I tug him away from the tree before I shift. My wolf might not be as big as his, but it's still bigger than his human form.

Get on. And I swear if you argue, I will pick you up and carry you in my mouth like a child.

He thinks about it for half a second, then he climbs on

top of me, curling his hands into my fir. He holds tight, nearly lying down and wrapping his arms around my neck.

"You're my hero," he mumbles into my back just as I take off. The noise of the compound grows louder as the search for us begins, but I don't slow down, and I don't look back. I weave in and out of the trees, messing up the trail as much as possible. But when I reach the caves, I don't stop. I keep running around the mountain and away from the compound.

Away from everything and everyone we know. Away from home.

* * *

WE'RE in some hotel room in some big town whose name I don't know. Rylan is in the bathroom, washing up. I took us pretty far away from the compound, even farther than Williamsburg, north and then west—not even in the direction of Hawthorne, which was where I desperately wanted to go. Once I shifted back, we hiked for miles, until we could hitch a ride. Rylan was in a near state of shock the whole time, but he was moving.

I can't even imagine how he's feeling, what's going through his head. My own wolf whimpers in sympathy, wanting to comfort as much as she wants to fight.

His wolf is gone.

Gone.

Whatever they were doing to us, it must've been the same kind of experiments they were doing on those other humans. It didn't seem to work on me, which is a puzzle for another time. But for him? Instead of becoming a rabid wolf, he's become the opposite. An ordinary human.

He steps out of the bathroom then, and heads for the bed. But instead of sitting on it, he sinks down to the floor, his back against it. I don't give myself time to hesitate. I walk over immediately, taking a seat beside him and reaching for his hand.

The small contact seems to settle him, if only a little. He grips my fingers like they're a lifeline, before he turns his attention to me.

"What now, Trinity?" he asks, and I can hear the pain him his voice. When we saw the Oracle, we had our wolf repressed for a short period of time and that felt like an eternity. Now? Rylan has no idea when he's getting him back. Only that he is, because I will turn the whole world upside down to find a solution to this problem. I stare at the tattoo that's grown in size, ideas spinning in my mind. There is one pathway that we should take that he's not going to like, but we have no choice.

"I think we should go to Hawthorne." He stiffens immediately.

"More witches?"

"The best witches, Rylan." I squeeze his hand. "I think they'll be able to help. Or maybe Jefferson could. We can't do this on our own."

"But we do, Trin."

There's something in his voice, something that he's not telling me.

"Rylan, I think it's past time for secrets."

"It's not a secret, Trin. It's what I can't get over. How did Paul know we were coming? How did he know who we are? Who you are? Our plans, our movements?" He pauses.

I think I know where he's going with this and I don't like it. Not one bit. But I need to hear him say it.

"What is it, Rylan?"

"Who told him that a True Alpha was coming into town? I think—" He turns and looks me straight in the eye, his gaze full of hopelessness but also determination. My handsome contradiction. "I think there's a traitor in our midst."

We stare at each other, as if he's expecting an argument. But I can't offer him one, because no matter how much I want to argue with this, I know he's right. Someone close to us is feeding the other side information, manipulating us for their own advantage, just like whoever messed with our memories did it all those years ago.

"So what do we do?" I ask, and I think I surprise Rylan by not arguing. He thinks it over for a moment, giving my hand a gentle squeeze.

"We figure out who it is, together, and then we make them pay."

"That's the best plan I've heard yet."

Our whole mission was a failure, but I suppose we walked away with a ton of information. We know that what's happening is definitely not only happening to the wolves in our territory. This is a much bigger issue and there are far more people involved than I would've liked. The first shifter is still a mystery, but we'll keep looking for him.

Rylan and I are no longer enemies, but something more. Something I never thought we would ever be, but always wanted. Still want. So much. We still don't know who messed with our memories, and now we have to figure out who's feeding information to the other side. We seem to have enemies on every turn. But I'm not scared.

I lean over and place my head on Rylan's shoulder, staring at our entwined hands and the tattoo that's peeking over. I am more powerful than I think I am, and I will figure it out.

Because I am not alone. When Rylan places his cheek against the top of my head, I vow to save him.

I will do whatever it takes to save him.

Get ready to see what happens next in the third installment of the White Wolf Saga, Shifter Hunted! Trinity and Rylan's story isn't over yet!

NEXT IN THE WHITE WOLF SAGA

There's nothing I won't do to save my pack.

With the danger tracking our every step, we have no choice but to make difficult decisions. Leaving the pack behind,

NEXT IN THE WHITE WOLF SAGA

cutting ourselves off from everything and everyone we love, we only have each other. And Rylan is not his best at the moment.

I will do whatever it takes to help him find his way back to me. I refuse to give up on him, I refuse to give up on us.

Shifter Hunted is book three in the pulse-pounding series by USA Today Bestselling author, Valia Lind. If you love fast-paced action, friends-to-enemies-to-lovers romance, snarky heroines and broody heroes, and found family, then this is a series for you!

* * *

Thank you for reading my book! If you have enjoyed it, please consider leaving a review. Reviews are like gold to authors and are a huge help!
They help authors get more visibility, and help readers make a decision!
And, if you'd like to stay up to date with all of my shenanigans, sign up for my newsletter today!

You will also receive the FREE prequel to Trinity's story!

You can find the link readily available at https://valialind.com/free-book/

Thank you!

MORE FROM THE HAWTHORNE UNIVERSE

If you'd like to learn more about the Hawthorne universe, including the witches and shifters at the town Trinity stayed in, you can check out three complete series:
Hawthorne Chronicles
Thunderbird Academy
Faerie Destiny

Find out more information at http://valialind.com

ABOUT THE AUTHOR

USA Today bestselling author. Photographer. Artist. Born and raised in St. Petersburg, Russia, Valia Lind has always had a love for the written word. She wrote her first published book on the bathroom floor of her dormitory, while procrastinating to study for her college classes. Upon graduation, she has moved her writing to more respectable places, and has found her voice in Young Adult and cozy mysteries.

ALSO BY VALIA LIND

The Skazka Fairy Tales
The Scarlet Rose (A Beauty and the Beast Retelling)
The Golden Slipper (A Cinderella Retelling)
The Poisoned Princess (A Snow White Retelling) - coming 2023!

The White Wolf Saga
Shared Dreams - FREE prequel
Moonlight Mate (#1)
Wolf Untamed (#2)
Shifter Hunted (#3) - coming 2023!

Thunderbird Academy
The Complete trilogy Boxset
Of Water and Moonlight (Thunderbird Academy, #1)
Of Destiny and Illusions (Thunderbird Academy, #2)
Of Storms and Triumphs (Thunderbird Academy, #3)
Of Holidays and Soulmates (A Christmas Novella)

Fae Chronicles
The Complete trilogy Boxset
Shadow of the Fae (#1)
Blood of the Fae (#2)
Revenge of the Fae (#3)

Hawthorne Chronicles

The Complete Season One Box Set

Guardian Witch (Hawthorne Chronicles, #1)

Witch's Fire (Hawthorne Chronicles, #2)

Witch's Heart (Hawthorne Chronicles, #3)

Tempest Witch (Hawthorne Chronicles, #4)

Crooked Windows Inn Cozy Mysteries

Books 1-3 Boxset

Once Upon a Witch #1

Two Can Witch the Game #2

Witch's First Zombie - FREE short story

Third Witch's the Charm #3

Witches Four the Win #4

The Skazka Chronicles

Hardcover Omnibus - 4 books in one

Remembering Majyk (The Skazka Chronicles, #1)

Majyk Reborn (The Skazka Chronicles, #2)

The Faithful Soldier (The Skazka Chronicles, #2.5)

Majyk Reclaimed (The Skazka Chronicles, #3)

Blackwood Supernatural Prison Series

Witch Condemned (#1)

Witch Unchained (#2)

Witch Awakened (#3)

Witch Ascendant (#4)

Havenwood Falls (PNR standalone)
Predestined

The Titanium Trilogy
Pieces of Revenge (Titanium, #1)
Scarred by Vengeance (Titanium, #2)
Ruined in Retribution (Titanium, #3)
Complete Box Set

Falling Duology - YA contemporary romance
Falling by Design
Edge of Falling

www.ingramcontent.com/pod-product-compliance
Lightning Source LLC
LaVergne TN
LVHW011948060526
838201LV00061B/4245